L.A. Woman

Woman

Cathy Yardley

RED
DRESS
I N K
™

L.A. WOMAN

A Red Dress Ink novel

ISBN 0-373-81082-2

© 2002 by Cathy Yardley.

www.RedDressInk.com

Printed in U.S.A.

To the family of my heart: Pat Johnson, Katrina Healey, Mike Johnson, Chris Becker, Greedi James. I love you!

And to Liisa and Joey, the coolest people I've ever known. Thanks.

Chapter 1

Waiting For the Sun

Sarah looked nervously around the apartment. "You know, this wasn't how I pictured this. At all."

She heard Benjamin sigh. "I'm at the office, sweetie. Is this going to be long?"

Sarah sighed. "I just…felt a little lonely. Felt like calling."

"Well, you've been down in Los Angeles for a whole week. How are you doing? Feeling, you know, acclimated?"

"There are cardboard boxes up to the ceiling, but at least the bed's in. Thank God Judith and David were able to help me." She paused. "That wasn't…I mean, I understand you had to work last weekend, too.''

''Don't even get me started.'' She heard an impatient rustle of papers. ''Judith...who's she again?''

''She's my friend. From college. She got married to David, moved down here—let's see, that'd be three years ago. Remember? I took you to her wedding.''

A pause. ''The Chinese girl?''

Sarah rolled her eyes. ''That's the one.''

''Huh. Well, anyway, it's not like you're *completely* alone down there.''

Sarah leaned against the arm of the couch. ''It's not the same, and you know it,'' she teased, glancing out the window. It was looking fit to storm, she noticed. She thought that it never rained in Los Angeles. Maybe that was a myth. She hoped it wouldn't storm. ''I just can't wait until you're down here, tucked up in bed with me—picking out some more furniture, this place is *very* bare—you know. Settling in.''

As soon as she said the words, she winced. She hadn't meant to say *settling*. This wasn't about pressuring him to marry her...even if they had been engaged for four years. This was about her being a good girlfriend, helping him out.

Really.

''Well, what I'm saying is, sure, you miss me...but it's not going to, you know, *kill* you or anything.'' He laughed, warmly.

She felt a prickle of alarm. She knew that laugh. She'd been at a business party, and he'd made that laugh to one of the decision-makers of a computer company he was trying to sell semiconductors to. He'd walked away with the account.

"I'm not going to *die* if you're not here, yeah, but I'm going to be miserable," she said, hoping that didn't sound too whiny. On second thought, she was in a city with millions of people she didn't know. A little whining was probably not out of place. "So, how did Mr. Richardson take you going through with the transfer, anyway? You figured he'd be mad, but you thought once you'd signed with the L.A. office, there wasn't anything he could do…"

He sighed deeply. "Turned out I was wrong there, actually."

The prickle turned into a pang. "What happened?"

"Richardson's being a dick," Benjamin replied, his voice acidic. "He *knew*. He knew I'd try to sneak out of the office. With numbers like I bring in, though— I underestimated what he'd do to keep me here. He doesn't want to lose one of his highest Northern Cal reps to Southern Cal."

"But there isn't anything he can do about it, right?" she pressed. "You've already agreed with the sales manager, what's-his-name, right?"

"Sarah, he pulled the vice president in…and *he* told me, point-blank, that if I tried to leave Fairfield, I wouldn't be moving to another district—I'd be moving to another company."

Sarah blanched, and quickly sat down on the couch. "But…you've already signed a lease down here!"

I wouldn't have moved down if you hadn't!

"He knows it." Benjamin's voice dripped bitterness. "He pulled me aside privately and said that he'd work on Richardson, but they're, you know, *friends*." He all but spat the word out. "He said just give him a little time."

"How much time are we talking about?" Sarah tried to keep her voice calm. She gripped the cordless phone like a life preserver. "A few weeks?"

"More like two months."

"Two months!"

"You think I'm happy about this?"

Sarah started pacing. "Two months. Okay. That's like…that's like summer vacation. That's not too bad."

"Actually, it might be three," he corrected. "It all depends on Richardson. Goddammit!" He paused, then lowered his voice, obviously remembering he *was* at work, even if it was a weekend. "Goddammit. I'm so sick of this little town!"

She looked out the window. The clouds were definitely heavy-looking, and some drops pelted the window. She turned on a light. "I don't suppose…well, couldn't you just get *another* job down here? Does it have to be with Becker Electronics?"

"Are you crazy? The job market's terrible. I'm a proven commodity here," he said, harshly. "I'm not giving all that up and starting over!"

"Just a suggestion," Sarah replied, heading him off. *I just want you down here.* That wasn't going to happen—not on his end.

"I could break the lease, move back…"

"You already gave up your apartment."

"I could move in with you…"

"Sarah, the apartment's in my name. I don't want you fucking up my credit that way, okay?"

Well, it wasn't my idea in the first place to sign it, now, was it?

She didn't want to fight. She'd just have to make the best of things. "Okay. Three months by myself. That's not so bad," she said, even though it sounded more ghastly every time she thought of it. "I guess I can get a lot of things planned in the meantime." Like the wedding. He'd promised that it would be by the end of this year. He hadn't mentioned specifics, but she knew he wouldn't, so no sense rubbing his nose in it—especially with this Richardson business.

"Four at the absolute outside," he said, not helping at all. "Man. I envy you."

"Really?" Sarah smiled. "Why?"

"By the time I get down there, you'll practically be a native. You'll know all the places to go, you'll already have a job, you'll be genuinely…"

"Wait a second," she interrupted. "I don't know that I'll find the job I want in three months, Benjamin, so you might not have a leg up on me there."

He laughed—it was that selling laugh again. "I know you wanted to take some time to figure out what you're really interested in doing, but that's hardly realistic now, is it?"

She paced a little more quickly. "But that was part of the agreement. I'd move down to L.A. and get your house ready for you, and then you'd cover the bills for a few months while I figured out my, er, direction.''

"After three jobs in four years, honey, does it really *matter* now if you get a job you don't like?'' His voice was smoothly persuasive. "You can always quit it later, when I finally move down.''

Sarah felt like banging her head against the wall. "The point is, Benjamin, I don't *want* to keep quitting jobs. I feel so…planktonic!''

"Planktonic?'' This time, the laugh sounded more natural. "Is that a word?''

"I just want to stop floating around,'' she said. "I want some stability.''

He sighed, more irritably this time. "That's not exactly something I'm supposed to provide for you, Sarah. Is it?''

"You're missing the point.'' She frowned at the phone. "I'm usually so *unhappy* at work. I mean, there's got to be something out there I actually enjoy.''

"Nobody really enjoys their job,'' he dismissed out of hand. "Okay, maybe me. Still, it's not like you're going to be able to pay rent without a job, right? So now's hardly the time to be picky. And bills…they'll be coming up soon, too.''

"How much will you be able to help out?''

Another one of those long pauses. She was beginning to really hate those.

"Sarah,'' he said slowly, "I'm not living there, remember?''

She blinked. "But you said…''

''Things have changed.'' His tone was just this side of curt. ''You wouldn't honestly expect me to pay for the rent when I'm not moving down there.''

''Yet,'' she said, bristling. ''You're not moving down here *yet*.''

''I mean, you wouldn't think that,'' he continued stubbornly.

''You're right, Benjamin.'' Her voice was cold. ''I would have moved down here with what little savings I have, on a whim, all ready to pay rent even though *you* said you'd cover it, not knowing you wouldn't move down here until I'm already unpacked and signed to a year lease. Of course! What was *I* thinking?''

''I paid the deposit and the first month, so *please* don't give me that 'I'm stranded here!' bullshit,'' Benjamin answered. ''You're the one who was saying, 'Oh, L.A. will be so much *fun*'! You were the one who told me you'd love to move down there!''

That's because you *wanted to, you idiot!*

She'd already let her temper get too far ahead of her. She didn't want to fight...especially not with eight hundred miles and a telephone connection being her only hold on him. ''I'm sorry. I...it was unexpected. I wasn't expecting you to pay for everything.''

''Yeah, well, imagine how *I* felt.''

She was trying to. Very, very hard.

Three months—and getting a job. In a city where she didn't know anybody except Judith.

Sarah closed her eyes, breathing deeply. She wasn't

going to cry. He hated her crying and could sense it in a few seconds. "So are you going to visit me?"

"I'm in the middle of a killer quota, and we're not even to threshold, much less target this year…"

Meaning no.

"Sarah, I can tell you're getting upset about all of this. Believe me, you'll be so busy, you won't even *think* about me."

Considering every decision she'd made up to this point was for the sole purpose of getting him to move in with her—to get him *that much closer* to the altar— that seemed highly unlikely. "I miss you already," she said.

He sighed. "You know, I think this will probably be really good for us," he said instead.

"How do you figure?"

"I mean, you were spending all of this time with me. We were together *all the time*."

"Not all the time," she protested. "Not with you working as much as you do."

"But every time I came home, there you were. Now, you'll have a chance to do outside stuff."

"You want me to use this as, what, some kind of survival training?" She tried to make it sound like a joke, but her voice had other ideas.

"Well, it'll show me how long you'll last without me there."

She gasped a little at this. "What are you saying?"

"Nothing…nothing. It's just that, sometimes you can be a handful, Sarah. I feel like I'm taking care of you. Now you hit me up with the 'how much can you help with rent' and 'when are you flying down to visit me?' stuff, and I just wonder—how can you expect to survive L.A. without me at this rate?''

"I didn't realize I was going to have to," she snapped back.

"See? That's *exactly* what I mean!"

She sighed. "Benjamin..."

"I've got to go. These sales figures aren't typing themselves into the spreadsheet." She guessed he was trying to make a joke, too. Like hers, it came out wrong.

"I'll get a job," she said hurriedly. "And I'll make it just fine."

"I really have to go."

"Jam," she said, relapsing into her old nickname for him, "you know I love you."

"I know, Sarah," he said. "Talk to you next week."

He hung up.

She stared at the phone, until it made that annoying *beep-beep-beep* and she hit the off button.

Lying naked on her back, feeling the soft strokes of his fingertips on her skin, Martika felt truly, utterly bored.

"What are you thinking?" he asked, his blue eyes huge and curious.

She glanced at him. "That's a woman's question."

"You're so mysterious," he said, and she supposed he was complimenting her. It might help if he'd stop mooning over her like some Regency poet. "I always wonder what you're thinking."

I'm thinking, why the hell am I still here?

She'd been staying with…Andre. His name was Andre, she reminded herself, watching the way his blond hair hung slightly in his eyes. It used to charm her. Now it just made her fingers itch for scissors. Anyway, she'd been staying with the man for the past five months. He'd been starting to pressure about things like "where are we going with this?" and hinting around "permanent relationships." She thought he was about two years younger than she was chronologically—about five years younger emotionally, and about fifty years older when it came to things like marriage. She tried not to roll her eyes.

"So what are you thinking?" he pressed.

She winced. "I'm thinking that I'd like to go clubbing. Maybe hit Sunset."

He frowned. "You've been out three nights this week. I thought we could spend tonight at home." He grinned, his dimples pitting his cheeks. "In bed."

She was getting bored there, too…and bored in bed meant a hasty exit, stage right. "I really felt like going out."

His frown turned into a scowl. "Fine."

She huffed impatiently. "You don't have to pout."

"Sometimes, you can be such a bitch, Martika."

She pulled on a loose black silk robe. "No 'sometimes' about it," she agreed, grabbing her cigarettes and heading for the balcony. She was two steps toward it when she heard the high-pitched trill of her cell phone. She swiped it up on her way, shutting the glass door behind her as she hit the green *answer* button. "This is me. And you are?"

"Are we drinks?"

She grinned, leaning back and patting the cigarette package, pulling one out with her lips. It smelled like rain...and looked like it. Fat drops were haphazardly hitting the pavement. She hoped it would storm. "Taylor, you are my white knight. I thought I was going to have to bite my own leg off to get out of this place."

"Oh, Tika," he said, with a slight note of disapproval. "Have we hit that point, then?"

"If you mean the leaving point, yes, we've hit it and run through it."

"Damn. He's got such a great body."

"I know." She lit the cigarette, taking a long drag. "Too bad he's not a mute. Still, even then, I could only put up with those soulful looks for so long."

She glanced back through the glass door. Andre was still sitting on the bed, naked, sulking.

"So. What's the ETD?"

She grinned. "No departure date yet, Taylor...but soon. I feel like it's coming up soon." She took another drag on her cigarette. "Fuck. I hate moving."

"Strange, for someone who does it as often as you do," Taylor pointed out dryly. "You're like the Bedouin Dater. Maybe you should try living with somebody you aren't sleeping with."

"I *have* lived with people I haven't slept with."

"Your family doesn't count, darling, and that was how many years ago?"

"Touché." She didn't think about that, really. "But there was that guy...what was his name? Robbie?"

Taylor laughed. "The other restriction—you need to live with somebody *I* can't sleep with. Remember?"

She chuckled. "Ooh. Right. God, what a fiasco that was."

"Maybe you should try a girl next time."

"What, to sleep with?"

Taylor huffed. "Roommate, silly. Although..."

Martika cut him off. "I don't think so. Girls don't like me." She unleashed a feral grin. "Probably with good reason."

She heard a rap on the glass, and looked over. It was Andre, obviously unamused. "Are you going to be out there all night?" he mouthed through the glass.

"Maybe," she mouthed back, then turned back to look out on the road. "Taylor, there's the warden. We are more than drinks tonight, sweetie, we are *club*. Sunset?"

"Oooh. Let's be trashy and do martinis at the Viper Room."

She grinned. "This is why I love you, sweetie. I think I want to full out this time—so add about an hour to my usual grooming regime, 'kay?"

"I'm going to go eat first, anyway, and then say hi to Kit."

"Okay. So Viper Room, around eleven." She made a kiss noise. "Byee."

She clicked the phone off, and opened the door.

"Don't tell me," Andre said, his arms folded across his naked chest. "Now that the other man in your life calls, you'll be off running?"

"I can't believe you're jealous of a gay guy."

"I'm starting to think they're the only men you *could* love."

She smiled at him, cruelly sweet. "I see. So is that why you're acting so bitchy? So I'll think you've crossed over and fall madly for you?"

"Dammit." His gorgeously chiseled chin rippled as his jaw tensed. He looked like the model he was. *Okay, give me angry! Angry!* Martika almost laughed at the thought. "Martika, I think I'm in love with you. But I don't want you to go out with Taylor tonight."

She gave him a lazy once-over. While ordinarily she'd be applauding his growing a spine, he'd hit a hot button. Taylor was her best friend. Nobody fucked with her friends—or told her who she could and couldn't see.

"I'm going out tonight, Andre. You can go with me if you want..." She paused. "No. On second thought, you *can't* go with me. I am going out with my friends to try to ignore the idiocy that's just transpired here. You can throw a tantrum, or you could do something productive. Sleep. Watch TV. Write an angst-filled sonnet. Frankly, I don't care."

She stalked over to the bathroom, started the water running in the shower. She took off her robe and stepped into the stream, adjusting the heat. It felt good. Relaxing.

He followed her in, pulling open the door. She saw him, his handsome face obscured by the steam. "Maybe...maybe you shouldn't live here anymore," he said, and took a deep breath. His blue eyes were both angry and pleading. If he'd started crying, she wouldn't be surprised.

She sighed. "I'll be out by the end of the week." She shut the door.

Standing in the rain, Sarah glanced up at the sign: *Basix Café*. If she were going to start exploring the city, and getting used to it *by herself*, then this was as good a place as any. Granted, it was two blocks away from her house, but the fact that she was outside the apartment, among strangers, was a step in the right direction.

Of course, she'd tried calling Judith and seeing if she could meet her for dinner, but she'd only gotten the message machine. It had only taken her another half hour to stir up her courage to come here by herself.

The place was crowded, with a patio area that was closed in with clear plastic curtains and those butane heaters that looked like torches. She made her way toward the inner restaurant, feeling self-conscious. She wondered if she'd see anybody famous. This was Hollywood, after all. Okay, West Hollywood, but still...

The "host" looked her over, smiling slightly. "Good evening. How many?"

"Just one."

"Right."

Was it just her, or did he give her an appraising once-over? Not the sexual kind, either, the way men might at home. It was more like…something was wrong with her, or something.

She discreetly checked her jeans zipper.

Maybe it's because I'm here by myself, she thought. She noticed there were at least twosomes at most tables, usually more.

Next time, she told herself, she'd bring a book. If there were a next time.

He took her to a minuscule table in the corner, half obscured by a potted plant. She took a menu and sat. At least from her duck-blind vantage point she got to look around, which was nice. Nobody famous yet, but it was only, what, eight or so? She imagined they'd probably come out later. Somewhat like vampires.

The thing she noticed immediately was that the restaurant was predominantly filled with men…all well dressed, she noticed, in that stylish, edgy way that seemed very "MTV." You wouldn't see guys dressed like this in Fairfield. At least, not in a café, for dinner.

She turned her attention to the menu. Her stomach grumbled. The place smelled wonderful, and the desserts…what she could see in the glass case looked so good, she briefly considered having a dinner of chocolate cake with a side order of éclairs. Still, she was running on empty—she needed real food first, or she'd be twitching on the carpeted floor with a sugar rush all night.

"What do you mean, there's no table for me?" a

flamboyant voice pierced the rumble of conversation. All eyes turned to the new arrival. Sarah turned, too, then gaped, momentarily ignoring the menu.

He was one of the biggest men she'd ever seen. He had short hair that was obviously curly in its natural state—it waved over his forehead, obviously calmed by gel of some sort. He had big, dark eyes, broad shoulders, and like everyone else here, it seemed, his clothes were stylish. He was wearing black, shiny cargo pants and an almost metallic looking red shirt. He had two earrings in his right ear, and to her surprise, he had on black nail polish.

"But I'm *starving,* Mitch," he said, in a melodramatic whine, then winked at the maître d'. "Besides, I'm clubbing with Tika tonight, so I can't wait two hours for a table!"

The giant glanced around, then suddenly descended on her. "Is anybody sitting with you?"

Goggling, she gathered enough presence of mind to shake her head.

"Great. Then I'll just have dinner with you. Hi," he said, pulling up a chair and sprawling down heavily on it. "I'm Taylor."

She nodded, feeling overwhelmed. "S-Sarah," she said.

He beamed. "What a delicious voice! Like a Powerpuff girl. I love them. Did you know they were originally called the WhupAss Girls when they were just a student film? But of course, Cartoon Network wouldn't let them stay that way…but I digress." He looked at her. "You haven't ordered yet, have you?"

"Uh…no." She glanced back down at the menu. "I've never eaten here before," she ventured, "so I hadn't decided."

"Never?" He sounded delighted. "Well, then, you're in for a treat. Start with the corn bisque, then have a pizza…the barbecued chicken and gouda. It's fantastic."

Her stomach growled, and she pressed a hand to it, embarrassed. "That sounds great."

"Obviously!" He looked her over. *What was it with that look?* But he was less disparaging, and smiled. "You're not from around here, are you?"

You think? "Well, I am now." She smiled weakly. "I just moved in. Up the street."

"Really?" She wondered if he ever sounded disappointed about anything. "That's great. I live right up the street, myself! Oh, hold on a sec. That's a friend of mine." He got up and maneuvered his way across the room, managing to catch the eye of every person in the restaurant. Which, Sarah supposed, was the point. "Michael! It's been way too long. Why weren't you at Beer Bust?"

Sarah watched in amazement as he exuberantly hugged the man in question, who was presenting another man to her dinner companion.

Well, it beats eating alone.

The waiter walked over to her. "Made your decision?"

She nodded. "Corn bisque," she repeated dutifully, "and the barbecued chicken pizza."

He smiled again, that sort of slick, polite smile.

"Oh, but he's sitting with me," she said, as the waiter started to walk away. "He hasn't ordered yet."

"He doesn't have to," the waiter said, with a little sneer in his voice. "He gets the same thing every time."

"Oh." The food here had better be damned good, she thought, because the service definitely leaves something to be desired.

Taylor was back in a matter of minutes. "Great guy, that Michael."

"He seemed nice." Sarah didn't know what else to say.

He grinned at her, then winked. "Next time, I'll have to introduce you. We're practically neighbors, after all." He sighed gustily. "I've been going on and on. You look like a little drowned rat, no offense, with not a friend in the world. So what's your story, little girl?"

"I didn't know it rained in L.A.," she said in her defense, "or I would have brought an umbrella."

He grinned at her. "So you don't know L.A. Where are you from?"

"Fairfield."

His brows raised. She wondered briefly if he had them plucked—they looked like perfect arches. "Fairfield? Where is that? Out in the valley?"

She shook her head. "No. It's up by Sacramento, sort of. Well, closer to…well, it's in Northern California," she said, realizing if he thought it were in "the valley" he didn't know the area at all.

"Oh, Northern Cal," he said, rolling his eyes.

"Well, that explains the clothes, at least. So you just moved down today? Are you...no, you're not an actress."

"How do you know?"

"Not a high enough bitch factor, to be perfectly honest. I mean, you *could* be an actress, but I doubt you're a very successful one...of course, L.A. is full of those, too. Besides, you look like you have too much money."

She didn't know if she should be insulted by Taylor's reasoning or not, so she chose not to be. The corn bisque had arrived, and she sampled it, sighing deeply.

"Told you," Taylor said smugly.

"It's *wonderful,*" she said, trying her best not to gobble it down. She didn't want to know what Taylor would say about deplorable table manners.

Taylor looked at her, his head tilted to one side. "You know," he said, taking a spoonful of his own bisque and tasting it, "I've decided to like you."

She smiled, the aches from moving momentarily forgotten. "Thanks. That's nice."

"And of course, you're going to like me, so there it is," he said, and she laughed...she couldn't help it. He motioned for the waiter to come over. "I like her," he said expansively. The waiter simply smiled, much more friendly and simpering, Sarah noted. "We're going to need some wine."

Sarah stopped him, alarmed. "Oh, no, really, I couldn't..."

He stared her into silence. "Nonsense. You're getting a Tayler welcome to L.A. Get me a bottle of that Ravenwood cab, would you? Thanks,'' he said, dismissing the waiter, who just nodded and turned silently.

''Now then,'' Taylor said, all but rubbing his hands together. ''Being such good friends and all, you need to tell me your whole life, beginning to end. Leave out no detail. I want to know everything.''

The master bathroom in Judith and David's house had two sinks: his and hers. It was a sign of how well David was doing. He'd be making partner any day now. His side of the sink reflected that: an organized display of toiletries, from his silver toothbrush holder and razor holder (no disposables for David), to the little silver mug that he lathered his shaving cream in, right down to the way he folded the towel that hung on his own towel rack, for his own use. He kept the toothpaste and other tackier items hidden in the drawer, even if the toothpaste was Rembrandt and not something cheap like Colgate.

Judith's side was almost clinical looking. There was a complete line of Dr. Hauschka skin care, sitting companionably with its almost generic labels of white with a thin band of orange. Cleansing milk, cleansing cream, toner, moisturizer—daily and Rose Cream, for problem areas. Her toothbrush was sitting in a ceramic cup, a creamy white. The toothbrush itself was orange.

She went through the ritual: brush, wash, tone, moisturize. Search for wrinkles, even at twenty-five, even with her moisture-plump Asian skin that people at work continually proclaimed an envious miracle. Remove hair band. Brush lustrous black hair, fifteen measured strokes. Throw clothes in hamper, put on cotton nightgown. Climb into California King bed, on the right hand side, by the wall. David liked sleeping on the side by the door. She rolled and picked up the book she'd left on his nightstand. *The Oz Principle.* Something for work. She wanted to get a leg up on it—the next few weeks would be busy. Her Filofax was pretty full.

She barely registered the noises of David going through his ritual: long span in the bathroom, evacuating that night's dinner (in this case, Ahi tuna appetizer and braised lamb chops from Chinois) with a book in the bathroom before brushing his teeth and surveying the wrinkle situation, a larger possibility considering he was thirty-two. She felt rather than heard him checking his hairline for signs of losing ground—a tiny buzz of apprehension before the shrug of denial. He wouldn't stoop to doing a full nightly regimen including moisturizer, but she'd walked in on him trying some of the Dr. Hauschka. Judith planned on picking up some more bottles in preparation for the eventuality. She felt sure he'd keep his hidden in the other drawer, or in the medicine cabinet.

He lumbered toward bed in just boxers, and she handed him the book. He rested it on the nearby bookcase. David in just boxers signaled sex. She took off her nightgown and panties, handed them to him, as well. He stripped out of his boxers, and climbed into bed, settling the covers around him.

It would take about five, ten minutes of conversation for him to be ready.

"So. Anybody call while we were gone?"

"Sarah," Judith said. "She wanted to know if I wanted to see her for lunch tomorrow. I think I'll go visit…she sounded a little lonely."

"Sarah. She was one of your friends from college, right?" He toyed with her shoulder, then absently with one breast.

She smiled. "She was my best friend from college. She was like my little sister. We roomed together as freshmen, in the dorms."

"Little sister? Is she younger than you?"

Judith shrugged. He was stroking a little more insistently. "She always seemed younger. She changed her major four times," she said with a laugh. "She just always needed to…I don't know. She had trouble getting it together."

He laughed, his deliberate caressing sidetracked for a moment. "You two must have been the *Odd Couple,* redux."

"I helped her, a little. She's nice. You just want to give her a hand." Judith stared at the ceiling. "Still, I was really glad that she got involved with Benjamin. He is a very stabilizing force for her. Now, if she could just get him to the altar…"

David looked at her for a moment. "You say his name funny. Like it's a title or something."

"Do I?" She thought about it. "He's the consummate salesman, from what I can tell. I've never met anybody more driven in my life.''

''Not even you?'' He resumed stroking. She ignored the ticklish sensation as he traced across her stomach, and consciously moved so he'd tickle elsewhere. He didn't notice.

''He went through his M.B.A. program in record time, but he still went for sales—something about his personality. Very charismatic.''

''The guy's got some redeeming features, right?''

That would be jealousy. Lately, David's ego was bruising a bit more easily. Judith made sure some of her skin rubbed lightly against his developing erection.

''He's loyal, I think.'' Even as she said it, she wasn't sure. ''At least, I hope so, for Sarah's sake. He shouldn't be long in moving, anyway. A man shouldn't be left to his own devices for very long.''

''Why not?''

''He's young, attractive, good income, good car, going places. Women target men like that—and men like that find women who target hard to resist, I get the feeling. Sarah would be smart to keep an eye on him, until they're married.''

The erection was still hovering at semihard, and Judith studied him to gauge possible problems. This might be a blowjob night. Damn.

He was staring at her with a look that was part fascination and part disgust. ''Target, huh? That sounds downright eerie.''

''I don't make the rules.''

"You just live by them, right?"

She inched away from him, irritated. Why couldn't he just enjoy this and go to sleep? "I didn't say that."

"You didn't have to."

He needed coddling, apparently. She should have chosen more appropriate foreplay conversation, but work was pressing her a little too hard recently. She needed to get back into her meditation. With a sigh, she concentrated harder. Leaning over, she kissed him rather thoroughly. "I landed you, didn't I?" she asked, and was glad to feel the familiar press against her inner thigh.

If it were that easy, he couldn't be too upset.

"That's right. You did land me. Damned good choice on your part." There was that overtone of the cocky lawyer back in his voice. He'd be energetic, she thought as she angled away from him. Chances were good he'd be relatively quick.

Within moments, he'd shut off the light. In the darkness, he felt him reach for her. Minutes after that, she was being pressed into the soft, enveloping mass that was her mattress pad, foam egg crate, and gently resilient Sealy-Posturepedic mattress. She deliberately moaned, getting louder when his breathing picked up pitch.

When he groaned against her, she closed her eyes.

He rolled off of her and handed her her nightgown and underwear. She could feel his weight pressing down on the bed, his maneuvering his boxers back on, clumsily.

His breathing turned to snores not long after.

She put her clothes back on with a bare minimum of movement, careful not to wake him. She could picture her Filofax in her mind, mentally scheduling a call to that meditation coach after her 10:00 a.m. meeting. Canceling her manicure. Seeing if there were a job opening for Sarah somewhere…maybe account management or H.R.

By the time she mentally got to the section of the day labeled Go To Bed, she fell asleep.

Chapter 2

Take It As It Comes

The next morning, it took Sarah a few minutes to figure out where she was. Sunlight was pouring in cruelly through the bedroom window. Los Angeles, she thought groggily. She was in bed, in her new bedroom, in her new apartment.

She had absolutely no recollection of how she got there. Or why her head was pounding.

She glanced down.

Or, to add to matters, why she was wearing her clothes.

The doorbell rang, and she groaned, stumbling out of bed. Well, the door was locked, even if the dead bolt wasn't, she noticed. Small blessings. She hit the intercom. "Hello?" she croaked.

"Sarah, darling? It's me, Taylor."

Taylor? She flipped through her mental Rolodex. "Taylor…"

"Gorgeous man who tucked you in yesterday, sweetie. Come on, be a good girl and open up…oh, never mind, here's a gentleman getting the door. Up in a second."

She stood there, listening to the door shut with agonizing loudness. Her heart started beating a little faster.

How could you have been so stupid?

Last night was a blur, but she did remember the stylish giant she'd had dinner with. At least, she remembered him to a point. She closed her eyes, swaying a little as she did so, fighting to remember. She'd managed to knock out a bottle of Ravenswood Cabernet with a six-foot-five stranger. He'd helped her to get to her door…she seemed to recall being carried part of the way, or did she dream that?

He *had* tucked her in, she seemed to remember. He'd given her a kiss on her forehead, and said he'd be back in the morning.

She hastily went over to her purse, pawing through it. Well, the credit cards were still there, as was her cash.

How could you have been so stupid? She'd let a complete stranger, no matter how "nice" he was, into her house! And let him lock up after himself! After getting drunk with him!

A sharp knock on the door rapped her out of her thoughts. Her heart pounded painfully in her chest.

He could be some kind of serial killer. Don't you open the door!

"Sarah? Sweetie, open the door, it's just me."

She stayed silent for a minute.

"Sarah." She heard him let out an irritated sigh. "Come on, I know you're there, and I've got something that will fix you right up."

She thought about going to the kitchen, getting a knife or something. She couldn't lock the dead bolt without being…

Without being what? Rude?

There was a long pause. "Oh, baby, don't be this way," she heard him finally say, obviously pitching his voice deeper. "After you slept with me last night, I thought…"

She gasped, and before she could think the better of it threw open the door. "I did *not* sleep with you!"

She looked up and saw him grinning at her. "Well, *obviously*. But I figured you'd open the door if I said you did."

She was blushing. She knew she was blushing.

"Mind if I come in for a sec? These are a little heavy."

Without really waiting for an invitation, he walked in, followed by another man. She eyed them both nervously.

Taylor was resplendent in a sparkling white T-shirt and jeans that looked like they were pressed, with various holes that were obviously cut in the knees for artistic effect, not worn-out naturally. He was carrying what looked like two cases of soda. "I figured eleven was late enough to come over. Kit? Could you give her the coffee?"

The other man was lanky, with sandy-brown hair tucked under a backward baseball cap. He wore a gray T-shirt and a pair of khaki cargo pants which sported holes that were probably from actual use, as well as a scuffed pair of suede sneakers. He looked short next to Taylor, but she guessed he was maybe six foot. "Welcome…to Jurassic Park," he said, and handed her a foam cup with a lid.

She looked at Taylor nervously, and he rolled his eyes. "You'll get used to Kit. He's my DSF."

"DSF?" she asked.

"Designated Straight Friend."

"So nice to fill a quota," Kit said, shrugging.

She smiled weakly, then sipped the coffee. It was good. The headache retreated a few millimeters. In fact, she would have felt a lot better if the doorbell hadn't chosen to ring at that particular moment.

"Yes?"

"Sarah? It's Judith. I was in the neighborhood, so I thought I'd take you to lunch."

Sarah glanced at the dynamic duo in her living room. "Um…it'll take me a little bit to get ready…"

"Just let me in, Sarah. I'll wait."

Sarah buzzed the entry button, then glanced at the men. "That was my friend Judith," she explained.

Taylor smiled, obviously not getting the point—that

she wanted them out of there. "So, this is your place?"

"Such as it is," she said. "There's two bedrooms and a bathroom."

"Heaven." Without being asked (much like when he entered her apartment) he peeked into both rooms. "Spacious. You wouldn't happen to be looking for a roommate, would you? I know someone who's looking…"

"No," she said emphatically, then rubbed at her temples. *Okay, less emphasis. On* everything *this morning.* "I'm…my boyfriend is moving down."

"Oh, right. The guy you mentioned last night." He sent a skeptical glance to Kit. Sarah scowled.

"I'm sure he'll…"

Judith stepped in the half-opened door. "Sarah? Hi. I thought, since it's eleven, it wouldn't be too…" She stopped stock-still, and took in Taylor and Kit. "Oh. I didn't realize you had company." She arched one inky-black eyebrow at Sarah. "Friends of yours?"

Sarah looked away. "Well…"

"I'm sorry, I should have introduced myself. It's what I'm best at," Taylor said, offering one of his huge hands. Judith was surprised into shaking it. "I'm Taylor, one of Sarah's neighbors. This is Kit." Kit didn't shake hands with Judith, he simply nodded. "Kit is just Kit."

"I see. And how well do you know Sarah?"

Taylor's expression was almost gleeful. "Oh, about as well as someone can get to know another person after getting completely plastered with them. Sarah's a cutie-pie,'' he pronounced, and if he reached over to pinch her cheek, she wouldn't have been surprised. ''I think we'll keep her.''

''Sarah?'' Judith was looking more anxious than disapproving now.

''Taylor's okay,'' Sarah said, and realized that she really did believe he was. ''Taylor, thanks for stopping by and, um, checking on me.''

''No problem.'' He ignored Judith's stares, and sidled up to Sarah, dropping to a mock whisper. ''No offense, my dear, but you might want to jump in the shower and change before you brunch with Ms. Mom. You'll feel much better.''

''I was planning to,'' she said.

''Oh, and here.'' He handed her a can from the case of soda he had carried in and put on her kitchen table.

''What's this?''

''Fabulous stuff. Buy it in Chinatown by the caseload,'' he said. She realized she couldn't read the label—she thought the label was Chinese, or possibly Korean. ''I like to call it Hangover Remover. You chug that down like a good girl. Do you club?''

Her eyes widened. ''Um…''

He smiled, and it was like being smiled on by a benevolent god. ''You are so sweet! Well, we'll stick to dinners first, but I *like* you,'' he said expansively. She liked him, too, she realized. ''Here.'' He reached into his back pocket, and pulled out a business card. She read it: ''Taylor Mayerling. Marketing Communications Manager, Demille Plastics Company.''

''Plastics?'' she said.

Kit grinned. "There is a great future in plastics."

"*The Graduate*. That's *so* easy." Taylor frowned at him, then turned back to Sarah. "Well, it's not sexy, but it's a paycheck."

"I hear you," Sarah said, then winced again.

"Gotta run, but you call me and we'll do dinner. I'd ask for your number, but…" He looked at Judith and smiled. "Well, some other time. Oh!" He took the card back, grabbed a pen off of her table and wrote on the other side.

She glanced at his hasty scrawl. "Martika?"

"That's her number. If you change your mind about the roomie thing, give her a call."

He hugged her, and it was nice—even if Judith was frowning. Kit just gave her a friendly half nod, and the two of them trooped out, closing the door behind them.

"Who *were* those characters?" Judith said.

Sarah smiled, looking down at the card. "Friends," she said. "My first friends here."

Judith's lips pursed. "You really need to be more careful, Sarah. They could be dangerous."

"Do you really think so?"

"Sarah," Judith said. Now that the men were gone, disapproval replaced fear. "Honestly. This isn't Fairfield."

"So. We're having brunch?" Sarah didn't want to be reminded, or lectured.

"I know you're looking for *the perfect job,* but I thought you might want to try advertising. I mean, you've done P.R. and a little ad sales, so why not try the agency?''

Ordinarily, Sarah would have considered the agency on the same level as, say, becoming a free-lance sump pump service tech. But she didn't have a lot of options. ''I'm a little less picky than I thought I'd be,'' Sarah replied.

Judith smiled. ''I thought we'd eat and go over your résumé. I seem to remember a spot opening up on Account Management,'' Judith said, all business now. ''I don't have any particular restaurant in mind, but I'm sure there's going to be something fairly close by. This is West Hollywood, after all.''

''What, is that a good restaurant part of town?''

Judith sent her a little puzzled grin. ''Sarah...don't you *know* about West Hollywood?''

Sarah frowned. ''What about it?''

''Your friend Taylor is a shining example of the residents of West Hollywood,'' Judith said.

''So what?'' Sarah huffed impatiently. ''I like Taylor. And he's right, I need to shower and change my clothes real quick...''

''Notice how many men are around here?'' Judith interrupted. ''Good-looking, well dressed....''

Something tugged at Sarah's hangover-fogged consciousness. A very faint light went on. ''Wait a minute. You mean, I'm living in the...''

''Gay district,'' Judith said, nodding. ''I thought everybody knew.''

"Oh." Sarah blinked.

Benjamin wasn't going to be thrilled about this. She could just tell.

Just get the job, Sarah.

Sarah stood in Becky Weisel's office, in the ad agency where Judith worked, albeit on a higher floor. It was a corner office, the kind that looked out over the city, with glass windows rather than walls. She had a full cherry-wood desk set, complete with credenza and bookshelves. Sarah could see little placards and inspirational quotes engraved on chotchke. Sarah waited while Becky finished the phone call, holding her portfolio awkwardly in front of her like a high school student.

She hated the interview process. Still, as Benjamin pointed out, those bills weren't going to be paying themselves.

And I don't need him to pay them for me.

Becky impatiently motioned her to take a chair, which she did.

"John, I didn't ask for the numbers for first quarter sales to be on my desk by Monday. I asked you to get them to me *today*." Becky paused slightly. "That was this morning, John. You don't need to whine at me, I know what the time difference is. Just do it, okay?" She sighed, obviously listening to whoever was on the other end of the phone. "Listen, would you rather deal with Stefan? I can patch him over the next time he calls to chew my ass out." She waited again, then smiled smugly. "Great. I'll look forward to seeing them tonight."

She hung up the phone, then looked at Sarah, as if trying to reorient herself. "Right. Who are you, and why are you here?"

Before Sarah could answer, Becky snapped her fingers. "Oh, *right*. You must be...let's see...Sarah." She reached across the desk, shaking Sarah's hand with a firmness that bordered on painful. "I'm Becky Weisel. I'm one of the Account Supervisors here at Salamanca Advertising."

She leaned back against her leather seat, surveying Sarah. Sarah sat up straighter, trying to make the best impression possible. It was *Let's Make A Deal*. She was doing everything except holding a sign that said "Hire me! Hire me!"

Sarah smiled at the thought. The friendly gesture seemed to give Becky pause.

"So...why do you want to work at Salamanca Advertising?"

Because I like paying my rent. "I've read it's a great firm, really up-and-coming, with cutting-edge advertising and a lot of high-tech clients..." At least, that's what the Web site had mentioned. Sarah had had only a few minutes to go over it prior to the interview.

Becky smiled. "Done your homework. Like that. And friendly. That always helps."

"Thank you."

"And polite." Becky looked like she was buying a car. Sarah hoped she wasn't going to kick her tires, as it were—or check her teeth, to mix metaphors. "All right. You're better than most of the applicants

I've seen, I've got to tell you that.'' She glanced down at the copy of the résumé Sarah had faxed to her. She made a few inarticulate noises of acknowledgment. Sarah sat quietly. ''Hmm. P.R....and some education...kind of all over the place, aren't you?''

Sarah felt her stomach drop a little. ''I'm still narrowing my focus,'' she explained. ''I have a lot of interests...''

''How old are you?''

Sarah blinked. That was an illegal question—this woman ought to know that.

Becky's smile turned crafty. ''You don't mind me asking that, do you?''

Sarah felt stunned, but found herself shaking her head slowly. ''No, of course not,'' she said, thinking about her bank account...the way the savings number slowly decreased. Rent was coming due soon. ''I'm twenty-five.''

''That's not so old,'' Becky said dubiously, then laughed. ''You've got plenty of time, I guess. And maybe advertising is just what you've been looking for.''

Sarah took a deep breath, feeling as if she'd somehow passed a test. ''That's what I'm hoping.''

''Great. How's your Excel? PowerPoint? We do a lot of presentations here.''

Sarah nodded. Now she was on familiar ground. ''I've got a lot of experience in all of the Microsoft Office Suite.''

''How do you feel about overtime?'' Becky asked.

"We work on big projects for important clients here, Sarah. I need somebody I can count on."

Sarah felt her spine straighten, and she nodded her head proudly. "I am willing to work overtime if a project needs finishing. I want to do the best possible job I can." She wondered if that last touch was a little too kiss-ass, then decided she didn't care. Besides, a little overtime wouldn't kill her. It wasn't like she had a social life to speak of in this town.

Becky's eyes flashed. Sarah had obviously jumped through the second hoop. What else... "We ask people to do things that are outside of their job description here. I'm going to need you to be versatile, and really think outside the box. Are you willing to do that?"

Sarah nodded. "Of course." Outside the box. Good grief. Next thing, she'd be saying, *We need someone who's a people person and a team player who displays over-the-line accountability.*

Becky leaned back, all but putting her hands behind her head as she smiled triumphantly. "I don't usually do this, but I have a really good feeling about you, Sarah. What would you say if I offered you a job, right now?"

Sarah goggled, then got a hold of herself. "We might want to discuss pay," she said instead, feeling shaky.

Becky laughed. "Well of course! Well put, shows you're paying attention." She named a figure. Sarah did some quick math. It would cover her rent...if she lived very, very spartanly.

And, say, didn't turn on her lights.

I don't know what the next job offer's going to be, either. Or when. And Benjamin isn't going to help me.

Sarah weighed, decided. Nodded. "That seems fine."

Becky's quick smile sealed the deal.

Sarah would be starting work that following Monday. It was now Thursday. Rent was coming due Tuesday.

She needed help.

How do you expect to survive in L.A. without me? Benjamin's voice rang in her head.

She'd find help somewhere else.

There, on the coffee table in her barren-looking living room, sat Taylor's business card, with "Martika" written on it. Taylor's friend, Martika—the one looking for a roomie.

Possibly the help she was looking for.

She finally dialed Martika's number. It rang five times. She was about to hang up on the sixth when she heard a deep, sultry voice say, "This is me. And you are?"

"I'm sorry?" Sarah looked at the number. "Maybe I've misdialed…"

There was a pause on the other line. "Maybe you have. This is Martika."

Sarah winced. This was not starting off well. "Um, Taylor asked me to call you…"

"Taylor! That bitch, he hasn't called me, *and* he missed Beer Bust. Well, you can't be his new flame, unless something weirdly radical has changed in his life that he's not telling me," she said, all in a rush. Sarah thought she could hear her puffing cigarettes…there was a crackle, and Sarah realized that she had called Martika's cell phone. "So, what did he want you to call me for?"

Sarah paused. "Well, ah, he seemed to think you might be looking for a place to live, and I'm looking for a roommate…"

"Great! As a matter of fact, I am," she said. "Where are you?"

"Santa Monica and Robertson."

Martika squealed. Sarah had to pull the phone away from her ear. "Perfect! I'm right around the corner…and this is my spot. I hadn't realized Taylor would find me something so convenient. How do you know Taylor again?" Sarah started to answer, but was quickly cut off. "Dumb question. I'll be over in ten minutes. What's your address?"

Numbly, Sarah gave it to her, then heard her say "Be there in a sec. Byee!" and quickly clicked off.

Please, let her not be a psycho.

She still didn't quite know why she trusted Taylor as much as she did…maybe it was still gratitude at the fact that he'd at least given her one positive experience in this strange new world. She would have had a truly miserable night if she hadn't bumped into the flamboyant giant.

It was less than ten minutes when her intercom buzzed, and Martika announced her presence. Sarah buzzed her in, praying even as she walked to the door. When she opened it, she felt her jaw drop.

Martika was an Amazon. Easily five-ten, she had deep maroon hair that cascaded in curls down past her shoulder blades. She was wearing a pair of hip-hugging bell bottoms in a deep black, and a maroon top of a sort of silky material that sported some sort of Indian embroidery design at the bottom. She had on a black leather coat over it. She was wearing sunglasses perched on her head, ostensibly to keep the curls out of her face. Her face…it wasn't necessarily pretty, not in the vogue sort of way. She had large hazel eyes and a pug nose that looked odd on her. She had a strong chin, and a round face. She stared back at Sarah.

"I don't bite," she said pointedly. "At least, not until I get to know you."

Sarah shook herself. "Oh! Sorry. You must be Martika."

"I must be," she drawled, and walked in, her stacked heel half-boots making her stride seem even more impressive. She gave Sarah a little questioning look as she walked in, then let out a low whistle as her attention shifted from the owner of the apartment to the apartment itself. "Nice. Empty, but we could fix that in a minute. All yours?"

"Um, yes. Although it'd have to be month to month…"

"I wouldn't have it any other way," Martika said, eliminating that possible bone of contention. She went out to the balcony. "I guess this would be my smoking area...I can't stand smoking in the house, strangely enough. I like smoking, but hate smelling it all the time.''

"Okay," Sarah said.

Martika turned around, and studied Sarah again. Sarah felt...dowdy. And old, although she knew the woman was probably older than she was. "And you're Taylor's friend?" Martika asked.

"I know," Sarah said. "I have trouble believing it myself."

Martika laughed, a leonine laugh that matched the rest of her. Sarah was torn between admiring her and being intimidated by her. "So which room'd be mine?"

Sarah showed her. "I'd move the boxes, of course..."

"Oh, this would work out *fine,* just fine," Martika pronounced on the spot. "Great! So when could I move in?"

"Um..." Apparently, this was more of a done deal than she'd expected. "Don't you want to ask any questions about me?"

Martika looked at her, a sarcastic, wry expression on her very expressive face. "You look like..." She paused, as if editing her words. "Let's just say I trust you to pay your bills on time, sweetie, and leave it at that."

Sarah knew that wasn't a compliment, but didn't know what she could say to counter it. "I might need a little time to think about it."

Martika looked at her, curious and amused. "You don't like me, do you?"

"I don't even know you," Sarah protested. "How could I not like you?"

"I can just tell that about people. They get this poochy-faced little look that says, 'I may not know you, but you're definitely not my kind of people.' You haven't gotten that look yet," Martika said, ducking her head to meet the level of Sarah's face, "but you're working on it."

"I don't know what you're talking about," Sarah said, even though she did. "I just...I'm new to L.A."

Martika laughed. "I'd guessed, sweetie."

Sarah glanced around, trying to buy some time. She needed a roommate, but she'd already made one snap decision out of desperation this week. She was starting to develop a habit.

"It's just that I'm very linear," she said slowly, looking at Martika. "I get the feeling you're very... organic."

Martika stared at her, then burst out into another round of raucous laughter. "Oh, sweetie, if you keep popping out with gems like that, I may *have* to live here!" She chuckled. "No wonder you're a friend of Taylor's. You're so cute, I could eat you up with a spoon."

Sarah wasn't sure how to handle that comment. Things were already getting less linear by the minute.

"This will work out perfectly," Martika said with a flourish. "I'll have Taylor and the boys move me in on Saturday. Do you have a spare key?"

"Wait a second. I hadn't decided yet."

Martika shot her a skeptical look. "You've got rent on the first, right?"

"Well, yes."

"Where else were you thinking of looking for a roommate?"

Sarah fidgeted. "I hadn't…well, I'm still in preliminary stages," she hedged.

"In other words, you don't know," Martika said, cutting through her excuse. "Let me fill you in—if you advertise in the *L.A. Times,* you're going to get the crème de la crème of freak shows. If you go through an agency, you'll get the freaks that are willing to pay some clerk at a Mailboxes Etc. to put their name on a list…and you'll have to pay to find them. If you're going for someone who's willing to go month to month, you'll get somebody who probably likes to turn young Asian boys into patio furniture in his spare time." She did a slow twirl. "Or, you can get me—who's vouched for by Taylor."

Sarah winced.

"I don't even really think it's a question, do you?" Martika said mildly.

Sarah sighed. "I…er. I've got the spare key somewhere."

Martika smiled sweetly. "Wise choice."

Sarah smiled back uncertainly. *Glad one of us thinks so.*

Chapter 3

People Are Strange

"Well," Martika murmured, "it's not much, but it's home."

"I think we moved you in record time," Taylor drawled, surveying her new digs with the air of one bored with the process. "What, five hours?"

"I've unloaded a lot since last time."

"You mean, *besides* Andre?"

"Let's not be bitchy," Martika chastised, then stuck out her tongue at him before arranging her peacock feathers in a tall wooden vase in the corner. This looked much more homey. The way this Sarah chick had decorated—ick. It looked like corporate housing.

She was surprised the girl hadn't put a Sanitized For Your Protection banner across the toilet.

Kit glanced around, muttering incoherently.

"Sorry?"

He half smiled at her. She didn't think he ever full smiled. "I said, there's no place like home."

"*Wizard of Oz,*" Taylor said promptly.

Martika simply rolled her eyes. "You two still playing that game?"

Kit shrugged. Taylor started babbling. Martika grabbed her last moving box, labeled Private in big block print, and moved to the bedroom. This was always the last part of her unpacking ritual—the nightstands. She wondered how Andre would fare tonight, getting his bed out of storage, since the three pieces of furniture that she had since she was twenty-two was a California king bed and two nightstands. *Girl's gotta have her necessities,* she thought. She loaded up the nightstand on the right of the bed with condoms and a variety of oils and other lubricants, her handcuffs, and a few other knickknacks she'd picked up along the way. The one on the right was always for guests. The one on the left…she put her chicken-scratch-filled journal, loaded with the most disgustingly self-pitying poetry ever spouted on earth, a few Chunky bars, several boxes of cigarettes, a vibrator and a pack of gum.

That drawer wasn't for anybody else.

She closed it with a nod, and headed out. The guys were on the couch. Sarah was giving them glasses of lemonade. *How very Martha Stewart,* Martika thought with a grin.

This was already weird. She hadn't roomed with a girl in longer than she could remember—and a girl like this, the native version of F.O.B. She supposed Sarah was F.O.F…Fresh Outta Fairfax. Or whatever the name of her Podunk town was.

"Well, looks like I'm all settled in," Martika said.

Sarah was nodding as she looked around, clearly bewildered. "It's…more than I expected."

Was that disapproval? Martika smiled. God, she hoped so. "Well, when I move someplace, I like to…"

"Take it over?" Luis, Taylor's boyfriend, commented with a nasal whine.

Martika grinned at him, feeling her anger start to turn over a little. She usually couldn't take Luis for longer than, oh, fifteen minutes. She'd now been with him for over six hours, and if the man realized how close to death he was…

She shrugged it off, searching for lemonade. At least the asshole moved the bed in. You made allowances.

"Well, everything looks great," Sarah said in a soft voice behind her.

"Thanks." Martika smiled a little more easily. Kid's shy, she thought, but there's potential there. "I'm a graphic designer, did I mention that?"

"No."

"Well, I am. I like to have artistic things around me." She noted that almost all of the prints up were hers. "It's all about atmosphere, presentation...you know."

Sarah nodded, although Martika doubted she understood a damned word. She was doing that agreeing-to-be-agreeable thing.

"I mean, what did *you* think you were saying with the apartment before?" she pressed.

"Um...." Sarah blinked, very deer-in-headlights, at being put on the spot. "This space for rent?"

Martika laughed. Definite potential.

She wandered back out to the living room. "Well. I'm starving." Translation: We are now going out to eat. She looked around expectantly.

Taylor looked happy at the proclamation, Luis looked sour at spending time with her (*ah, but I'm so looking forward to bonding with you!* she thought with a smile), and Kit...well, Kit just looked the same as he usually did. She had tried getting him to sleep with her, but she suspected he must actually bat for Taylor's team, no matter what Taylor said about him being a DSF. She just had a feeling about this sort of thing.

"So. Where are we eating?"

Luis spoke up. "Why not Trader Vic's?"

She shot Taylor a glance. He shrugged, embarrassed. She rolled her eyes, communicating quite clearly: *Well, you're the one fucking him.* She shook her head. "Let me try this again. So. Where are we eating?"

"What? What?"

"Too tacky," Taylor explained.

"If I wanted to spend that kind of money to see a bunch of old white men, I'd go to Le Dome," Martika added, causing Luis to pout.

"How about Le Dome?" Kit put in sardonically.

She thought she heard Sarah giggle at that, again softly, but when she turned around Sarah's face was impassive.

"Hmm…obviously I'm going to…ooh! How about L.A. Farm? I haven't been in ages." There! A viable alternative. "They've got a great vegetarian spread."

"So you're vegetarian this week?" Kit asked.

She frowned at him. "Like you're even going, Kit."

Kit shrugged. "Nope. Working a shift at the coffeehouse."

"Didn't anybody tell you? The grunge scene is over."

"It's retro."

Taylor shook his head. "Working at a coffee shop on a Saturday night seems just *wrong,* somehow. Going to the club with us later? I thought Asylum, just for kicks."

Kit shrugged. "I guess. I'll catch up with you later."

"Lovely. So L.A. Farm it is," Martika said, and glared at Luis, who looked ready to dissent.

"Sure," Taylor said, and Luis did *not* look pleased. "Just give me time to run home and change…I'm not going all sweaty and stinky like *this.*"

She laughed, then looked at Sarah. She was standing there, very wallflowerish. Well, now was as good a time as any to test the new girl. "What about you? I'll give you forty minutes to get ready, but only because I'm going to use the bathroom first." She winked, to show she was kidding. Although she really wasn't.

Sarah cleared her throat. "No. I'm sorry. I'd love to, but I can't."

"You're just saying that," Martika said. Sarah sounded so polite it was painful. "Come on. It'll be fun, and I really do want you there. Think of it as an initiation ritual."

"Like hazing," Kit offered. "I name you...Pinto."

"*Animal House,*" Taylor interjected.

"Shut up." Martika studied Sarah's face. "So how about it?"

"I really can't," Sarah said, and there was a trace more firmness in her voice. "My boyfriend—that is, my *fiancé,* is going to be calling me tonight."

"Oh?" She raised her eyebrow, then glanced at Taylor. He rolled his eyes, and formed a small "W" with his thumbs and index fingers. She didn't think that Sarah caught it, and even if she did, she doubted she'd put it together.

Whatever, Taylor was telling her. And he'd fill Martika in on the rest of it later, no doubt.

"Fine," she said, shrugging. So her new roommate was...boring. Well, hell. It's not like she had to sleep with her. "Wouldn't want to get in the way of true love. I'm going to use the bathroom, sweetie, so if you've got to pee, better do it now...I could be a while."

"I'll be back here in an hour, Tika," Taylor said with a tone of warning.

"I'll be ready," she said, shuffling the boys out the door. After she closed it, she turned to Sarah, only to find her still staring. "You sure? You could always call him back later. Or tomorrow."

Sarah just gave her a cool smile. "Thanks anyway."

She shrugged, then headed for the bathroom, remembering belatedly to shut the door before she started stripping. She doubted Sarah would be amenable to her relatively exhibitionist ways.

Well, Martika thought as she stepped into the shower, I've shacked up with a nun who's pining away for some absentee boyfriend. Joy. Fun.

Two choices: get ready to move again, which was unpalatable. Or start corrupting the girl.

Martika smiled against the force of the water hitting her face. Like there was even a question there.

It was Saturday night...rather, it was Sunday morning, Sarah thought, blearily looking at the clock. She had woken up, and initially she wasn't sure why: 3:00 a.m. What the hell?

She hadn't had a great Saturday night, frankly. She had waited for Benjamin to call...then had left a message on his machine at work and at home, and still waited. By eleven, she had made herself a hot chocolate, thought about it, dumped a little rum in and went to bed. She'd plowed through *Bridget Jones* and enjoyed it thoroughly, then switched gears and was now reading *Harry Potter.* She had gone to sleep, curled in a ball by eleven o'clock. Now, 3:00 a.m., and she was...

"Oh... *Oh...* Oh, yeah, baby, like that..."

Sarah went still, like a frightened mouse. The sounds were growing louder. They reminded her of Martika's shower singing, all low and throaty.

Sarah got up and crept to her half-opened bedroom door. She peeked out. It was dark, and Martika's bedroom door was closed. She could hear the bedsprings creaking wildly, picking up in speed.

Horribly embarrassed, Sarah shut her door quietly, all the way. In the deathly stillness of the early morning, she could still hear the noises, which were starting to gain a bit in volume. Looking around, she saw her fuzzy terry-cloth bathrobe hanging from a hook on her closet door. She threw it down across the crack of the door, hoping to muffle some of the sound. Still no help. She crawled back into bed, yanking a pillow over her head and pushing it against her ear. And the flannel and fleece lap blanket her mother had given her for Christmas from Costco, saying that it did get cold at nights.

Martika, Sarah reflected, might not have been the great idea Taylor thought it'd be.

On that Thursday night, almost a full week of work at Salamanca and a paid month's rent behind her, she felt downright jubilant.

"Benjamin Slater."

"Jam, it's me. Sarah."

"Sarah." She thought she could hear the smile in his voice. "Hey there. How are things going in L.A.? I was going to call you Saturday."

"I figured I'd jump the gun," she said. "Guess what? I got a job!"

"I knew you would," he said. "What are you doing?"

"I'm an assistant account executive at Salamanca Advertising Agency. That's where Judith works, but I'm not working with Judith—she's in production. I'm on the account management side."

"That's great, honey."

"I've been really busy, and it's only been the first few days..."

"I've been swamped, myself," he said, with a heavy sigh.

She paused. "Any luck with Richardson? I'm not trying to push."

"None. I have to make the assumption that Andrew—the V.P., you know?—that he's making good on his promise to get me out of there. So Cal could use somebody like me. That's what he said."

"That's great, Jam."

"So just a few more months, and then I'll be able to move down," he said. "I just have to make it up here in the meantime."

"I'm sure you will," she said warmly.

"Actually, I can't talk long," he said. "Paul Jacobs and, well, some people from the L.A. office are up for a visit—I promised I'd go out for a few beers with them. You know, blow off some steam."

She bit her lip. "Um, okay."

"It's just a few beers, Sarah." He sighed again, this time a little more irritably. "It's not like I'm going out and boinking a bunch of coeds."

"I know that!" she replied. What, did she expect him to stay in every night, just because she wasn't up there with him?

Still, a little more pining would be comforting, she thought, then brushed the thought aside.

"Sarah! *Saaa-rah…*" Martika called from the frame of Sarah's bedroom door. "You wanna come out with us? We're drinks."

Sarah frowned, then motioned to the phone that she held to her ear. Martika huffed irritably, then retreated to the living room.

"Sorry," Sarah muttered.

"Who the hell was *that?* I thought you were at home."

"I am," Sarah replied. "That was…well, I couldn't quite make rent just on my salary. So I took on a roommate."

There was a pause as Benjamin digested that fact.

"It wasn't my idea," Sarah assured him hastily. "Besides, Martika knows that it's month-to-month…"

"Martika? What the hell sort of name is that?"

"I don't know. Danish, I think." Okay, that was a shot in the dark.

"I told you that I'd make it down to Los Angeles as soon as Richardson gives me a goddamn chance, Sarah. I didn't tell you to get a roommate."

Sarah frowned. ''What you *told* me was that I had to cover rent on this apartment—this *considerably more expensive apartment,* I might add—by myself. Since you're not living here yet. Really, realistically, what would you have had me do, Jam?''

''Dammit, Sarah, I didn't…don't get all touchy on me, okay? I *really* don't need this right now.''

Like I do?

She sighed. ''I'm just saying I didn't have a lot of options.''

''I see.'' He made a low grumbling sort of sound. ''Well, you're right, of course. It's better that you got a roommate. Just… Did you do a thorough search?''

Sarah crossed her fingers—childish, granted. ''Sure I did. She's a friend of a friend of mine, so it wasn't like getting a complete stranger.''

''Huh. What's she like?''

She thought about Martika's late night sex-a-thons. ''Um, she's very social.''

''Social?''

''Yes,'' Sarah said hastily, ''but responsible. I mean, she's kicked in for half of the bills already, on time, and she's a graphic designer.''

''I see.'' He didn't, obviously—his tone said that much. ''Did she just say something about drinking?''

Sarah shrugged. ''I think she wants me to go out with…them.'' She was going to say *her and Taylor,* but she suddenly didn't want to explain Taylor. That whole incident was something Benjamin would definitely frown upon.

Too late. "Well, I think you might want to consider before you go out."

"Consider what?" Sarah felt a little burn of anger. "You're going out for beers with the guys. I'd just have, I don't know, a drink or two with Martika."

"L.A. isn't Fairfield, you know. It's a more dangerous city."

Sarah thought of Martika and Taylor, the imposing duo. "I think I'll be fine."

"You're so naive sometimes," he said. "Fine. Do whatever you think is best. I have to go."

"I'll be sure not to boink any coeds," she replied, wanting to lighten the conversation a little.

He laughed, as she hoped he would. "I'll talk to you next week."

"Love you," she said quickly.

"You, too," he said. He clicked off.

What was *that* all about? Sarah hung up the phone, pensive. She wanted to believe he was just being protective—but part of her felt like he was just maintaining some sort of double standard.

He's going out and having beers with the guys. Why shouldn't I go out?

After all, he was the one who said that she just clung to him like a vine. If anything, this would be…asserting her independence, she thought.

She went out to the living room. Martika was in the labor-intensive process of lacing up her knee-length black leather boots. "Martika?"

"Mmm?"

"Is that invitation still open?"

Martika looked up from her boots. "Really? You'll really go?"

"Just for a little bit," Sarah hedged. "I've got a big day at work tomorrow."

"It's Friday. Who does much on Fridays?"

Sarah bit her lip. Maybe this *wasn't* such a good idea.

"You don't do anything much your first week," Martika said, as if countering Sarah's resistance. Then she flashed her a quick, mischievous grin. "Besides, I told Taylor you weren't going to come anyway. You'd probably just curl up with a book and be asleep by ten or whatever."

Martika was doing everything but calling her chicken. She really didn't... "What, do I have 'Shirley Temple' written across my forehead or something?"

"You don't need it," Martika answered with a wink. "You practically introduce yourself that way. So, out to 5140 with me and Taylor? Just a few drinks, and I promise we'll get you home early since it's a school night."

"All right," Sarah said, ignoring the tail end of Martika's statement. "Just let me get my coat."

"This is historic," Martika said from the living room. "Next thing you know, I'll have you dancing with male strippers."

Sarah came back, tugging on her coat and then clutching her purse. "Just a few drinks," Sarah hastily added. She didn't want to do anything that would make Benjamin right about her being naive. "No strippers, nothing like that."

"Careful, Shirley," Martika said with a wicked smile. "You're backsliding."

"Maybe 5140 wasn't the best place to take her for her first time out," Taylor said with a note of concern.

Martika leaned back against the slick red vinyl cushion of the booth they were sitting in. The lights were dim enough to cause your pupils to dilate like dinner plates. Sarah sat huddled against one corner, trying as hard as she could to blend into the scenery.

Martika sighed…5140 was a fairly rough-and-tumble bar, nice and seedy, with none of the Holly-wood club kids or the college pricks from West L.A. and Santa Monica. As good a testing ground as any.

"So, can I get you another drink?" Martika asked as politely as she could, considering she needed to yell to get over the blasting jukebox.

Sarah shook her head vehemently, clutching her piña colada with a weak smile. "I'm fine. Thank you, though," she said politely, doing her Martha Stewart impression again. She glanced around, as if she were sightseeing in a demilitarized zone.

Taylor scooted next to her. "Don't worry, girlie-girl, Martika just likes dives." He grinned at her. *"Trashy."*

"Drama," she said back, blowing him a kiss. "I do like dives. Less pretentious." She turned her gaze on Sarah. "What do you think?"

Sarah bit the corner of her lip, looking around.

"It's...surprisingly roomy," she offered, with a hopeful look.

"Roomy," Martika repeated, as Taylor roared with laughter. "That's a good description. Roomy. Well, I'm going to go see if I can't make it over the vast expanse to the bar," she said, tilting her empty glass. "I could do for a refill. Taylor?"

"Another currant martini, please."

She smiled, heading over to the bar, noticing several of the guys at the bar were watching her as she walked. She was used to it, sending them a killer smile then ignoring them.

She'd finally taken Taylor's advice and decided to live with somebody she wasn't planning on sleeping with, and she wound up with a virgin schoolgirl. Irony. Like a continual cosmic joke.

Still, the kid had potential—and she got the feeling that that phone conversation Sarah had been on was with her boyfriend/fiancé/whatever. And that it hadn't gone well, if she was going out with Martika & Crew.

"One watermelon shot and one currant martini," she said to Bill, the bartender. He nodded, quickly making up the drinks. "Oh, and another piña colada," she said. "Strong."

He added the third. "You gonna pay off that tab anytime soon, Tika?"

"I get paid next Friday," she said, with a wink, and deftly balanced the three drinks, carrying them while still managing to wiggle her hips. She put them down on the small table in front of the chatting Sarah and Taylor with a plunk. "Bottoms up, people."

"I've still got half a drink," Sarah protested.

"Well then," Martika drawled, "you'd better hurry, huh?"

Sarah's eyes grew round.

"Taylor...would you care to show her how?"

Taylor grinned. "Not really, as I'm forced to drive during this excursion. Besides, I'm supposed to see Luis later this evening, and he hates it when I'm plowed without him." He sipped genteelly from the martini glass instead, then made a florid gesture at her own shot glass. "You show her. You're the pro, anyway."

Sarah said, "You want me to just chug this, don't you?"

Martika was surprised into a real smile. *"Chug?"*

"I know. I'm not *that* sheltered," she said. "I'm not good at that sort of thing, though, I have to warn you."

"Well, show me what you've got."

Sarah screwed up her face for courage, then took the half-drunk piña colada and finished it off in about eight manful swallows. Martika grinned at Taylor, watching the debacle.

Sarah took a deep breath. Her pale cheeks were flushed and pink—from the alcohol or from the time that it took her to drink it without pausing for air, Martika wasn't sure.

"There. I did it."

Taylor made a polite golf clap. "Brava."

"Now the other one," Martika said. "A little faster, this time."

"But…I have to go to work tomorrow!"

"Two piña coladas isn't going to put you under the table," Martika said, with an exasperated sigh. "Besides, we haven't even gone to a club yet. This is just warm-up."

As Taylor started to protest that he needed to make this an early night (*"I promised Luis!"*) Martika noticed that Sarah was going from flushed to pale.

"I think I'll just nurse this one."

Martika shrugged. "Suit yourself." She took her watermelon shot, and with a quick snap of the wrist threw it back, feeling more than tasting the quick tang of Midori before being hit with the slight flame of alcohol. She put the glass down, smiling at Sarah. "One piña colada, and you're trashy. This is downright epic."

"I didn't say I was trashy. I just said I had to go to work tomorrow."

"What is it you do again?"

"I'm an assistant account executive," she said. Her dilated eyes *were* beginning to look a little out of focus. "At Judith's…that's my friend." She took another sip of the piña colada, as if she weren't thinking about it—like she was just thirsty. "My friend Judith, who you haven't met."

"I have," Taylor said, also noticing that Sarah was slowly working down her drink. "Judith makes this one look like you."

"Wow. Guess I'll have to not meet her, then."

Taylor chuckled. Sarah sipped.

In an hour, Sarah had sipped her way through another piña colada and was getting surprisingly talkative. The club idea was out—the girl was weaving as they got her into the car, something Martika thought completely hysterical and Taylor found "charming."

"I've gotten so used to you stereotypical Irish two-fisters that it's been a while to see a ladylike, girl-drink-drunk," he said. Martika frowned at him.

"I'm ladylike."

"Sure," Taylor patted her cheek. "And I'm Keanu Reeves."

"Good night, Keanu!" Sarah said, and abruptly started hiccupping. "Oh, God. Hope I don't yuke."

"You and me both, sister," Martika said, propping her up in the elevator. "Four piña coladas and you're a mess. This is so funny."

Martika guided her back to the apartment. She was still talking in that little girl voice of hers.

"So I'm waiting for Jam to move back," Sarah confided earnestly. "Well, not back, it's not like he's lived here before. But you know what I mean."

"Sure." She grinned as she undid the top two dead bolts and finally got the door handle. "Although, if I hadn't heard the details from Taylor, I'd guess that Jam was your invisible friend rather than your fiancé."

"Well, he's sort of my invisible fiancé," she said, with a hiccupy little laugh.

"You said it," Martika pointed out, closing the door behind the wobbling Sarah. "Not me."

"I know. I don't mean to complain. I just *miss* him, that's all. Sometimes it doesn't seem like he misses me," she said. The tone was so matter-of-fact, Martika felt a pang of pain on her behalf. She wondered if Sarah were sober if she would have felt the pain. Then she realized—if Sarah were sober, she wouldn't be saying all of this. "So why do you stay with the guy?"

Martika knew she probably shouldn't counsel her roommate on her love life—but hell, she counseled all of her friends. And if anyone ever needed a mentor, it was this little drunk girl with the long blond hair—like a misplaced Norwegian waif.

Sarah stopped by the arm of the couch, in the middle of a very amusing tableau of trying to kick one shoe off with the other foot. "Why what?"

"If he's invisible, and you miss him, why do you stay with him?"

"Can't walk away," she mumbled, finally successfully kicking off one shoe and sighing. "I mean, you can't just give up on something like that. Besides, I love him. I couldn't walk away from somebody I loved."

"I can understand that," Martika said. Not about relationships. But say Taylor—she'd never walk away from him. "But the question is, does *he* love you? He seems to be hurting you an awful lot."

Sarah seemed to sober for a moment—like a kid at a high school party who had suddenly realized that her parents had come home. "He's not hurting me," she said, struggling with the other shoe. "He just... he's just busy. He needs me to understand. I'm trying to be very, very understanding."

Martika was understanding this whole thing a bit, herself. She frowned. The guy was an obvious asshole. Sarah really ought to dump him, move on. Maybe she'd start that campaign, too, as well as her campaign to "corrupt" the kid. "Well, as long as he's away, it doesn't matter how often you're out, right?"

Sarah thought about this for a minute, then grinned. "Nope. Doesn't, really. I'm sure he might mind if it were like every night or if it were interfering with my career..."

"Well, it won't."

"I'm just saying," Sarah said...then slumped into the couch. "I think I'm going to sleep right here."

"Oh, no, you're not," Martika said, tugging her to an upright position. She'd never seen somebody decompress quite this fast. "Shit. Come on, Sarah. You take Martika's advice—a few vitamins, a few aspirins and one huge glass of water. Then brush your teeth, and go to bed."

"What day is it?"

"Thursday, sweetie. Remember?"

"I think I have something important to do tomorrow, but I can't remember what."

"You'll remember tomorrow," Martika promised. "I swear, honey. Now get up and brush."

Chapter 4

Unhappy Girl

"Walker! Where the *fuck* have you been?"

Sarah stood stock-still, as if she'd been shot. Her slight headache made her feel as if she *had* been shot. "I beg your pardon?"

"I told everybody they needed to be in here early today!" Becky's eyes were glinting like gunmetal, and if she'd shot red lasers out of them, Sarah would have been no less surprised. "Early! What time is it?"

Sarah glanced at her watch, unsure if that was a rhetorical question or not. "Eight?" she said, glad that she'd set the alarm before she went out on the town.

"Goddam *eight.* Jacob has been in here since seven. Michelle has been here since goddamn *six.*"

Jacob and Michelle had not been hazed at 5140, either, Sarah reflected. She *knew* there was something she was supposed to do today. "I'm sorry," she said instead. Just when she was trying to make a good impression, too! She needed this job. She really, *really* needed this job!

Becky was not appeased. "I need you to input all of these—and *double check* this time—and Raquel's going to be busy doing copying for me, so I need you to go to the cleaners and get my suits. Goddam presentation is first thing Monday morning, we've got absolutely nothing worth showing yet, I need to pull off a goddamn miracle. If you're not careful, Sarah, you're not going to be staying here. Off the top of my *head,* I can think of twenty people who'd give their right arm to work for a place like Salamanca."

Oh, no. Sarah felt herself go clammy with shock. "I'm really very sorry," she breathed. "I know you've got a lot to do, and I want to make sure that everything gets done. No matter how much overtime it takes, I'll make sure you get what you need. On time."

Jacob and Michelle were staring at her with expressions of abject horror. Becky, on the other hand, looked speculative.

"Now there's team spirit. Much better," Becky said, with a smooth, pleased tone that gave Sarah the willies. "Why don't you come to my office after I finish up this conference call, and we can talk about that?"

"Sure," Sarah said, but Becky was already on her way. Once she'd left the room, Jacob turned to Sarah.

"Are you out of your mind?"

Sarah shrugged. "I'm trying to get a little more in my paycheck. I'm not going to prove anything by coming in hungover," she said, rubbing at her temples. "I'm just trying to show that I'm good at my job."

"You could come in here with a gun and they wouldn't fire you," Michelle said. "You're in for a world of pain, Sarah."

"You've got absolutely no idea," Jacob said, in sepulchral tones. "Brand review is coming. You're going to be in hell."

Sarah shrugged. "Aren't you exaggerating just a bit?"

Michelle looked at Jacob. "Cavalier little thing, isn't she?"

"You can't say you weren't warned," Jacob replied to Sarah instead. "I put five dollars on you cracking like a walnut in two weeks."

"I give her a month," Michelle said. "She looks like a scrapper."

Sarah sighed. "I'm going to go scrounge up some Tylenol before she gets finished with that call. And believe it or not, I'm going to make it."

Sarah was walking away as she heard Ernest down the hall call out, "Put me down for two months."

* * *

By the end of the fifth week, Sarah was bleary-eyed. She left the office at eight, Friday night, surprised that it was suddenly April. Thank God she did her taxes early this year…she didn't even know it was coming.

"Good night," she said to Schuyler, the portly security guard. He no longer asked her to show her badge. She'd been there the past five weekends and late every single night. He knew her on sight, and regularly asked her "how it was going."

"You get some rest, Miss Walker," he called after her.

She drove home, exhausted. It was only about twenty minutes back to West Hollywood from the Mid-Wilshire district, if that, but tonight traffic seemed particularly bad. She'd be back in at ten tomorrow morning—Becky was letting them have a little sleep-in before cracking down on yet another pointless presentation, complete with requisite numbers and velo-bound reports. God, she hated velo-binding.

She parked her car, noted that Martika's car was not there and sent up a little prayer. Probably out with Taylor, searching for this weekend's Random Fuck, as she so colorfully put it. She and Martika were not working out as well as she had hoped. Martika had tried to invite her out again, but after having her job threatened, Sarah made it a point of not joining Martika on her excursions. Martika was sort of hurt by this, and consequently cold, but there wasn't anything that could be done. Benjamin had been right—she was naive.

Now, Sarah would stumble in just as Martika was striding out, or sometimes at the same time as Martika stumbled in, with or without a companion. They only spoke about things like the utilities. Sarah had hoped to have a bit more friendly relationship with her room-mate. Now, she just prayed that Martika would pipe down and maybe put some WD-40 on her box springs.

She closed the door of her Saturn, hearing the alarm beep on. She made her way to the elevator from the parking garage and hit three, then leaned her head against the door as it slowly creaked its way upstairs. A bath. No, food. No, a bath, and then food. If she had food then the bath, she'd drown.

She stepped out of the elevator, then stopped abruptly. A figure, a *male* figure, was hovering by her doorstep. He had a dark coat, and his blond hair was...

"Jam?"

He turned, and his face was like a storm cloud. "I've been here for hours," he said, without preamble.

"I'm so sorry!" The response was automatic, like saying ouch when you stubbed your toe. "I didn't know. Why didn't you tell me you were going to come down?"

"I didn't really know myself. Screw up at the L.A. office...and they brought me in to 'consult' on some possible solutions to getting their numbers up. It's going to be soon, I'm telling you. The flights were delayed, so I figured I'd stay over a night and see you."

She wanted to feel more elated by the whole process, but felt weary as she fumbled for her keys. She let him in the apartment. "I'm so glad you made it," she said, wondering even as they spoke what kind of food she had around. They could do a restaurant. Of course, it was Friday night in WeHo. They were going to have a hell of a time getting a table. Maybe she could order a pizza.

"So this is the apartment. Huh. I haven't seen it since I signed the lease."

She paused, before hanging her key on the set of hooks under the pretty white wooden cabinet-looking thing that she used to separate mail for herself and Martika. Her mailbox had a cheerful yellow daisy on it…Martika's, a sticker of one of the Powerpuff girls. "Home sweet home," she said, wondering what his tone was all about.

"Hmm." He was studying the place minutely. Then he shrugged. "Pretty good sized. Seems like a nice enough neighborhood."

Sarah let out a breath she didn't even know she was holding. "I like it."

He scowled. "I think some guy was hitting on me in the lobby, though."

"Really?" Now was obviously *not* the time to explain West Hollywood to him. "How odd."

They wound up staying in and ordering pizza. Sarah wished she could take that hot bath, but he seemed in the mood to talk. They talked at length about his job, and she told him about the hell that was her boss and the ad agency. "I've got to go into work tomorrow, too," she said sorrowfully.

He didn't seem very sympathetic. "Honey, I've told you before...you've got to pay your dues. You didn't just think they'd give you some six-figure job you loved right out of school, do you?"

She hated it when he got patronizing, but she knew he was just trying to be helpful. "I didn't think that. I just didn't think I'd have to work every single day for a month going to a job that frankly makes me want to vomit every time I go in in the morning. Honestly, when I get sight of the building, my foot eases up off the accelerator."

He shook his head. "It's normal. If it were fun, you wouldn't get paid for it."

"Don't you think that's sad?"

He shrugged. "I think that's reality." He smiled, and it was one of his indulgent smiles. "Honey, you just want a little dream world."

"Guess I'm in the right city," she said, and went over to the bedroom.

He followed her in, sighing heavily. "Don't be this way," he said, in a voice that was persuasive but she knew could turn stern at the drop of a hat. "I've come all the way down to L.A. to see you. Do you really want to waste what little time we have fighting?"

She immediately felt the wave of guilt hit her, and she sighed. "No. I'm sorry."

"Then let's make up." He stroked the back of her

neck, then reached forward to unbutton her blouse. Within minutes, she was naked, on her back, while he went at her a little more quickly than she'd have liked. Of course, she'd been so tired lately, it wasn't like she was even really in the mood. She went through the motions of being interested as best she could, when all she could picture was her deep tub and scalding hot water. Maybe some lavender bubble bath. Mmm, she thought, smiling over his shoulder. Bubble bath. God, that sounded good.

Still, she was glad he was there, she thought as he shuddered and groaned, pushing against her. It had been a while. Besides, it was only twenty minutes out of an otherwise very long day.

Sarah turned over the next morning, and immediately gasped. *Shit, ten o'clock, ten o'clock, ten o'clock!* She prayed that Becky wasn't coming into the office this morning. She sort of doubted it…Becky usually had plans on the weekend, and she left the work to her "able team." Sarah grabbed her toothbrush, smeared toothpaste on it as she turned the shower on, then jumped in, brushing and getting her hair wet at the same time. Screw shaving, no time for that. She jumped out and was toweling herself off when she realized that something was missing. It wasn't unusual to wake up alone, she realized, but this morning she had, and she shouldn't have. Benjamin had been snoring in her ear when she'd dozed off last night around one.

She came out in a towel. "Honey…?"

She stopped, abruptly. Martika was sitting at the kitchen table, eating cottage cheese straight out of the carton with a spoon. "Sweetie?" she said, mimicking Sarah's tone.

Sarah blinked at her, surprised twice in the past five minutes. "I'm sorry. I thought…did you see my fiancé here? Tall guy, blond…"

"Bit of a prick?" Martika calmly spooned up some more cottage cheese, then put the cartoon down and drizzled honey over it. "He was leaving when I got home. I tried to introduce myself, but he looked at me like I was some sort of thief until he realized I was your roommate. Then he looked at me like I was a potted plant. Grunted something incomprehensible, left in a hurry."

Sarah's heart fell.

"Real prince you got there."

"You could tell that from just five minutes," Sarah said sharply. "You don't know him. You don't even know *me,* and I live here."

"Good!" Martika smiled, a bitchly-sweet sort of grin. "I was starting to wonder if you were dead. You know, that's the loudest and clearest I've ever heard you speak? And what exactly is so wonderful about Mr. Personality, that I seem to have overlooked?"

Sarah didn't even grace it with a response. She was already late, it was ten, and her boyfriend had left her without so much as a goodbye. She just sort of harrumphed in Martika's general direction. Sarah conjured up a vision of him, stumbling around in the dark, getting ready and trying not to wake her up, kissing her gently while she slept. No, Martika didn't know him, and she did. After being engaged to him for four years, she ought to know, dammit. She pulled on jeans and a T-shirt, dumping her towel on the floor. Dammit. Dammit, dammit, *dammit.*

Sarah was still thinking about the exchange on Sunday, the first day off she'd had in...hell, too long. They were testing the building for asbestos or something, so Becky couldn't force her to come in. Though she'd tried.

Sarah sat at a lunch table at Il Trattorio on Melrose with Judith. It was nice to see a friendly face that didn't want a mound of paperwork done.

Sarah toyed with her salad. ''Judith? Do you think Benjamin...I mean, does he strike you...''

Judith sighed, putting her own salad fork down. ''This has your roommate Martika written all over it. What's the so-called problem with Benjamin now?''

''You don't think he's a prick, do you?''

Judith goggled. Sarah didn't think she'd ever heard Judith say ''prick'' in her life, now that she thought about it.

''No, I most certainly do *not* think he's...that.'' Judith straightened out her napkin on her lap with a cluck. ''Just because he's not some sideshow freak or a candidate for that Jim Rose tattoo show doesn't mean the man's a...'' Judith glanced around, seeing if any of the other tables were noticing the inappropriate turn this conversation was taking. ''Well, he just isn't.''

Sarah smiled, suppressing the urge to say "Prick! Prick! Prick!" and watch Judith turn purple.

"Why do you ask? Do *you* think he is?"

Sarah looked down at the table. "I've been sort of unhappy lately."

"Well, that's understandable," Judith soothed. "You've been apart for a while, and you guys haven't been separated since college, for pity's sake."

"I know, I know," Sarah said. "It's just…"

She paused.

"Spit it out already."

"Well, don't you think it's sort of…well, *prickish* of him to be completely behind me moving down here, to help him out, and then all of a sudden he can't help me make ends meet with the rent?"

Judith looked at her inscrutably. "You mean, when he found out the promotion he was counting on suddenly fell through?"

Sarah continued doggedly, "Okay, but…he never calls, and he's only visited the once, and it always seems like it's all about *him*…"

"When it ought to be all about you?"

Sarah glared at her. "When it ought to be, you know, more *even*."

Judith shook her head, then took a sip of her iced tea. "Sarah, what exactly do you think he's done to you that's so 'prickish'?"

"He just doesn't seem supportive at all." Sarah knew that was a lame way to put it, and her carefully thought out argument, the one that made so much sense when she ranted to herself in the car on the way over to this lunch, suddenly seemed like a cross between a whine and a wail. "I mean, I know he's busy and all—and he has a set career, while I'm still bobbing, but…but I mean, I've been working really hellish hours…"

"That he's been working all this time," Judith interjected.

"Judith, you're not helping!" Sarah finally burst out.

"Sarah, I'm trying to. I'm trying to help you put this in perspective." Her voice had the cold logic of Mr. Spock. Sarah bit back on a pout, feeling like a complete and utter idiot. "He's been working really hard to try to get down here to be with you. He's been working crazy hours for years, while you've flitted from job to job. You volunteered to help him out by moving down here. Now, are you going to help him out or not?"

"I thought you'd be on my side, is all," Sarah finally grumped. "I'm being a complete baby about this, aren't I?" Strangely, she felt a little better—like she wasn't dating a loser prick, as Martika was intimating.

Judith smiled. "You're just losing perspective a little, that's all. You've become really independent lately, and that's a big change."

Sarah sighed. "Work has really been grating on me."

"You'll get used to it."

But I don't want *to get used to it!*

Sarah sipped at her Diet Coke. "Well, does it get any easier?"

"Yes. After a while, it's like you've been doing it all your life. It'll be like...brushing your teeth, washing your face. You won't remember a time when your life wasn't like this. Here's a bit of advice from a greeting card I once got..."

"Judith," Sarah warned.

"I like it. It said, 'Not shelter from the storm, but peace *within* the storm.' You just have to look at life like that. Recognize how everything is, and be okay with it."

That was depressing enough to send Sarah to the dessert tray with Chocolate Suicide in mind.

Chapter 5

Break on Through

Peace within the storm, peace within the storm,
Sarah thought, as she made copies in the office. It was
three in the morning. She was here, alone, with a temp
from CompuPros. He was working furiously on one
of their stronger graphic design computers, doing
some complicated presentation with animation and
music and movie clips. He hummed the theme to *Star
Trek* to himself incessantly as he ate Chee•tos and
drank Mountain Dew. "Highest caffeine of any regular brand," he confided in her, producing a two-liter
bottle from his knapsack. "I don't like the taste of
Jolt. Those are a hell of a lot of copies," he noted, as

the computer whirred, processing something. "Why don't you send it out to Kinko's?"

Sarah rubbed at her eyes, waiting for the bleary, blurred vision to clear. After a second, it did. "My boss wants me to keep an eye on it. Kinko's screwed up her last order."

"Must've been pretty bad." He shrugged.

"It wasn't entirely their fault," Sarah said, trying not to lose count. At least the conversation was keeping her awake. "But...well, you met my boss."

"Briefly." The man's tone spoke volumes. "She always like that?"

"She's been stressed..." Sarah started to make the excuse, then sighed. "Yes. She's always like that." She took a deep breath as she hit the stapler with a little too much force. She pulled out the crumpled bit of metal and tried again, more carefully. "She threw such a fit that the Kinko's manager said not only would he not help her, he was going to send her picture out like a Wanted poster to all the other branches in a fifteen-mile radius. I thought Becky was going to have an aneurysm."

"So you're here by yourself."

Sarah nodded. She was doing the binders, and revising the spreadsheets, and revising the presentation notes, and making sure that all the arrangements for the team offsite that Becky was planning was going according to schedule. Raquel, their admin, had lost her marbles over the weekend, and had quit by sharpening a pencil to a spike point and driving it through a note on Becky's desk that said *I QUIT* in a quavery red line. Sarah prayed it was ink.

"That's gotta suck."

"Not so bad," Sarah said stoically, frowning. She'd lost count. She went through the piles again.

She was trying to hold on. She really was. She spoke with Benjamin every Saturday religiously, and didn't bother him during the week. The promotion was on the cusp, he told her, just weeks to days away. He would be coming to L.A. And, like the caterpillar says in *A Bug's Life,* "then things would be much better." She just had to take Judith's advice, grow up and hold out.

"Man, I'm tired." The CompuPro guy leaned back, taking off his glasses and rubbing at his eyes.

"When do you think you'll be done with this?" Sarah asked hopefully. When he was done with the mechanics, she could proof it, do the notes and stills from it, and then get some sleep, herself.

"Oh, man. Not too much longer."

"Great." Sarah breathed a sigh of relief.

"I figure not later than six."

"*Six?*"

"Yup. You said you wanted it done by tomorrow, that's before workday tomorrow," he said defensively, as he saw Sarah's ashen face. "Maybe sooner."

"Please, God," she murmured.

Good as his word, he was done with the presentation just as the sun rose. It was six on the dot. "I'll send the bill on," he said, yawning. "God, I'm glad I don't have an assignment today."

She hurried him out, then looked over the presentation. She had hit a nice buzz...her second wind (or perhaps third wind) had struck at around five, and she was moving on a pleasant little high. She went through the presentation. It looked pretty good to her—but then, a Crayola presentation would look pretty damn slick at this point, she reasoned. Becky would be in the office in about an hour, she thought. She briefly considered going home, then decided against it. Something of the martyr was creeping up on her. *If Becky sees that I've stayed here all night,* Sarah reasoned as best she could in her sleep-deprived mind, *then she'll see how dedicated I am. She'll go easier on me. I'll have paid my dues.*

With this, Sarah collated, made calls and got a good chunk of her to-do list done. By seven, she was frenetically wiping down her desk with Windex when Jacob came in.

"Have you been here all night?" he said, eyeing her clothes...studying her eyes.

"Yes, I have," she said, noticing her hands were shaking a little when she stopped doing something with them. She took another sip of Mountain Dew, sighing as the caffeine and sugar hit her bloodstream. That CompuPro kid wasn't lying. "I've gotten a lot done."

"You certainly have," Becky said.

Was that a pleased tone? In her delirium, Sarah smiled, sure that it was. "Those are all the packets," she said proudly, "and these are the graphs and the reports and sales figures and media charts you wanted. And here's the presentation." She handed Becky the chart, the pièce de résistance. *And now, can I please go home and go to...*

Becky looked at the disk like it held the plague. "What the hell is *that?*"

Sarah stared at her. "It's...the presentation," she said. Seeing Becky's blank stare, she reminded her, "You said you wanted it to be really snazzy, remember? You authorized us to bring in a temp from CompuPro to add animations and...and music, and..."

"Yes, yes," Becky said, with an impatient wave of her hand. "But where are the *slides?*"

Sarah stared at her like she'd lost her mind. "They don't come with slides," she said, trying desperately not to add *you stupid slut.* "You use the LCD projector...it runs right off the laptop."

She should have known better. Becky's eyes rolled back in her head like a terrified cow just at the mention of *laptop.* "Oh, no, I'm not," she said, angry and accusing. Jacob, Sarah noticed, vanished. "I'm not using a goddamn laptop to give this presentation. Why didn't anybody mention this earlier? I've got to give this fucking thing at two o'clock, why didn't somebody mention it earlier?"

How precisely Becky thought that you could add moving images to a piece of plastic with ink on it, Sarah wasn't sure. But obviously that's exactly what she thought. "I...didn't realize that you didn't know about the LCD projector,'' Sarah said slowly, feeling that delicious euphoria start to fade and the cold hard reality sink in.

"Listen here. I want *slides* printed up. *SLIDES!*"

Sarah did mental calculations. The meeting starts at noon. Presentation at two. It was now eight. It took about a minute a slide…there were one hundred and twenty slides…she could get them all printed out with an hour to spare. Plenty of time.

"All right, Becky," she said. *Peace within the storm, peace within the storm…*

Becky had picked up one of the booklets…one with the printed stills. She glanced through it quickly and to Sarah's horror, picked up a pen.

"Also, I'm going to need some changes."

Sarah quickly saw the mountain of velo-bound presentation folders, the slides, all of it, getting shot to hell. *Peace within…oh, suck.*

By noon, Sarah had moved from euphoria to hysteria. She had already burst into spontaneous tears at her keyboard not once, but twice. Jacob was her godsend, fetching her Jolt and Mountain Dew. He would have set up an IV if he'd known how. She flashed through the changes Becky made, then sent him with the prints to make the note pages and velo-bind the presentation stuff. She printed out each slide, removing the animation stuff that would leave the little icon. *Stupid cow, stupid cow, stupid cow,* she thought. The "peace within" mantra just wasn't working, and the stupid cow one at least gave her enough fuel to continue going. She was seriously considering taking a cab home…or saying fuck it, and going to sleep under her desk. She'd probably go with the cab. At least she'd be away from Becky…

"Sarah, how's it coming?"

Sarah glanced at the printer, which was moaning like it was going to die a horrible electronic death. She picked up the last sheet of acetate. "Last slide," she said, putting it over the last white sheet of paper with a flourish. "And the overhead is all set up in the conference center."

"And you ordered lunch, of course?" Becky's eyes narrowed. "I know I didn't ask you to, but I figured you should know…"

Sarah smiled with an exhausted sort of smugness. "I ordered lunch. Maria's. They delivered at eleven forty-five."

"You're tired, aren't you?" As if she had only just noticed, Becky squinted her eyes, studying Sarah's face.

And about to remedy *that,* Sarah thought. "Yes, I am."

"You shouldn't stay at that keyboard."

"My thoughts exactly."

"You should get up," Becky said thoughtfully. "Walk around. Definitely pick up some lunch. I'll be out of my meeting at three, and maybe we could go over the Veggi-round TV spots they're shooting next month."

Sarah didn't believe she'd heard correctly. "You mean…you want me to *stay?*"

Becky looked at her like she was from Pluto. "It's *noon,* Sarah. You did a good job, and all, but I wasn't going to give you a half day."

"A HALF DAY?" Sarah felt like she was channeling the voice that was yelling. "I was here *all night!"*

Becky blinked, obviously not expecting her docile A.A.E. to start shouting. "And I appreciate it," she said, in that sickly smooth voice that Sarah hated.

"I am going home," Sarah said, grabbing her coat. It tangled when she tried to stick her arm through it…she slowly realized she was putting it in the wrong hole. She straightened it out. "I am leaving here. I'll be lucky if I don't wrap my car around a telephone pole from here to Santa Monica Boulevard. Are you out of your *mind?* I am going *home!"*

Becky sighed wearily. "Oh, all right. There is just one more thing I need you to do, though. It'll be quick, and it'll be on your way." She shot her an accusing glare. "You said you'd do anything to make my job easier, you know."

Paying your dues, peace within the storm…

"What did you want me to do?" Sarah said instead. *Sainthood, here I come.*

Becky rummaged around in her pockets, pulling out a key. Sarah stared at it. "This is the key to my apartment. I just need you to take care of Charlie. You remember Charlie, right? The cat I asked you to feed over the July Fourth weekend, when I was out of town?"

Sarah sighed. "You want me to feed Charlie."

"Not…well, no." Becky shrugged. "His litter box is just behind the…"

"*NO.*"

Becky looked at her. "Well, it will get you out of work early, won't it?" she said like she was conferring a favor.

Sarah stared at the key, at the pile of presentation booklets, at Jacob who was staring at Becky like she was possessed. She didn't even have any inflection in her voice when she spoke.

"Becky, I quit. I completely, utterly, totally *quit.*" She grabbed her purse. "I'm *through* paying my dues, I'm *not* growing up, and *fuck* peace within the storm!"

Sarah made it home safely, guessing that it was probably due to whichever saint it was that watched over drunks, tramps and stupid twats who stuck to jobs long past the point of abuse. Martika was blessedly still at work when she got home at twelve-thirty. She took off her clothes and burrowed under her covers naked. She wandered through the living room at around three naked, to pee, then promptly went back to sleep. She finally emerged at around seven, realizing she was hungry. She'd been crying in her sleep…she'd left makeup on, and there were rings of mascara around her eyes. She looked like she'd been beat up.

She rummaged through the fridge. There was some Chalula, the hot sauce that Martika used on pretty much everything, and a few takeout containers. God knows how long they'd been in there. There weren't even any ingredients to cook anything. She rattled through the cupboards, finally producing mushroom-flavored ramen. She cooked that on the stove, yawning as she tied her terry-cloth robe more tightly around her. She then picked up the phone, dialing Benjamin's work number.

"Benjamin Slater."

"I quit my job."

She heard him sigh, and she sighed in return. "What happened?" he asked, in an exhausted tone of voice.

She went through everything, from the copying to the litter box. "I can't believe she asked me to do that," she finished, repeating "I can't believe" for about the fiftieth time in the whole story. She still reeled from the shock of it.

"Well, it's obviously a done deal," Benjamin said, still with that tired note in his voice. She knew he'd been working hard, but dammit, a little more righteous indignation was called for, a little voice told her. "So now what are you going to do?"

"I don't know," Sarah said woodenly. "Find another job, I suppose."

"That would seem like the best course of action."

"You could be a little more...I don't know, helpful," Sarah complained.

"I don't know how I can be," he said. "I mean, you just quit your job with no notice and walked out saying something about 'fuck inner peace' or whatever. I don't know how I can help you out of something like that."

This was so *him* Sarah thought, then she was starting to fume. "Why don't you try telling me something cheerful, then?" she suggested acidly. "You know, like 'I really miss you' or 'I'll see you soon.' You know. Boyfriend-fiancé kind of stuff."

"I miss you," he said. "And actually, I will see you soon." He took a deep breath, and his voice took on an intonation of pride. "I got it. I got the promotion."

Sarah shut the burner off with a click. "What?"

"I got the promotion. I'll be head of the L.A. office."

Sarah beamed. "Oh, honey! That's wonderful!" This was it! Her shelter…no, her *peace within the storm.* This was the answer. He'd move down, and Martika would move out. No more noisy sex bouts to put up with, how 'bout *that?* And she would have the financial resources to rest with…she could look for a job she liked, since Benjamin made more than enough to pay the bills. And he'd said once they got married that she could stay home with the kids…rather insisted upon it, in fact, since he appreciated the upbringing his mother gave him as a stay-at-home mom. At any rate, she could use the break until then. "So when are you coming? I'll need to give Martika notice." She said it, almost crowing.

There was a pause. "Um, Sarah…I've done a lot of thinking."

"So have I. I figure we don't have to have both desks in the second bedroom, just yours would be fine. It's a lot bigger than mine, anyway and…"

"Sarah, I'm not living with you."

He might as well have been speaking Swahili. "What? What?" Her mind went numb.

"I'm not going to live with you." He sighed. "You're just a little too much of a distraction, and frankly, I've gotten a lot done…I can't afford to screw this up. I really need to focus."

The peace she envisioned shattered like a glass bottle dropped on a hard tile floor. "You need to focus," she repeated carefully.

"I figured I'd get my own place, and you could visit me every weekend, just like you used to do when you lived up here. Hell, we could probably see each other more than that. We practically lived together our final year of college, remember?"

But never in actuality, she thought, again with that sheen of numbness. It reminded her of her state at five that morning. "So, you're moving down here, but you're not going to live with me, so you can focus on your job."

"That's it," he said encouragingly, since she wasn't reacting with any emotion. He sounded relieved. "That's it exactly."

"Martika was right," she said, with a voice of growing wonder. "You *are* a dick."

"What?"

"You…are…a…dick." She said the words slowly, with exaggeration. "Which word don't you understand?"

"Thanks a lot, Sarah," he said, his voice freezing cold. "Thanks a fucking lot. I tell you about my promotion, and this is the best you can do? Thanks for being happy for me, I mean, what else could I expect from my girlfriend?"

"Oh, don't play that shit with me," she said, leaping up from the chair she'd sat down in. "Don't *even* try to guilt me. I pulled a twenty-nine-hour straight *day* working for an idiot. I could have been killed. And your idea of boyfriend-type support is that I should *grow up and pay my dues?* And now, after being engaged for four *fucking* years, you're going to move to the city that I moved to—" she took a deep breath "—JUST TO GET YOU A PLACE TO LIVE, AND NOW YOU'RE GOING TO LIVE SOMEWHERE ELSE? JUST BECAUSE I'M A FUCKING *DISTRACTION?*"

"Don't yell at me. I mean it, Sarah," he said, his voice full of dire threat. "I don't have to put up with this shit."

"No, you don't. Not ever again." Her voice wavered, and she knuckled her tears out of her eyes, smearing the liquid down her cheeks with the back of her hands. "Go find someone else who knows how to be your *girlfriend,* dickhead. And *fuck off!*"

She hung up on him. Within a moment, the phone rang again. *"What?"*

"We're through, Sarah," he said. "And don't ever hang up on me again." With that he promptly hung up on her.

She sat, shaking, unable to believe what had just transpired. She was now unemployed, she thought, and now single again, a state she hadn't been

in...God, had it been five years? She'd been twenty.
And she hadn't been much good at dating, even then.

She realized she was rocking back and forth, and
stood up, walking around. She felt like screaming, or
doing something similarly crazy. She felt like vomit-
ing, but nothing came. She cried a little more—it
helped, but not enough.

She needed to vent this. She needed to get a grip
on it. Somehow.

What, she thought, crazily, *would Martika do?*

After a moment's thought, she went to the freezer,
and got out the bottle of Stolichnaya Vodka that Martika kept stored there. She then got out the cranberry
concentrate which was also in the freezer. Then, with
the care of a chemist, she poured the vodka directly
into the pitcher of cranberry concentrate, and mixed
it. She got herself out a glass and filled it to the rim.

"Peace within the storm," she said, with determination, and emptied the glass in one long, extended
swallow.

I am sick to death of that tight-assed prig.

Martika got back to the apartment around ten or so.
She was trying to stay away from it more and more
lately, which was usually a sign that she'd be moving
again, fairly soon.

She didn't know what Taylor had been thinking.
"She's sweet," he'd gushed, in that oh-so-Taylor way
of his. "She's like a little *doll.* You just want to stuff
her in a backpack and take her home, put her under
glass on your mantel. And a voice like a little cartoon

girl...you know, one of those Japanese ones, where every other word they say is 'Oh!' with eyes as big as dinner plates."

"And I would be interested in continuing to live with her *why?*" Martika had responded, smoking her Dunhills outside Tacos Tacos after a night of clubbing at Revolver.

"You'd be a *good influence,* darling," he'd purred, knowing that her maternal instinct was a weakness, damn him. She was the goddamn "den mother of Santa Monica Boulevard," self-appointed. The idea of training a real daughter instead of her wanna-bes *was* a little appealing.

When she first met Sarah, she really thought she could do something. She was so...so funny, in a clean, prepackaged kind of way. She was a lot of good raw material. She had to ditch the Eddie Bauer catalog crap that she was wearing, to start, and she had to have that stick up her ass surgically removed, but otherwise, Martika had some high hopes.

Those hopes had diminished over the past few months. Now, going back to her apartment was like going back to Bosnia, when her home was supposed to be her refuge from the pricks, both literal and figurative, of the outside world. She had gotten nowhere with the Bitch, as Martika now called her. It was time to give notice.

She got home, and there were no lights on, so she almost jumped out of her skin when she heard Sarah's voice. "Tika? That you?"

Martika made a sharp gasp, then grumbled. "You

scared the *shit* out of me, Sarah,'' she said. One more thing to add to the Bitch List, as she'd referred to Sarah's various flaws when speaking with Taylor. ''Why are you sitting here with no lights on, anyway?''

''There aren't any lights on, are there?''

Was it her imagination, or was Sarah slurring? Rummaging around, Martika turned on a light, and gasped again.

There was a pool of red on the table, around an empty glass, a pair of scissors, and Sarah's arms. To her relief, it was too thin to be blood. One sniff suggested it was her emergency Stoli.

''Sweetie, what…'' Martika started, then gasped again as she got a good look at Sarah. ''Oh, *shit*. Sarah, what did you *do?*''

''Huh? Oh.'' Sarah's fingers went to her head. Her hair was now shorn unevenly, sticking out in comical waves and tufts. ''Did you know that there are Native American tribes that cut their hair to mourn people?'' she asked, as if she were merely discussing a casual topic of conversation. ''I always thought that was sort of cool.''

All thoughts of leaving fled Martika's head. From the looks of it, this little girl had done some serious damage to a fifth of strong vodka, and cut off all her hair. This was some deliciously juicy trouble, and the type that was right up Martika's alley. *Man* trouble.

''Don't worry,'' Martika said, sitting down while shutting off her cell phone. The Bitch was dead, thank God—and Martika had some work to do with this poor little girl. ''Just tell me everything, and I promise, we can make it all better.''

Chapter 6

The Changeling

Sarah woke the next day, with her mouth tasting vile and her head pounding. She seemed to recall waking up and staggering to the bathroom to throw up, which she did with enough force and momentum that the toilet seat fell on her head. She also seemed to remember Martika being there, like a watchful mother hen—which was strange, since Martika didn't even like her. Did she?

Well, if she didn't, she'd probably like her even less, now…flashes of last night came back to her in bizarre, disjointed cuts that reminded her of a really bad art house movie. Her, telling Martika about how

she met Benjamin, and then proceeding to tell her
entire life story and how it related to men and sex and
oh God, why hadn't Martika shut her up? Probably
thought she was psychotic—best to humor her, Martika had probably been thinking, or else Sarah might
have gotten violent. Sarah rubbed at her temples. Of
course, that might have happened. She'd never been
in quite the state she'd been in last night.

She was wearing jammies, at least, she thought,
looking down at her T-shirt and shorts. Then realized
that wasn't her T-shirt, although she recognized the
shorts as a pair she didn't wear anymore. She'd probably gone to throw up naked, or something. Good
God. It just got worse and worse.

She looked out to the living room gingerly, wincing
as light poured in through the balcony doors. God it
was bright. What time was it? A glance at her clock—
six o'clock. Where the hell did the time go?

Her gaze fell on the kitchen table, and she smiled.
Walking over like an old woman who'd forgotten her
walker, she shuffled her way to where three of Taylor's Hangover Remover sodas sat, with a note:

Thought you'd need this.
Be ready to be picked up at 7:00.
We're going to see Joey.
MARTIKA

Sarah read the note, slowly, three times. She then
opened a soda and drank every drop, having remembered the positive results it garnered the last time

she'd gone out with Taylor. She didn't know why she was being picked up…and she had no idea who Joey was. However, it gave her an hour to get ready. She figured that she owed Martika that much. After all, she'd put up with a really amazingly nasty scene the previous evening.

She wandered into the bathroom, yawning slightly, looking forward to brushing her teeth…then turned on the light, looked in the mirror, and screamed.

She looked like a cross between a punk rocker and a scrub brush. Whole hunks of her hair had been cut short, while other layers of locks had been left at their original length, just past her shoulder blades. Her fingers reached up, and her mouth rounded in a circle of disbelief.

Oh my God.

She just kept brushing her fingers over the bizarre modern art that used to be her hair, tickling her fingertips with now wavy, now sticking-straight-out locks.

She seemed to vaguely remember thinking at one point the previous evening about Native Americans— God, what sort of train of thought had brought that on—and she'd remembered in the crap-trap that was her mind something about them cutting their hair. The scissors seemed to move of their own accord, like something out of *Alice in Wonderland.* She had literally not thought a thing about it since that moment, and now…holy shit, she looked like a mutant, she ought to be dragged out and shaved bald…

She brushed her teeth, trying as best she could to

brush the terrible taste out of her mouth while simultaneously and religiously avoiding looking at herself in the mirror. Just a glimpse made her want to cry. She retreated to the shower, pulling the decorative curtain Martika had bought in front of the glass shower doors so she wouldn't have to see even the frosted reflection of her head. She stayed in the shower for a long, long time, waiting for the bathroom mirror to get good and coated with steam before stepping out to the fluffy bath mat. She wrapped her head in a towel-turban, then dried off and went back to her room. She got in jeans, a T-shirt, and rummaged around for a hat. She was still looking for one—she was sure she brought one from Fairfield—when she heard Martika come in the house. "Sarah! Sarah! Sweetie, are you ready? Are you okay?"

Sarah found a floppy denim hat that she only wore when gardening back home. Grabbing what straggly long hair remained, she stuffed the whole thing under the brim as best she could. "I just have to put on my shoes," she called.

Martika gave her a studied look, then grinned broadly. "You look like you're about ten years old."

Sarah frowned. "You don't have to rub it in. I can't believe I did that to my hair."

"I can, and it's about time. Not for you to cut your hair," she corrected, waiting patiently as Sarah pulled on a pair of Keds with no socks. "I mean, obviously you've been storing that little episode up for some time. Now that you've let it out, I think you'll be much healthier. I almost called you today, to make sure you were all right, but I wanted to make sure you got enough sleep…you were up puking half the night.'' It sounded odd, all that maternal caring coming from an hourglass Amazon like Martika, but at the same time it was very, very comforting.

Sarah stood up, feeling awkward. ''I wanted to say thank you, Martika. You were really…you've been so…''

''Don't even worry about it. I've been waiting for you to become, well, interesting since I moved in here. I was starting to give up hope,'' Martika said, laughing in that rough-scratchy way of hers. Sarah, surprisingly, did not feel insulted. ''At any rate, we're going to see my hairdresser, Joey. You're lucky, he usually needs an appointment at least a month in advance, but he owes me a few favors, so I'm finally cashing in on one.''

''Thank you…''

Martika smiled. ''Sweetie, this is just the beginning. You're single now. You just wait…this is going to be so much fun!''

Sarah felt about ten when she walked into the salon in Beverly Hills. Martika had zoomed them there in her midnight-blue BMW convertible in about half the time it would have taken Sarah to go across the street, it seemed. Sarah tried as best she could to surreptitiously grip the car door handle while Martika managed to put on lipstick, talk to Taylor on her cell phone and negotiate traffic on a busy Wednesday night. ''Taylor, sweetie, you've got to meet me at the

salon. Joey's salon, silly. We've got a *project* going
on. Yes, Sarah is with me.'' She smiled at Sarah even
as she narrowly avoided plowing into a VW bug.
Sarah smiled back nervously, feeling her palms grow
sweaty. "We'll be there in about…oh, here we are.
Gotta run. We're drinks later, right? Maybe Sarah will
come with.'' She winked at Sarah, then seemed to
float the car into a parallel parking spot. "Later.'' She
beeped off her cell phone, then gestured to a very
posh-looking salon storefront. "Voilà. Let's go get
you girlish.''

Sarah looked in, anxiously. She saw her reflection
in the mirror, as well as Martika's. Martika was wearing a micromini in some black stretchy material, a
black sleeveless sweater-top, and knee-high black
boots. She also wore sunglasses, pushed up to act like
a headband for her crazily tumbling maroon curls.
Sarah, on the other hand, really did look like a ten-
year-old in her jeans, T-shirt, Keds and floppy denim
hat. If Martika looked older, she probably would have
passed for Sarah's mother, for pity's sake. She followed behind Martika, head down, trying to avoid the
gaze of other patrons who were all swathed in soft
pink robes and who were staring at her expectantly.

"Joey!'' Martika did a trademark squeal, then went
over to air-kiss a man who was wearing black leather
pants and a crisp white T-shirt that Sarah could have
bounced a quarter off. "Sweetie, it's been *ages!*''

"You bitch. Tell me somebody else did your hair
color, and I'll strangle you,'' he said, though his tone
didn't sound at all threatening. In fact, it sounded like

some sort of compliment, in a weird, femmy sort of way. "It looks good, but you know I can do better."

"L'Oreal Hydrience, can you believe it?"

"*Eyew*. Box color." Joey rolled his eyes. "So, where's your project?"

Sarah wasn't sure she liked being referred to in these terms.

"Here's our girl," Martika said, gesturing to Sarah as if she were Vanna White turning letters.

He looked at her, and his eyes widened so far that his pierced eyebrow twitched. He made a low whistle. "Hmm. I don't suppose...I just signed on for hair, Tika, I didn't sign on for a full-day here..."

"No, no, hair to start," Martika said. Okay, now Sarah was pretty sure she was feeling offended. "Sarah, sweetie, take your hat off for Joey, okay?"

Sarah obviously understood why it was necessary, but she still felt like Martika had asked her to strip. It would have been no less embarrassing. She slowly reached up, grabbed the brim of her hat, and tugged it off. The few long strands tumbled limply down her back.

Joey gasped. "Oh, my."

Martika simply nodded.

"Ah...well..." Joey was obviously trying to get a handle on this unexpected situation. He circled her like a knife-fighter. "Um. I see."

"I know you've seen worse," Martika said. Sarah wasn't sure how, but it sounded good when Martika said it. "I'm thinking chic, kicky, something fun.

Something that says 'I eat men like you for breakfast.' But still sexy.''

"I'm thinking something that says 'No, I didn't stick my head in my Mixmaster,'" Sarah said under her breath.

Joey heard it, and laughed. "Well, all right. Let me go to the magazines, I'm sure we can do something...you've got a good natural wave," he said, obviously getting his balance back. He sounded all business. "Kicky, sexy, fun," he muttered, as he wandered over to the magazine rack.

"Sarah, darling, I heard *everything*," Sarah heard Taylor's voice say from the front of the room, and she smirked. "I'm so very, very sor... *Oh my God what happened to your head?*"

Martika rolled her eyes, and Sarah laughed.

"Obviously you didn't hear everything," Sarah said, grinning.

"Obviously." He circled her, much as Joey had. "Wow. When you get drunk, you really get drunk, huh?"

"I don't know. I don't get drunk a whole lot."

Martika and Taylor gave each other challenging grins. "We'll fix that," they said in unison.

"Um, I don't know..."

"Right! Here we go. It looks kicky and fun."

Sarah, Martika and Taylor hunched together like football players in a huddle, looking over the magazine Joey presented to them. There was a woman in a sharp dress with hair that looked...well, like she'd just emerged with curls from a very sexy wind tunnel.

"I don't know…" Sarah repeated, but Taylor and Martika were already ushering her toward an impossibly thin young woman in black jeans and a white T-shirt, her hair pulled back in a severe bun. The woman nudged her into a changing room and handed her a pink towel, giving her head only the quickest glance and the most fleeting sneer. Sarah then shut up. She couldn't keep her hair the way it was, that much was apparent. And Martika and Taylor seemed to know what they were doing. Right?

She sat down and allowed Joey to wash her hair in something that smelled deliciously like apricot. The whole time, Martika updated Joey on the Benjamin fiasco. Sarah didn't mind…after all, if you couldn't share with your hairdresser, who could you share with, right? With every sentence, Joey seemed to get more irate…and more convinced that he would make her a masterpiece. "This one's going to be an ass-kicker," he said, eyes narrowed and eyebrow ring glinting. "That prick, that absolute *prick.*"

It felt good, Sarah realized, as several pink-clad women deliberately eavesdropped, then started giving their opinions. There was something about salons, good salons, that was like group therapy and a very nice slumber party all rolled into one.

But as they continued to talk about Benjamin, it hurt her heart…yes, that prick, that absolute prick. Four years engaged, five years together, and he couldn't live with her? That was disturbing. She felt tears welling up, and tried to think of other things,

but she couldn't and gave up. The women simply nodded to her and shared stories, which helped slightly.

"Don't waste any tears on that asshole," Martika
said firmly. "You've been doing fine all these months
without him, right? And to be honest, he's just been
using you."

"I know," Sarah said, trying not to move her head
as Joey snipped and yanked at her hair. "It's just that
I'm *used* to him using me."

"Oh, honey, I know that one," an older woman in
the chair opposite chimed in.

"Well, now you can get used to being independent," Martika said, and several other women nodded
firmly. If they'd all stood up and broken into a spirited
version of the new Charlie's Angels song, Sarah
wouldn't have been the least surprised, it was that sort
of day.

Taylor smiled with delight. "You know what this
means. *Wardrobe.*"

"I'm unemployed now, Taylor," Sarah pointed
out, then it suddenly occurred to her...she was in a
salon in Beverly Hills. She had heard rumors that
somebody had paid one hundred dollars for dim sum
for one in this town. Good God, she was going to be
on a budget from here on out. What the hell was she
doing?

As if reading the panic in her eyes, Martika put a
strong hand on her shoulder. "You won't be unemployed for long."

Taylor put a comforting hand on her other shoulder.
"We know it's hard," he said, and his voice was

soothing. "Still, at the very least let us *think* about what you ought to be wearing. No offense, girlie, but every time I see you in that Eddie Bauer denim dress, I just want to cry."

"For me, it's that sundress with the flowers," Martika volunteered. "The Laura Ashley PTA one."

Sarah pulled her lips tight, offended. "I don't see anything wrong with what I wear."

"Of course you don't. I'm sure Benjamin approved of all of it."

Martika had her there, so Sarah kept her mouth shut.

Like a couple of excited schoolkids, Martika and Taylor tore through old magazines that Joey was about to throw away, only keeping the most recent of everything. Lots of them were in Italian or Czechoslovakian, with women that looked like cats and shot hateful glances at the camera. "What do you think of this?" they would say periodically. Sarah kept saying she wasn't sure. Apparently, they thought that meant "perfect!" because that would be inevitably yanked out.

She spent the better part of an hour under a hair lamp with foil on her head. Joey had now entered the insanity with Martika and Taylor, and was tearing out magazine pictures and comparing things. Sarah couldn't hear what they were saying, just watched as they gesticulated wildly. Patrons were taking sides. It was turning into a free-for-all. Sarah tried to read the magazine in front of her and pretend she had nothing

to do with all the proceedings. After a grueling long
time, Joey finally pronounced her done.

"It was not easy," he said, in a tone usually re-
served for Oscar acceptance speeches, "but I think
we can all agree that it was worth it."

Sarah looked at the mirror, and her mouth dropped
open.

She looked *frosted,* was the only way she could
describe it. Her usually ashy-honey blond hair now
had all these streaks, like she was running through a
perpetually sun-dappled meadow. She knew she had
wavy hair, but this was *artistically* wavy, not the
Sonic the Hedgehog tangles that she was used to.

She, too, had gone into a sexy wind tunnel and
lived to tell about it.

"How long will this last?" she said, her fingers
reaching up but only touching the aura of her hair, as
if by touching the hair itself the whole thing would
vanish in a puff of smoke and she'd be reduced to the
hedgehog looking thing she'd resembled when she
walked in.

Joey laughed. "You just need to do a few simple
steps," he said. "I'll give you some molding mud,
and you need to put that at the roots…then some of
this mousse at the tips…you just go like this—" he
tilted his head upside down, pretending that his
closely-cropped hairstyle matched hers "—and then
like this, swing your hair up, and it's just that easy."
He grinned. "And tell everyone you came here, naturally."

Martika and Taylor could not have been prouder if

they were her parents. "Let's hit the town," Martika said, and in that moment, Sarah could have said yes.

Taylor nay-sayed. "What do we always say in Marketing? It's all about positioning. The haircut is a *fabulous* start, granted. But we've still got to draw up a game plan." He grinned, taking Martika's arm. "I say, dinner at El Torito with absolutely *tons* of margaritas."

"I concur." Martika linked her arm in Sarah's, and Sarah smiled. Martika saw the hat in her hands, frowned and took it, tossing it in a tall artsy silver trash canister. Sarah still smiled.

"You did what?"

Judith watched Sarah calmly eat her salad, her hair glinting platinum and honey-blond in the afternoon sun. "I dumped Benjamin."

"Would this be before or after your emotional pyrotechnics at Salamanca?" Judith asked. "Because if it was before, maybe I could negotiate to get your job back. Sort of like temporary insanity. I mean, Becky herself has been under some emotional strain and would probably cut you some sort of slack, especially as she's shorthanded now…"

"I don't want to go back," Sarah said firmly. "I'm sorry if it made you look bad, Judith."

Judith smoothed her napkin in her lap, glancing out the window. "It did cause some commotion. I mean, I did recommend you."

"And I'm sorry, but I couldn't work for that horrid woman one more day," Sarah said, her green eyes earnest. "She wanted me to clean out her cat box, Jude. I swear, the woman was a nightmare."

"You could have handled it better, Sarah," Judith corrected her gently. "You could have simply told her no."

Sarah sighed. "I don't think you'll be able to understand."

"I've been there," Judith said. "We've all had nightmare bosses. You just pay…"

"Don't say pay your dues," Sarah said, her voice uncharacteristically steely. "I mean it. I'll scream."

Judith was so surprised, she put her fork down. "Sarah, what's gotten into you? First the outburst at Salamanca, then dumping Benjamin—and what really happened there, anyway?"

"He was being a *dick*. Don't even try to argue with me on that point."

Now Judith openly gaped. "What do you mean?"

Sarah pushed radicchio leaves from one side of the broad white plate to the other. She looked like a bored starlet with that hair, Judith noticed. "I mean, he's been so insensitive. Here I am, working thirty hours in one day, and all he can say is I have to pay my dues, keep my chin up. Everything I was doing was for him, Jude," she confided. "Everything was to convince him that I could make the cut, that he wouldn't be making a mistake in marrying me. Can you believe that?"

"It can't have been that bad."

"Couldn't it?"

Judith couldn't believe the bitterness in Sarah's

voice. "Sarah, moving to a new city is hard—and working at an ad agency in Los Angeles is brutal. You might have lost some perspective, but it's not impossible to pull off. I mean, I do it. I've been able to balance a husband and a work life for the past few years."

Sarah pushed her salad to one side. "I don't know how, honestly."

"Well, good organization and keeping your priorities balanced, basically," Judith said. "I'd love to help you out. I can give you the name of my meditation coach…"

"I'm unemployed right now, Judith," Sarah said. "I don't think I can afford him."

Judith looked away. It would help if Sarah wasn't so *negative* about the whole thing. There was always a solution. "You know what…I'm going to loan you a book that might help you."

"Really?" Sarah said unenthusiastically.

"*Seven Habits of Highly Effective People.* It's been a godsend in my life," Judith said.

"Judith, can I ask you a question?"

Thinking it was about the book, Judith smiled. "Certainly."

"Are you really happy?"

Judith blinked. "What a question!" She paused. "Of course I'm happy."

Sarah looked at her suspiciously, then shrugged.

Judith waited for clarification—when Sarah didn't respond, she finally asked. "What brings that up?"

Sarah shrugged again. "I don't know. It's just

that—well, you always seem to be in a hurry to do something, you know? You've got everything neatly compartmentalized. I'll bet you've got me written down in your notebook as a to-do item. You know, something like 'get explanation from Sarah' or 'get Sarah to take job back.'''

"Don't be ridiculous," Judith said sharply. It was listed in her "friends/family" section as "provide emotional support." Sarah would understand when she read the book—no point in mentioning it to her now.

"Anyway, I guess you're right, to a point," Sarah said. "I let my life spin a little out of control. I was totally focused on Benjamin, what he was thinking, what he *would* think—and then I was totally focused on work, because I thought it would help me prove something to Benjamin. Well, not this time around. I'm going to have some *fun*."

Judith didn't like the sound of that. "And get a new job," Judith said.

"I figured I'd temp," Sarah said casually.

Temping? Judith hid a wince. She'd had temps work in her department. They all seemed like submorons. Sarah certainly deserved better, after all her education. "Well, I'll look around, too," she promised, wishing she could write it down in her organizer. She would when she went to the ladies' room, she decided.

"I'll find something, Judith. Don't worry."

Well, obviously one of us needs to. "Read the book?"

Sarah sighed, then smiled. "Sure, Judith. After all, it's worked like a charm for you. Who am I to argue with success, right?"

Judith smiled. "Right." *Worked like a charm.* Of course it did.

Of course she was happy.

"Waiter?" She stopped the man walking past them with a little hand gesture. "You know, I think I'll have a little glass of wine after all."

"Sarah, are you ready yet?" Martika called.

Sarah adjusted her outfit…a bra-strap styled tank dress in pink. She thought it looked good with the new haircut, and she hadn't worn it out yet. Frankly, she wasn't sure about the straps, but she was in L.A. Hell, she was *frosted* in L.A. A little bra-strap tank dress was probably just the thing.

She stepped out. "Ta-daah-ah-AH!" The fanfare announcement turned into a disconcerted wail.

Martika was wearing a vinyl dress that ended somewhere just below her pubic hair, from the looks of it. It looked like she poured herself into it. She was wearing leather knee-high boots that were supported by absolutely mountainous black platform heels. Her hair flew out in a bloodred nimbus that made Firestarter look like Alfalfa. She had everything but the whip and zippered mask.

Sarah quickly looked around. Nope, no accoutrements that she could see. She counted herself lucky.

Martika looked her over with a disdainful eye. "I thought I told you we were Goth clubbing."

Sarah choked.

"Hmm. Well, we can see if I've got anything you can borrow." She grabbed Sarah by the arm and tugged her into her room. Compared to Sarah's relative neatness, Martika's room looked like a war zone. She dug into her closet with relish. "Let's see…it'll have to be something small—you're on the short side, aren't you?"

"Five-six," Sarah said. "Average."

Martika laughed. "Average is never something to aspire to, darling…ah! Here we go." She handed Sarah a plaid micromini with a white crop top that said "boys suck" on it in rhinestones. "If you're going to go with the little girl look, be slutty about it."

"Who said that? Betsey Johnson?"

Martika laughed again. She looked like some evil arch nemesis of, say, Wonder Woman. "Go on. And put some makeup on."

"I have some makeup on!"

Martika rolled her eyes and followed her into the bathroom. "For God's sake, we're clubbing. You can't wear Bobbi Brown neutrals clubbing!"

Sarah grumbled something. The miniskirt fell just above her knee…God knows where it fell when Martika wore it. She pulled the crop top on. It was less crop than Martika seemed it should be and she had to stop her from cutting it to make it shorter.

"Maybe you could wear the netting top…"

"No!" Sarah's arms crossed protectively in front of her chest.

"Oh, all right, Sister Sarah."

A half hour later, coated with a healthy shellacking of Urban Decay and enough eyeliner to give Cleopatra a run for her money, Sarah was pronounced "slutty enough." She tottered on her highest high heels next to Martika, who made it look like she was born in stilettos.

"Just think attitude...attitude..."

As opposed to thinking "sharp, agonizing pain." Sarah limped after her.

"We're picking up Taylor, and then we're going to Perversion. God! It's been ages."

They got into the Martikamobile, and went to Taylor's place. Then they drove to Hollywood, Sarah doing her usual "brace yourself!" against Martika's version of Offensive Driving.

When they parked, Sarah said a small prayer of thanks for arriving in one piece, then followed Taylor, wearing what looked like rubber lederhosen, and Martika the vinyl war goddess. The two of them looked like vampires, she noted. She must be the character of the little blond girl that Lestat changed. She snickered at that, until she saw the line to enter the club.

Oh, my God. Apparently, the memo had gone out to the other vampires, because they were there in full force. You couldn't throw a dart without hitting someone with black clothing, pale skin...and a scary expression in his eye, for that matter. Sarah took a protective step behind Martika.

"It's not that bad," Martika admonished. "Come on!"

Martika and Taylor chatted while they slowly

moved forward in the line. They were greeted by an absolutely huge guy in a yellow shirt with bold block letters that said SECURITY, for those who couldn't have guessed. He was wearing one of those speaker-headphone things, like Madonna wore on the Blonde Ambition tour.

"ID?"

Sarah dutifully produced her awful driver's license photo. He scrutinized the license, then her face. She expected some pithy comment, like "Related to Tammy Faye Baker?" but instead he just waved her on. She paid the cover, and then followed Martika and Taylor into a large, darkened hall.

The first thing that struck her was the music, and that almost literally. It had all the force of a cannon blast, and it kept going.

Martika turned and said something to her—she couldn't make out what it was.

"WHAT?" she yelled.

Martika pointed to the bar, then broadly panto-mimed getting a glass and tossing back a drink.

"OH." Sarah shrugged. "HOW ABOUT WA-TER?" she bellowed into Martika's ear.

Martika looked at Taylor, then rolled her eyes and dragged Sarah to the bar. She said something to the bartender. Sarah was then unceremoniously presented with a vodka and cranberry, which Martika paid for.

"To your first night clubbing!" she said, clinking her own drink against Sarah's.

Sarah nodded weakly, then took a sip. It was strong enough to set her coughing. The cranberry was simply there for coloring, apparently. The bartender winked at her. She quickly looked away.

After a few minutes, Martika had finished her drink and was staring at the floor. It was eleven o'clock, late by Sarah's reckoning, but apparently "when things got going." Everything in Martika's posture said that she wanted to dance.

"Come on, come on!" Martika nudged at Sarah impatiently.

Sarah forced down the rest of the drink, then fought off another fit of coughing. She was still feeling the burn of the alcohol in her chest as Taylor and Martika dragged her out onto the crowded dance floor. Taylor and Martika started to dance to the music. It sounded like a man singing…harsh and guttural enough to sound like some sort of German. Sarah couldn't make out the words, but apparently the lyrics were secondary to the pounding electronic beat.

Taylor and Martika cut a stunning figure. Sarah, herself, felt like she was just shuffling. Other people jostled her. She felt an elbow prod into her side.

"Hey!"

She turned, only to see a man with one white eye and one red eye stare back at her.

"Sorry," she muttered, and hastily turned back to Martika and Taylor.

She could've gotten into the music, maybe, but the bodies on the floor were crowding closer. Martika and Taylor were close dancing, to Sarah's surprise…*really* close dancing. And nobody else seemed to notice. The other dancers were either all over each other, like

Martika and Taylor, or else aggressively asexual, dancing like it was some sort of pagan ritual. Sarah, who was doing just above the high school version of a two-step and narrowly avoiding getting mauled doing it, was now distinctly uncomfortable. When Martika signaled for a drink, Sarah followed her with relief.

"So what do you think?"

Sarah shrugged. "I don't know."

Martika sighed. At least, it looked like she sighed. She did the little bosom bounce and shoulder heave thing. "Sarah, aren't you going to even let yourself try to have fun?"

Sarah looked down at her drink. "I am trying to have fun," she answered, then repeated it since Martika couldn't hear her.

"Not from what I can see. You're free! You aren't dating that Neanderthal dickhead anymore!" She studied Sarah appraisingly. "Believe me, *he's* probably more than fucking aware of it, Sarah."

Sarah's chin jutted up. "What do you mean?"

"Sarah, do you honestly think he's saving himself for you?"

Sarah's eyes widened. She hadn't thought about that.

Sarah approached the dance floor with a vengeance. She closed her eyes, trying to feel the music, rather than just be deafened by it. She moved with an aggressive sensuality...all hips, boobs, everything. Martika was right. She wasn't saving anything for that...that Neanderthal dickhead! If he was out haunting some sports bar or something, hanging out with the boys at the office, then she could sure as hell have a good time in what Benjamin would definitely call a den of iniquity. And who cared!

She noticed a man, fairly close, staring at her. He was attractive, in a Children-of-the-Night sort of way…long dark hair, waxy-pinkish skin. *At least his eyes are the right color,* she thought, trying not to be too obvious. She glanced away, continuing her sensuous dance, and when she looked back he was still staring at her.

No, more than staring at her. *He was headed her way.*

Play it cool, play it cool, she thought, continuing her dance. She wasn't sure how she felt about this. It's not like she had to sleep with him or anything, she reasoned. Just dance with him. There wasn't any harm in that. She noticed she was slowly moving away from him, and then stopped, continuing to dance in place, letting him approach her.

He said something to her. She stopped dancing. "What?" she mouthed. She figured mouthing was probably sexier than yelling. Not that she had to have sex with him, she reminded herself. She wasn't Martika, after all!

He frowned, and repeated it. Forget sexy. "What?" she yelled.

He leaned close to her ear. "I said, you've stepped on my girlfriend's foot twice now. Could you please fucking watch it?"

She pulled back, eyes wide. "Oh, my God."

He motioned to a woman with long jet-black hair with two streaks of silver, á la Frankenstein's bride. She was favoring one foot and glaring at Sarah like a curse.

"Sorry! Sorry," she mouthed, making the apologetic hand movements, like Moses calming the waters. The woman nodded curtly.

Sarah quickly retreated to the bar. Oh, my God. Oh, my God. She stood there, looking for Martika. Martika wasn't far behind.

"What did that guy say to you?" Martika was in mother hen mode, glaring at the guy from the side of the bar. "Did he frighten you? I'll kick his ass!"

"Martika, I have to go home."

Martika stared at her, aghast. "Home? It's only midnight! You've been here an hour!"

"I know, but..." Sarah didn't know how to explain. "I just...I have to get up early in the morning."

Martika stared at her suspiciously. "And do what?"

"I have to go to a temp agency," Sarah said reasonably. "The rent isn't going to pay itself, you know."

"You can go to a temp agency on Monday, and you know it."

"Martika, *please*."

Martika stared at her for a minute longer, then let out a lusty, unmistakable sigh. "Let me go tell Taylor. You are going to owe me *so* big time!"

Chapter 7

Roadhouse Blues

The desk in Judith's home office was heavy, expensive mahogany that she and David had searched for for months, right after he got hired at MacManus. As it turned out, David got tired of lugging the heavy case files and background from the office to home, and wound up camping out there as often as not. Judith brought work home occasionally, but she now had a competent staff and had her job so well in hand that all she had to do when she came home was go online. She had taken several classes that way, and it was easier than leaving the house and going to the

UCLA extension courses she had taken last year. Now, she was still searching for something else to sign up for. In the meantime, she had what she supposed *Newsweek* would label a ''cybercommunity'' of sorts. The computer hummed happily and her fingers flew across the keyboard, each stroke sounding like rapid machine gun fire.

She was glad for their high-speed connection as she signed on to her favorite discussion group, ''Busy People,'' a group ostensibly started for professionals looking for ways to make their lives more time efficient, but one that had turned into a combination venting hall and coffee klatsch. She typed in a greeting, and got a chorus of replies.

Feyn: Hi, Judith23!
Isabella749: Hello Judith.
Roger: 'Lo, Judith. :)
Ms. sexy exec: Hi there@!
Ms. sexy exec: Whoops! LOL.

She glanced over the few lines of discussion that she'd stepped in on—Feyn was ranting about something, as usual. Roger's lines were blue and short. Isabella was talking about being at home with her child. The rather ridiculously named ''Ms. sexy'' was trying to hit on Feyn (whom Judith doubted was even male) and Roger. Feyn was too busy ranting—Roger flirted lightly.

''Not real full tonight,'' Judith typed.

Feyn: No. But it's only Tuesday.
Roger: How are you doing, Judith?

Judith pondered that. Actually, she'd been doing all
right—she'd finally gotten back to her meditation, and
had managed to get the last set of ad comps out for
that big push for Becky Weisel's client, as well as
bring David's car into the shop and squeeze in (no
pun intended) an Ob-Gyn appointment. Her life was
a well-oiled machine, if she said so herself.

"Not so good," she wound up answering.

Isabella749: Why not?
Feyn: I'm telling you, cyber communities are replac-
ing face-to-face contact, and I'm happy for that.
Roger: Are you okay, Judith?
Ms. sexy exec: Roger—what are you wearing?

Judith read over the responses. Feyn and Sexy were
too wrapped up in their own conversations, which was
fine. "I had a friend ask me a weird question. She
wanted to know if I was happy."

Isabella749: And you don't feel you are?
Feyn: I have all kinds of people tell me that I'm just
a geek for having so many online friends.
Roger: What did you tell her?
Ms. sexy exec: I've been thinking of trying out online
dating. What do you think, Roger, Feyn?

"That's just the thing," Judith answered. "I said I was, but I had to think about it. I hadn't thought about it." She hit Send, then rapidly typed another question. "Are you happy?"

Roger: Generally, I'd say I'm happy. I mean, bad things happen, but it's just a matter of how you respond to them.
Isabella 749: I used to have periods of unhappiness, but then I found Paxsel. It's wonderful stuff...evens you right out. Are you on anything, medication?
Feyn: I'm very happy! I just don't see why so many people think that a face-to-face social life is the only kind of social life you can have!
Ms. sexy exec: What? Who's unhappy?

Judith sighed. *And pandemonium reigned.*

"Isabella—no, I'm not on medication. Roger—I agree with you, it's all about choices. Feyn—I agree, cybersocial life is just as good. Sexy—nobody's unhappy."

Isabella749: If you're not on medication, I'd recommend it. It's really good, not that heavy, sleepy feeling like the stuff they used to prescribe in the '80s.
Feyn: I mean, you guys are my closest friends. Well, not all of you.
Ms. sexy exec: This is boring. I'm going to another chat room. //wave

Judith was sorry she brought the subject up at all.

Her computer made a tingling bell noise, and she saw an Instant Message window pop up. It was from Roger.

Roger: Hi there. Sorry if this is getting uncomfortable. Are you okay?

"I'm fine," she typed back. She liked Roger, what little she'd seen of him. He was a doctor in Atlanta, and had an active social life. He was the one that recommended Filofax over the system she'd been using, now that she remembered it.

Roger: Really? Work going okay? I hear ad agencies are slave drivers.

She rubbed at her eyes. "Well, it's been tough. I mean, my job's going great, but I'm catching a little flak from a friend…got her a job, and then she quit. Rather spectacularly. People are casting a few aspersions."

Roger: {{{Hugs}}} That's bad. Sorry.

She smiled. "It's not that bad."

She was now ignoring the chat going on in the "Busy People" Room completely. A few other people she knew had entered, and were involved in a huge debate over whether or not Feyn should go on medication or at least rehab for his online tendencies and basic insecurity. They were also going into the pros and cons of various antidepressants and talking about how long they'd been in therapy. As her family didn't *do* therapy, she doubted she'd have much to contribute to the conversation.

Roger: So what happened?

"One of our Account Supervisors ran her pretty ragged, granted, but that was no excuse to quit the way she did. Besides, everybody works those hours, when necessary."

Roger: Even you?

"Especially me," she typed.

Roger: I just get the feeling you're more stressed than you're letting on. Otherwise her question wouldn't have shocked you quite so much.

She felt herself freeze at the comment. She wasn't the type to let her feelings project—not like some of her co-workers, who wore their frenzied expressions like badges of honor. *Yes, I really am so incredibly busy and important that I'm just this side of insane,* their faces seem to say. Not Judith. She preferred cool, competent, composed.

"Why do you say that?" she typed, instead of her usual oh-it's-nothing response. Roger usually had interesting posts and observations—maybe he'd have an insight she hadn't thought of.

Roger: The way you word things. Tight, controlled.

Judith smiled. "That was the idea."

Roger: Those sort of people usually have all sorts of private demons that they're keeping a lid on.

"I do not!" Judith said out loud, starting to type it, then backspaced. "Interesting theory," she sent instead.

Roger: Well, I like private demons. They're more interesting than the facade protecting it. I get the feeling you're an interesting person, Judith.

Judith read the message a couple of times, gauging his tone. She'd seen him flirt with others, nothing serious, and usually at their instigation. Was this flirting? It had been so long, she couldn't tell if she should be worried or just amused.

"You're running a line on me, aren't you?" she typed.

Roger: LOL! Is it working? :)

Judith laughed, then glanced behind her, as if David had suddenly come into the house invisibly and was frowning with disapproval over her shoulder. "Well, that's very flattering, but then my husband would hardly approve.''

Roger: I'm in Atlanta and you're in L.A. Somehow the idea of a clandestine affair between us seems...moot?

Judith frowned. He was right, of course. She was being ridiculous. He was three thousand miles away. Even if he were flirting with her, what difference did it make?

Roger: Judith? Sorry. I don't mean to make you uncomfortable. It's just the Internet. I figure, if I don't have to talk to people, it almost doesn't exist. Really sorry. Friends?

Suddenly, Judith felt foolish. ''Of course. Seduce away...somehow, I'll find the strength to resist.''

Roger: LOL!

Judith smiled, feeling better than she had in a long, long time.

Sarah sat at the desk at her temp assignment. It was a naked cubicle, with a standard issue desktop computer, a phone with a hands-free headphone set flanking it, and an ancient calculator with that ticker-tape thingy attached to it. She glanced over her brand-new organizer, the one Judith had nudged her toward, going over her mission statement until her new ''boss'' came to tell her the details of the job. She couldn't help but feel like the new kid at school, as people either looked at her curiously or ignored her completely.

It doesn't matter what they think. I am going to do this job to the best of my ability. Sarah smiled, making a little notation on the "daily" page.

Short term goal: get hired, full-time, permanent. She had always wanted to try working for a marketing department, and this was apparently an affluent one. She could work out a career plan from there. That was on her list of long-term goals: *develop a career plan.*

Under relationships, she had *regroup and decide on qualities of potential mate.*

She liked this system, she decided as she shut the organizer and zipped it closed. It gave her a sense of direction.

She tucked the organizer into her small, ergonomically correct knapsack, along with her lunch. It seemed a little more casual than a briefcase, granted, but somehow she doubted professionalism was at a high premium here. She was dressed more formally than most of the staff, who wore that brand of "office casual" that consisted of khakis for both sexes and polo shirts. She wasn't entirely sure what most of these people did, but unlike the agency, they didn't seem to be in very much of a hurry about it.

The office itself was like any other office she'd been in: the people sitting like ice cubes in trays of cubicles. Their cubicles sported pictures and cartoons, all the personal touches that made three walls a home of sorts. The amount of crap collected usually signi-

fied how long a person had been there. Sarah glanced
at the cubicle across from hers. She was surprised that
the woman in the vibrant tiger-stripe tank top and gold
colored slacks could fit in the overstuffed monstrosity.
Every square inch was covered with something, either
pinned to a wall or sitting on a shelf. The woman had
to have been there for years.

"Sarah?"

Sarah snapped her gaze up, feeling guilty for cube-
peeping. "Yes?"

"Great. It's good that you're on time. I'm Ms. Peccorino." The woman held out her hand, and Sarah
stood up and shook it. "My! Don't you look nice!"

Sarah self-consciously straightened her navy-blue
skirt and white blouse. She'd slung the matching
jacket over the back of her chair. It was just a Ross
special, but she felt like she might as well have been
wearing a prom dress in this casual atmosphere.
"Thank you."

"So few people here know how to dress appropri-
ately for the office." Ms. Peccorino shot a quick
glance over her shoulder at Ms. Tiger Stripe before
turning back to Sarah. Sarah noticed that the woman
in question flipped Ms. Peccorino off. Sarah kept her
eyes riveted on Ms. Peccorino, or Janice, after that,
terrified that she might burst out laughing and have to
explain it. Janice herself was dressed in a pink Cha-
nel-wannabe suit with black trim. Her blond hair and
dark eyebrows suggested that her coloring had nothing to do with nature, and everything to do with Miss
Clairol.

"I'm sorry—they didn't mention much at the temp agency, except that I needed to know Excel and PowerPoint," Sarah said, glad that her voice was steady.

"Oh, certainly. We've got plenty of projects here that need lots of help," Ms. Peccorino said, as if she were looking to Sarah to save her from drowning. "I'll show you your first one."

Sarah followed the woman through the maze of dun-colored cubicles, over to a bank of filing cabinets. Janice gestured to a stack of cardboard banker boxes, sitting three high and three across.

"We'll need all of these ad comps and direct mail pieces filed here," Ms. Peccorino said, with a voice of woe. "I'm afraid there's a lot of them. This could take you a while."

Sarah stared at the boxes. They were really long boxes. There had to be a couple hundred files there.

"And we need you to weed through all these files, as well. Anything older than a year needs to be archived." With that, Janice approached a cabinet, and reached for its handle.

The drawer exploded open. File folders were crammed in so tight that she couldn't see how the dumb thing stayed shut.

"Are all the drawers like that?" Sarah said involuntarily, aghast.

"I'm afraid so."

"And when was the last time these files were archived?"

Janice looked embarrassed. "Well…we haven't really had the time before, or the budget for a temp…"

In other words, Sarah thought, a sinking feeling in her stomach, *never.*

Sarah spent the whole day weeding through old files, getting paper cuts and cursing silently. Good thing I know all these computer skills, she thought to herself as she filled and labeled the tenth box that day. They're *so* coming in handy.

She glanced at her watch. It was twelve-thirty. *Is that all?* She felt like she'd been filing for the better part of a week.

"Wow. That's a lot of boxes."

She glanced up. A good-looking guy with black hair and really tanned skin was smiling down at her from where she sat on a rolling office chair. She squelched the desire to stand up. "Yup. Lot of boxes," she agreed inanely. *And one cute fella.*

For an inexplicable moment, she felt guilty—like she was cheating on Jam. She glanced down at the boxes.

"You're a temp, aren't you?"

"Is it that obvious?" she asked, then felt like biting her tongue.

He laughed. "Well, the suit is sort of a giveaway." His eyes studied her in a friendly but predatory way. "Looks good, though. If you don't mind my saying."

"Um, thanks." There it was again. Guilt pang!

"So…think you'll be busy later?"

Oh, my God. Cute guy asking her out. Guilt with a capital *G!*

"Um…what did you have in mind?" she heard herself ask. Stay calm. "I may be busy," she hedged. There. She was playing hard to get. Feeling guilty had nothing to do with it. Martika would probably even agree with that.

"Well, I can wait." His eyes were warm, almost hungry, even though his tone was casual as the rest of the office. "I'm sure you can help me with my particular problem, but I don't want to rush you."

She frowned. His particular problem? Ick! "Well, I certainly don't like to be rushed," she said emphatically. "I like to take my time with these sorts of things."

"I see." He quirked an eyebrow at her. "It's good to see you're so conscientious."

She felt like a spinster or something, but her lips still drew together primly. "Better that you know now. Up-front, I mean."

He shrugged. "Besides, my folders aren't going to go anywhere."

Suddenly, Sarah felt like she'd walked into a foreign film without subtitles. "Your…folders?"

"Yes. I need a whole mess of labels made. My filing system's a mess, and since you're doing so much work here, I figured you could help me with it."

Aha. Not what was she doing later socially…just when would she be done with the project.

"Oh. Well…I'm…I'll be sure to do it as soon as possible."

"Like I said," he explained, obvious amusement in his eyes. "No rush."

He walked away, leaving Sarah to blush unnoticed, her face was practically buried in the file drawer.

On the plus side, she didn't feel guilty anymore. She just felt stupid. A minor step up.

"I cut out of work early so I could watch this. This is my friend, Pink. She's got an absolutely *fabulous* eye for clothes."

Pink smiled demurely and removed her dark glasses. She was wearing a magenta car coat over a black body suit that would have done justice to Emma Peel. She wore black half-boots. The most striking thing about her, however, was her hair—a soft, baby-girl-pink pageboy that curled gently around her face. Her eyes were an icy gray-blue by comparison.

"I was named Pink before the singer was," she said, holding her hand out. "Had the hair color, first, too."

Sarah, who hadn't even realized there *was* a singer called Pink, politely shook hands. "Nice to meet you."

Pink then did the quick fashion-circle tour, just as Joey had. Sarah felt awkward, just as she had then.

Pink glanced over at Martika. "This is the one with the asshole ex, right?"

Sarah protested. "It's a long story…"

"Yes," Martika said unequivocally, frowning at Sarah.

"Got it," Pink said, jotting a few notes. "So. Basic

clothing type recommendations, keeping in mind guy-hunting component. So what I'm going to do is ask you a few questions, keep in mind your coloring and body frame, and then show you what I think you should be wearing.'' She gave Sarah a quick, almost clinical once-over. ''Great tits, by the way,'' she said off the cuff.

Sarah blushed scarlet. Now Martika laughed.

''I'm bi, I guess I'm as good a judge as any. So let's talk colors,'' Pink said, leaving Sarah to wonder if she'd really heard the first sentence correctly. ''What colors do you usually wear? What colors are you *drawn* to?''

''I, um...'' Sarah began, still hung up on the last statement, and surprised by the fact that Pink had produced a clipboard from her black patent leather bag and was quickly jotting down notes on some sort of form. ''I like pastels.''

Martika shook her head, but Pink nodded. ''Good. A jumping off point, at least. Any sort of pastels?''

Sarah glanced at her room. ''Blues, greens, lavenders.''

Pink saw the direction of her gaze, and stood up. ''Mind if I go in your room?'' she said, and walked in. Sarah followed her. Pink opened the curtains and glanced around. ''Ah. Monet water-lilies kind of colors. Got it.''

Sarah nodded.

''So you're a romantic-type,'' Pink said, jotting a quick note. She looked her over. ''We can work with it as a starting point, anyway. What do you do for a living?''

"I'm sort of between jobs at the moment," Sarah said, feeling embarrassed again.

Pink sighed. "Let me rephrase. How do you see yourself in a job? What sort of work do you *like* doing? What are you *good* at?"

Sarah paused, no longer embarrassed. Rather, she was intrigued. No one had ever asked her a question like that. Usually it was more, "What are you planning to do with your life *now?*"

"Hmm. What I'm like at work. What I like." She sat down for a second. "I handle crises, and I get people through them. I'm good at putting out fires and making people feel comfortable." She thought about it a second, then laughed. "I guess that means I should be wearing a fireman's hat and an apron."

"Not that kind of party, but it's a start," Pink said, all business. "Question 2: sex." She shot Sarah an inquisitive stare, expectant.

"Sex?" Sarah said weakly.

"You know. What sort of person are you trying to attract? What are you comfortable with? What do you like?" She saw Sarah's look of dismay, and chuckled. She turned to Martika. "You know, Taylor's right. She's absolutely Japanimation adorable."

"I know," Martika said, with that proud tone of voice. "With the right clothes, the right places..."

"I feel it," Pink said with a nod. "Well, Sarah?"

"Um...I like sex. I guess."

Pink and Martika looked at her, then looked at each other, then looked back at her.

"Houston, we have a problem." Pink started jotting notes down furiously, while Martika just stared at her.

"What?" Sarah stared back at them defensively. "What'd I say?"

"Honey, if you really liked sex…" Martika shook her head. "Suddenly, all that Eddie Bauer makes sense."

Sarah was torn between feeling insulted and feeling confused.

"Not a problem, not a problem. She just hasn't hit her groove, as it were," Pink said, in a clinical tone. "No biggie. Let's approach this from a different angle. What actors make you hot?"

Sarah blinked. She was definitely leaning more toward confused, now. "Um…"

Pink huffed impatiently. "Leonardo di Caprio? Russell Crowe?"

"Russell Crowe," Sarah said quickly, and felt a slight blush for no good reason.

Pink noticed the blush, and smiled. "Ah. *Now* we're getting somewhere. Are we talking Russell Crowe in *Gladiator,* or Russell Crowe in *Virtuosity?*" At Martika's curious look, she clarified, "You know. Younger, thinner."

"Gladiator," Sarah said, thinking about it, then smiled to herself. "And *L.A. Confidential.*"

"Totally," Martika said approvingly.

"Okay. And did you see him working with Kim Bassinger? Or that red-haired chick from *Gladiator?*"

"No," Sarah said, then was surprised at the quickness of her response. "I mean, I was glad he got together with them since he was the hero and all, but I don't really see him with those sorts of people."

"So who *do* you think he'd be perfectly cast with?" Pink probed.

Sarah thought about it. This was fun. Weird, but fun. She was glad they weren't talking about clothes anymore. "I don't know. I think I'd like to see him with…hmm. Not Gwyneth Paltrow…"

"God, I should hope not," Martika input, but Pink silenced her.

"Let her struggle it out," Pink reprimanded gently.

"Not Sandra Bullock…not Jenna Elfman…not Meg Ryan…"

"Thank you, God."

"Martika!" Pink said sharply.

"Sorry."

Sarah continued as if no interruption had occurred. "Didn't he used to date Nicole Kidman?" she asked, suddenly. "You know, that's perfect. Nicole Kidman."

"*Days of Thunder* Nicole Kidman, or *Eyes Wide Shut* Nicole Kidman?"

Sarah smiled. "*Practical Magic* Nicole Kidman."

"I see. The girl is good with her movies—has she met Kit?" Pink smiled, as if seeing Sarah in different clothes already. "I think I know what sort of style would suit. Stand up again."

Pink produced one of those cloth tape-measure thingies, and took down all of Sarah's measurements.

"Now, let's talk budget…"

"Um, I don't know how far I want to go with this until I get an idea of what sort of style you have in mind," Sarah said, not caring that Martika was shaking her head at her. "Martika, I am not blowing all my money on new clothes. It's just not happening."

Pink looked at Martika, her eyes sharp with predatory interest. "How much money is she not spending, say?"

Martika grinned. "Somewhere in the neighborhood of five grand."

Pink looked at her. "I could definitely get her a good foundation…fill it out a little more with chintzy stuff, but a good solid foundation is always worth the money."

Martika did a little strut, showing off her own bloodred silk suit. "Tell me about it."

"Five thousand dollars?" Sarah almost stamped her foot. "I am not going to spend that much money! I don't even have a permanent job yet!"

Pink looked at Martika. "Hmm. She doesn't seem as into this as reported."

"She will be," Martika assured Pink. She pulled Sarah into the kitchen under the pretense of getting Pink a glass of water. "What's the matter with you? It's not like you'd have to spend it all at one time. And you've got credit cards, haven't you?"

"I'm *not* spending five thousand dollars on clothes!"

"It wouldn't just be clothes," Pink called from the living room. "From what I've seen, accessories and makeup definitely need to be added to the list."

Sarah groaned, covering her face.

"Listen, Pink is here as a personal favor to me," Martika said, her tone slightly sharp. "You said you wanted to change. Is that true, or is that just bullshit?"

"It's just…too much. Too *fast*," Sarah countered. "I'll do a few things, but no big grand leaps, okay?"

Martika growled in frustration, then the two of them returned to the living room.

"I think I'll start with looking over what you have in mind, and then see how much I can afford," Sarah said diplomatically.

"She's being a pussy," Martika said, ruining Sarah's effort at tact.

Pink nodded, giving Sarah a quick, thoughtful nod. "This is new, I understand. It can be traumatic and not everyone can make the plunge all at once." *Like Martika and I can,* Sarah imagined her adding. "Tell you what—why don't we get you one outfit, and some new makeup, and then you can decide if it's a worthwhile investment?"

Sarah looked at Martika, who was glaring at her. "Okay," Sarah said, then quickly added, "but I'd like to put a—" she did some mental calculations "—two-hundred-dollar cap on it."

Pink looked at Martika, who rolled her eyes. "Hmm. In that case, let's just start with makeup. Next Saturday okay? Perfect."

Sarah was about to protest—*two hundred dollars for makeup?* But Martika's glare silenced her.

Pink stood up, and Sarah was shocked to be air-kissed by the Mary-Kay-haired stylist. "Don't you worry, chica, we are going to make you look, as Taylor would say, *imminently fuckable*." She smiled and put her sunglasses back on. *"Ciao."*

After Martika shut the door, she turned on Sarah. "What was that all about? I thought you said you were over him!"

Sarah blinked. "Who, Benjamin? I am over him! What does that have to do with anything?"

"If you're over him," Martika said, folding her arms across her chest, "what's the big deal about changing your look?"

"Five thousand dollars is a huge deal, Martika. Or would you rather I not pay the rent?"

Martika clucked her tongue impatiently. "You'll make the rent, Sarah. You've got credit cards that you could at least *start* with. This isn't about money."

Sarah sighed. "Maybe I'm just not ready. This is all too fast!"

Martika's eyebrow went up with a look of frustration. "Life's faster here, farmgirl. You might want to think about that."

Sarah stuck her tongue out at Martika's back as Martika retreated to her room.

"I saw that," Martika said, turning with a wicked grin. "Martika knows all and sees all. And believe me, someday you'll thank me."

* * *

Sarah took a deep breath. She'd been here almost a month, and she could honestly say she was hardly impressing *anyone,* much less making progress toward her short-term goal of getting hired. She needed to—how did they put it? Expand her Sphere of Influence or something?

At any rate, she really needed to get her butt in gear. This job had plenty of potential, if she'd just show a little initiative.

Potential for paper cuts, sure, Sarah heard Martika drawl in her head.

Sarah shut her eyes. Okay, she needed *not* to be hearing Martika's voice in her head, giving her advice.

Come to think of it, she really didn't need to be hearing *any* voices in her head.

"Sarah? Are you all right?"

Sarah looked up. It was Janice, looking at her with a mixture of kindness and apprehension. She wasn't quite sure how long she'd been sitting there, listening to the Martika-voice.

This wasn't looking like a good day to get any of her goals accomplished.

No, no, that's not the right attitude! Stay focused and positive!

Great. Now Judith's voice had popped up into her head. It was like dueling shoulder angels, with Judith in a prim white suit holding a gold organizer instead of a harp, versus Martika, in a red vinyl dress, replete with pitchfork and grin.

Okay, now she was imagining things, as well.

"Sarah?"

Sarah looked at Janice—whoops, Ms. Peccorino. Wasn't that a sort of cheese? "I'm sorry. I've just been a little preoccupied this morning. I was trying to remember if I had anything else to do for Jeremy."

Ms. Peccorino's eyebrow quirked slightly.

"I mean, Mr. Anderson."

"Of course." Ms. Peccorino's voice turned funny. "He hasn't asked you to do…*too much,* has he?"

Sarah looked at her, puzzled. "Well, there were a lot of folders…"

Ms. Peccorino still stared at her, then sighed. "Nothing. It's nothing. Do you have some time to work on a project, then? You'd be saving my life if you did."

Sarah smiled. Aha! The opportunity she'd been looking for! "Sure. I don't have anything on my plate that couldn't be, er, reprioritized." Which sounded better than *all the stuff I'm working on right now is stupid drone stuff, anyway.*

"Wonderful!" Ms. Peccorino trotted off, then came back with her arms laden with stapled papers, stacked three feet high. "I'll need you to input all of these report numbers into an Excel spreadsheet. You don't have to build it, that's been created already."

Sarah looked at the imposing pile. "Okay."

"And, well, I know this might be asking a lot, but—these are budget reports. If you see any sort of, I don't know, *trends*…do you think you could let me know?"

Sarah frowned. "Trends?" Simply keying these

monsters in was going to take time. And she'd hardly been involved in any kind of finance stuff.

Ms. Peccorino laughed a little. "Oh, you don't have to be all analytical about it, don't worry! I know you're not an accountant. But if you notice that there is any...repetition, say. Money being lost somewhere, money not being spent somewhere else. Don't worry, dear, you'll recognize it if it's there. And if it isn't, don't worry about it."

Sarah smiled. Frankly, she didn't plan on worrying about it. "No problem."

"Oh, and Sarah? I need it by—" she glanced at the clock hanging on the opposite wall "—five today. Is that okay?"

Sarah frowned. It was noon. Five hours to put all this stuff in? Much less that trend analysis thingy? "Well..."

Ms. Peccorino's eyes were pleading.

"Sure," Sarah said. Stay focused on your short-term goals, she thought. Increase your sphere. Or whatever.

That's the spirit, the Judith-angel said approvingly. *That's how you'll get a job here!*

Meanwhile, the Martika-devil snickered. *And then you'd get to do this all the time! And wouldn't that be fun!*

Sarah blew out a short breath, and got to work.

By four forty-five, she had slogged through all of the piles...and was noticing some disturbing trends. There were a lot more negatives than positives. If she were reading the sheets correctly (and she might not be—it's not like she'd been given any clear instructions, she thought bitterly) then the department was about to be several million dollars over budget. That didn't look good. Ms. Peccorino was right—if there was something wrong, and by all accounts there *was,* then she'd noticed it right away.

In the next fifteen minutes, she drew up a chart that showed where the money was hemorrhaging—and which accounts specifically seemed to be responsible for it. She added a little note that she would be able to figure out what sort of expenditures were causing it, if she were given some more detailed reports and another day or so. She wondered if that last part was too kiss-ass. The Judith in her said no.

She still had a minute to spare when Ms. Peccorino walked up to her, with that penguin-on-speed waddle of hers. "I hate to rush you, but…is it done?"

"Yes." Sarah resisted the impulse to buff her nails on her jacket. "It's done."

"So, everything looks…you know, all right?"

"Well, I wouldn't say that, actually." She called up the original spreadsheet, as well as her notations. "I could definitely do more with this," Sarah offered.

Ms. Peccorino's eyes never left the screen. "You're sure about this? Did you proofread the numbers? This can't be right."

Sarah sat up a little straighter. "When there's a loss that big, I naturally double-checked the numbers." And she had. Fifteen million had seemed like Monopoly money—she was sure she'd transposed numbers somewhere, only to discover on the third go-round that she hadn't. It really was that bad.

Ms. Peccorino had paled. "Well. This is…well."

She continued to stand there and stare, tapping the screen and moving the mouse. Sarah waited, silently. Fifteen minutes later, she finally cleared her throat.

"Sorry? What?" Ms. Peccorino finally looked at her.

"It's, er, after five," Sarah smiled hopefully. "I thought I'd go home for the day." She paused. "Unless you need help with this?"

Kiss ass, the Martika-devil denounced.

"No. By all means, go home," Ms. Peccorino said. "This is an excellent job, Sarah. Disconcerting—but really, excellent work. You've done a lot of work with computers, have you?"

Sarah smiled. *Now* she was getting somewhere. "Yes. The temp agency knew that you were looking for someone with good computer skills."

"Fantastic." Ms. Peccorino smiled weakly. "Well. I won't forget this. Have a nice evening."

Sarah went home in good spirits. Martika was already lounging on the couch, with a Green Tea Sobe in one hand and the TV remote in the other.

"So how was your day, dear?" she asked. "Did you make friends and influence people?"

She never should have left the books Judith loaned her on the coffee table, Sarah thought with a wince. "You know, I think I may have."

Martika lolled her head back, making gagging noises.

Sarah smiled. "So. You and Taylor hitting the town tonight?"

Martika made another rude noise, and her blue eyes were disparaging. "He's got to stay home and boy-friend-sit. I swear, I don't know what he sees in Luis. The man is beyond hopeless."

"Are you going to club by yourself, then?"

Martika contemplated the ceiling. "I don't know. Oval is still my club of choice, but it's been getting crowded lately. The club scene just sucks in L.A., have you noticed?"

Sarah raided the fridge, grabbing a Coke. "Hmmm. Maybe it's because you're getting…"

Martika raised an imperious hand. "Don't…even… say it."

Sarah grinned. "I was going to say 'jaded.'"

"Oh, honey, I've been jaded since I was twelve."

"Wanna go out to dinner?" Sarah smiled, taking a few quick sips of her soda. "I really think I made some progress at work today. Maybe enough to start getting a few pieces of clothing that Pink suggested." Sarah thought about her potential salary. "Okay. Maybe one piece of clothing. To start."

"This is a cause for celebration!" Martika grinned. "How about El Torito? I feel like getting a little *borracho*." She winked. Sarah laughed. Things were definitely looking up.

Chapter 8

Love Me Two Times

Sarah must have gotten a little teeny bit *borracho* herself…at least, that's the first thing that struck her when she answered the phone that morning at seven. Either that, or she was still dreaming.

"May I speak with Sarah Walker?"

Sarah blinked groggily. "Speaking."

"Sarah, this is Temps Fugit."

Her agency? Why would they…

A job. She must've impressed them more than she thought! "Hi. Is there…"

"You won't be going to your assignment today."

Sarah propped herself up on one arm. "I'm sorry?"

"You won't be going to your assignment," the voice on the other end said.

Sarah waited for an explanation, then realized the person on the other end was about to hang up. "Wait! When am I supposed to go back?"

There was a very long pause on the other end of the line.

"Hello?"

"I'm going to transfer you over to Monica," the voice said, and quickly Sarah was listening to a Muzak version of Ricky Martin's "La Vida Loca."

This can't be good.

"Sarah?"

"Yes," Sarah said eagerly, wide-awake now. "Monica? What's happened?"

"Sarah, this is very serious." Monica's birdlike twitter sounded grave, which in turn, sounded weird. "I'm afraid your assignment called with some rather unpleasant complaints."

"Complaints? About *what?*"

"Apparently, some large financial files got wiped out last night. It was last opened up on your computer, according to the I.T. people." Monica sounded like she wasn't sure what this meant, but it was *bad.*

A file…oh, shit. "They lost the *budget?*"

"Yes, I think they mentioned a budget."

"Well, I don't know how it got erased, but I'm sure they've got to have backups somewhere of all that information."

"Apparently not—even backup copies were erased from that computer, and then the computer being shut down so the daily backup didn't work or something...I don't know. There was even rumor of a virus. The whole thing was very distressing."

Sarah gasped. "Wait a second. Are you saying that I destroyed the files on purpose?"

Monica sighed. "Well, the company is calling it either criminal destruction of property or amazing stupidity, to be honest."

Sarah closed her eyes. The room was beginning to spin, and she knew it wasn't the margarita she'd indulged in last night. "Monica, you *know* me. You know what I'm capable of with computers!"

"Exactly, dear." There was another long sigh. "Which is why I'm afraid there's no place for you here at Temps Fugit, either."

"What?"

"We certainly don't need corporate espionage rumors haunting the place." Sarah could almost picture Monica, head bobbing, clothes rumpled. "No, indeed! So as of today, you're no longer a member of the Temps Fugit family. Your last paycheck will be mailed to you...no need to come in."

"Monica, you can't possibly believe this! I've got to be able to prove..."

"And there were some allegations that you were sleeping with one of the staff!"

Sarah gaped at that one. Her throat made a surprised, squawking sound.

"Frankly, I wouldn't have thought you capable of any of this, Sarah," Monica said mournfully. "I'm usually such a good judge of character!"

Like this was some sort of huge fucking insult to *her!* "Monica, listen to me..."

"No, I think we've had about enough. Goodbye, Sarah."

There was an almost immediate *click.*

Sarah hung up the phone.

Okay, Judith hadn't prepped her for this one.

Sarah was tired. She had to find another job, probably in retail or food service or something that paid minimum wage. *How did everything get this far awry,* she asked herself. She had it all planned out. She'd help out Benjamin. He'd marry her, loving her and supporting her decisions. She'd then naturally find a job that she adored, or be so wrapped up in having kids that the career thing would be postponed, depending. Now, she had nothing, just like Judith had warned. If she'd ever feared being a loser, she didn't have to fear anymore. She was a bona fide Varsity loser now, with a big flashing L-symbol on her forehead.

This was all Benjamin's fault, she thought.

She felt like screaming. She turned on the radio, dialing around until she hit a hard rock station. It was playing Limp Biskit's "Break Stuff." She felt like they were singing directly to her. She felt edgy, upset...raw.

The more Sarah thought about it, the more perturbed she started to get...and the more determined. Almost unconsciously she looked up Jam's company in the yellow pages.

Don't call. This is a really bad idea.

The litany continued in her head as she picked up the phone and started to dial. She knew it was a bad idea. However, it was the only idea she really had available right now. Besides, it probably was a hell of a lot more productive than going over to see Ms. Peccorino and Jeremy the Cute with a baseball bat.

"Becker Electronics."

"I'd like to speak to Benjamin Slater, please." She made her voice sound as businesslike as possible.

Apparently, that wasn't good enough. The secretary's voice was definitely suspicious. "May I ask who's calling, and what this is pertaining to?"

"This is Sarah Walker. He'll know what it's pertaining to." At least, she hoped he would. Or maybe she hoped he wouldn't—if he knew that she was calling to lambaste him, he'd hardly answer the call.

"One moment, please." Oh, the woman's voice was frosty.

She was put on hold, the cheesy music played some instrumental version of a romantic tune. It was ironic, considering her mood.

"Benjamin Slater."

His voice. Traitorously, her heart panged, just a little bit. "Hello, Jam."

There was a long pause on the other end of the line. "Sarah. You know, I wasn't even paying attention when Mathilde told me who was on the phone."

"I see." Okay, now she'd gotten him on the line. What was she supposed to do? Suddenly, her bad-but-only-option idea seemed like bad-and-what-was-I-thinking? The resulting pause seemed interminable.

Finally, Benjamin spoke. "What do you want to yell at me about, Sarah?"

The comment caught her off guard. "What makes you think I want to yell at you?"

He sighed. "I know you. You've probably been working yourself up for weeks. You obviously have something to say."

"I…" Well, she did. But what exactly? *You ruined my life? You're a selfish bastard?* "You haven't even called to see if I was alive."

Somehow, that sounded bad. Deflated. Downright wimpy.

"Well, you're obviously alive," he said, a little bit of a smile in his voice. No, she wasn't going to cave. The guy was…what was Joey's term for it? A prick, an absolute prick. "How have you been, Sarah?"

"Oh, now that's low."

"What is?"

"You sound all nice and concerned, when I know if I hadn't called, you probably wouldn't even have thought of me at all." Now she knew where she was going. "You selfish, rotten…"

"I do think about you, Sarah," Benjamin said quietly. "I think of you a lot."

That punctured her balloon of ire. "You do?"

"All the time, actually."

She thought about it. "What, do I owe you money or something?"

"That's not nice." His voice was coolly repri-
manding. "You know I care about you, Sarah. Just
because I didn't agree with what you did doesn't
mean I stopped caring about you."

Now Sarah felt like an idiot. An immature, whining
fool. She gripped the phone tightly. "You didn't support me. You made me feel all alone."

"I didn't make you feel anything, Sarah," he said,
in a calm and reasonable tone. "I just pointed out that
quitting your job—a job with a career path that you
were interested in, that your best friend stuck her neck
out to get for you—with no notice was really a bad
idea."

When he put it that way, yes, she did sound
pretty... *No. Stick to the subject at hand. Don't start
second-guessing yourself!*

"I was upset, Benjamin," she said, softly. "You
always shut me out or told me to grow up. You never
once paid attention to how I was feeling or why I was
doing what I was doing."

"Do *you* even know why you were doing what you
were doing?"

"Of course I did!" she countered passionately.

"So why did you quit?"

She rubbed at her temples. It all seemed so long
ago now. Why *had* she quit? "Because the place was
intolerable. They were verbally abusive, and I was
working all these hideous hours, and they were *never
happy.* And I was waiting for you to come down and
help me out, and then you just abandoned me!"

"You were waiting for me to rescue you, Sarah."

Sarah felt heat suffuse her cheeks. "You go to hell, Jam."

"I'm not saying that to make you feel bad," he said. "I'm just pointing out a fact."

"I don't need you to rescue me. I just need you to be there for me! And you never were—you were always too busy. Every single other thing in your life was more important than I was because I let you get away with it!"

She stopped, thinking about that. *Because I let you get away with it.*

"I'm more important than that. I *deserve* better than that." Her voice quavered slightly, and she took a deep breath, steadying it.

"I guess I did take you for granted, in some ways. You know how important the job is to me. I just wanted to get a good solid foundation..."

"I don't care."

She heard Benjamin sigh. "You actually picked an okay day to talk to me about this—things are under control. Why don't we have lunch, talk about it?"

Have lunch? Sarah blinked, pulling the receiver away for a second and staring at it. Talk about it? "Um, okay. I guess."

"My treat," he said. "How about...what's that place they keep talking about. Jozu?"

"Um, okay."

"I'll pick you up."

"Um...."

"That all right?"

She shrugged. "Sure." Spend your gas money, not mine. Why not?

She got dressed three times. The first was a dynamite, sexy outfit. Then she realized she didn't want him to get the message that she was trying to win him back, so she changed into jeans and a little T-shirt. Then she changed her mind again, thinking that was too obvious. She finally settled on a sundress that wasn't too risqué, but wasn't too casual. She thought, anyway. The door buzzer sounded.

"Yes?"

"It's Benjamin."

"I'll be down in a minute." She snatched up her purse and locked the door behind her.

He looked good, she thought miserably. He was wearing a suit, one she hadn't seen before. What worked in Fairfield probably didn't work in his L.A. office. She knew about that one. He looked serious, and a little too conservative. Then again, considering how much time she's spent at the ultracasual temp job and then around the likes of Martika, Taylor and Pink, who knew what was normal anymore?

He frowned at her. "You changed your hair."

"Yes."

"It's a lot shorter."

She frowned. "I like it. So do lots of other people." There! Let *him* decide who the lots of other people were. Probably men. Ha!

"I'm not saying I don't like it. I'm just saying it's a lot shorter."

She knew what he was saying. She shrugged and smiled. "Shall we?"

They went to the restaurant in relative silence. Once they got there, in the cool air-conditioned atmosphere, she began to relax. At least until he started talking. Then she gripped her water glass nervously. She wondered if it would be tacky to order something to drink. Like a Red Screaming Zombie. She figured she'd need superstrength muscle relaxants at this point, or her shoulders would be permanently pinned together.

"So why did you decide to call me today?"

She shrugged. "I don't know. I guess I had been thinking about it for a while."

"What's been going on in your life?"

She sighed. "Let's see. I work as a temp now."

"I see." To his credit, his voice wasn't all that smug. "I worried. I hoped that you were okay."

"Why didn't you just call me?" she asked, thinking of the times she'd felt lonely and horrible over the past four months.

He shrugged. "Hurt too much."

The words pinched at her heart. He was hurting. Because he missed her. She felt a little traitorous warmth, and had to force herself not to reach over like she used to and take his hand. She focused on the waiter instead, putting in her food order and asking for a glass of white wine. Within a short period of time, their meals arrived.

"So how has work been going?" she asked, more to change the conversation than anything. She knew it was a topic he'd warm to.

He shrugged again, to her surprise. "It's going well—but not like I expected. I'm not really a Los Angeles sort of person, I think," he said slowly. "I mean, I'm getting used to it, but it's not really my first choice of cities to live in." He looked at her speculatively. "Don't you miss Fairfield?"

"A little." Like when she was broke, when she'd quit her job and dumped him. Or when she had that horrible time at the club with Tika. Or, say, this morning. She shook off that thought with a shudder. "Sometimes. But L.A. has a lot going for it."

"Ha." His face was molded into that classic look of disdain Sarah remembered so well. "It's like an amusement park."

"You say that like it's a bad thing."

"I guess if you're just looking for a little fun, it's okay." He sipped his water. "We were going to talk about us, Sarah."

She frowned. "There is no 'us,' Jam."

"And whose idea was that?"

"I already explained why."

"Well, now I'm listening. I just think that you've kind of..." He paused, as if searching for the right words. "You went off the deep end there for a bit."

"I *what?*"

"You came down here, and you started changing. I mean, you were always sort of flaky..."

"*Flaky?*"

"You know what I mean. You never really settled on anything."

"I settled on you!" She had to deliberately lower

her voice, before she created a full-blown scene. "You were my *life*, Benjamin. I didn't need to have a career—you were a full-time job!"

He was silent for a second.

She felt like crying. All this time, and he didn't get it. He never got it. He probably never...

"I love you, Sarah."

She blinked. Inexplicably, she felt tears welling up. "What? What?"

"You heard me. I love you. You made me feel...you really were devoted to me, and only after I lost it did I realize what I'd been missing."

She looked at the walls, at the other diners—anything but him. "You can't be saying this to me now."

"Let me try making it up to you." He'd paid for the check, and was looking at her with eyes that were dangerously persuasive. "Spend the afternoon with me."

"Don't...don't you have to get back to work?" Sarah said, clutching at straws. *If going to lunch with him was a bad idea, getting anywhere where you might be tempted to sleep with him is a hugely bad idea.*

"I don't care. Work'll still be there when I get back. In fact..."

Sarah watched in dazed disbelief as he called his frosty secretary and let her know he was taking the rest of the afternoon off. "Yes, really, I am," he repeated. Obviously, the secretary couldn't believe it any more than Sarah could. He looked at her. "Want to see my house?"

She was about to say no before she realized she was already nodding.

Alarm bells rang in her head, but she ignored them. The fact of the matter was, she missed him. Her chest was achy with missing him. Talking with him, walking to his car with him, feeling the brush of his hand against her shoulders...all of that felt *normal*. This was what she'd planned for—being with him, a happy team. Not what she'd been living, with the uncertainty of being a temp or trying to fit into Martika's glam world. Sure, it was exciting, but it was temporary. All of it was temporary. Benjamin was solidity and stability and purpose. Benjamin was permanent.

By the time they got to his house, her stomach was fluttering in that nervous, vaguely-turned-on way that she hadn't felt in what seemed like a long time. And best of all, no guilt pangs, no feelings of infidelity/ insecurity. This was what she remembered, she thought as she stepped out of the car. This was *right*.

The house was a generic stucco job in West Los Angeles. They had passed Westwood, and UCLA was not that far away. He let her in, and her heart felt a different kind of pang. This was what she'd been expecting, when she moved down to Los Angeles. All of his furniture was positioned in various rooms, taking up all the space. She would have had him put the TV on the other wall, she thought, and move the couch. She noticed that the dining-room table looked stark, probably would have gotten him a runner and maybe a centerpiece. She saw that the kitchen, what little she could see of it, looked barren and utilitarian.

"This is it."

She sighed.

"Would you like to see the bedroom?" His eyes were low-lidded, and he smiled slightly.

Her conscience sent up one last warning.

She solidly ignored it.

"Honey? I've got to go...I'm supposed to do a business dinner tonight."

Sarah stirred. She was sex-sated and sleepy. Make-up sex really was best, she thought with a smile. "Oh. Give me a minute to wake up."

He chuckled. "That was pretty incredible."

"Mmm."

He got up, walking naked over to the bathroom attached to the master bedroom. She heard him shut the door, and then heard the running water of the shower. She got up, stretching, wincing at the discomfort she was feeling. It had been a long time since she'd had sex. She felt bruised, but not in a bad way.

She got up, stretching from one side to another, then slipped on her clothes. She'd be shame-walking. She hoped that Martika wasn't looking for her, that she'd be home a little later...Sarah knew that Tika would not approve of this latest development. Especially since it looked like she was walking on the road to reconciliation. Tika would just have to deal with it, Sarah thought with a determined nod. Besides, maybe she'd just move in with Benjamin...she was pretty sure he was renting this house, and it wasn't like she had a lot of stuff to move. Maybe Tika could just take over the lease.

The phone started ringing. "Want me to get that?" she called out.

Jam obviously couldn't hear her over the shower. She debated, then decided to just let the machine get it. She wandered out into the hallway, wanting to see how his home office looked.

She was halfway down the hallway when she heard the recorded greeting echoing loudly from the answering machine.

"Hi. You've reached Benjamin and Jessica. We're unable to come to the phone right now, but if you'll leave your name and number, we'll get back to you as soon as we're free. Thanks."

It was Benjamin's voice, she thought.

Who the hell was Jessica?

She quickly turned. Her heart was racing, her stomach's quivering turning to queasiness. Everything was Benjamin's...she recognized the furniture. She shot a furtive look at the door to the bathroom. The shower was still running.

She went to the closet: there were two sliding doors. She opened one and saw a row of suits, neatly lined up. She shut it quickly and moved to the other one.

Dresses.

Relatively petite dresses.

I love you, Sarah. The words rang in her head.

That bastard, she thought, feeling numb. That lying, cheating *bastard.*

Chapter 9

Strange Days

It was a Thursday night. Judith sat at her home office computer. She was wearing her nightgown—it was getting late, and David was still at work. Strangely, she still had her makeup on.

Judith stared at her computer screen, watching the chat transcript of the ''Busy People'' Room scroll slowly up the monitor. She was waiting for Roger to log on.

It's simply the Internet, she reminded herself. Silly, to feel like she was having an illicit affair simply because she had friends in cyberspace. And that she e-mailed one friend more than the others, maybe.

She had been getting e-mail from Roger steadily since she'd posed her "am I happy?" question in the "Busy People" Room, and they'd been growing steadily more—intimate. Not, as Seinfeld would say, that there was anything wrong with it. They were just kidding around. It was nice to talk to someone (even if it was type-talking) who understood her, that knew when she was having a bad day, that made her smile. She never felt like she could reveal the fact that she was having a bad day to David, for some reason. No, not for some reason—she knew precisely why she felt like she couldn't. Because compared to law, *nothing* was that important, or bad. If she was having a client giving her hives, he had a client who was going to lose $100 billion in fraud and was raking him over the coals. If she was stressed because of something related to the house, or balancing his home environment and her job and being the perfect wife, then he was even more stressed, bringing in the huge amount of cash that he felt she needed to have for the life she'd become accustomed to.

If she mentioned she was late in getting her period, she felt sure he'd somehow announce he was expecting triplets.

"So how are you, beautiful?" the instant message came over.

Judith sat down, inexplicably straightening her hair with her fingers, letting it tumble rakishly over her shoulders. "How do you know I'm beautiful?" she typed back.

Roger: You're Judith, aren't you?

She smiled at that. "Charmer."

Roger: Probably. So how's it going?

"Terribly." She sighed, leaning back farther in her office chair. "Work has been hellish, husband has been out a lot."

Roger: Not to be forward, but he should pay more attention to you. You sound tired. Whatever he's doing can't be that important.

She shrugged, even though he couldn't see it. "Nature of the business. Lawyerlyness is closer to Godliness."

Roger: I thought that was just us doctors. :)

She smiled. "One of those rich, good-looking George Clooney look-alikes, right?"

Roger: Yup. The type your mother wanted you to land, if you couldn't land a lawyer.

Judith felt anger burn in the pit of her stomach. "Of course, I was targeting an occupation more than a husband." There was a pause before she got a response.

Roger: I was just kidding, Judith. Just a joke.

She immediately felt badly, and oversensitive to boot. "Sorry. Trophy-wife disease." As soon as she hit Send, she regretted it.

Roger: I've always wondered how they fit you gals on those little stands with the engraved plate.

She knew he was trying to make her feel better for her gaffe. "I wouldn't say I'm a trophy wife. David and I understand each other, and we care about each other very much."

Roger: You really don't need to tell me his name.

She blinked at that. "Why not?"

Roger: Because then I'll feel bad for him when I go to L.A. to sweep you off of your feet and have you live a life of naked splendor with me in Atlanta.

She glanced over her shoulder, inexplicably. "Bad man."

Roger: LOL. It's been mentioned from time to time.

She pictured him, a tall, blond-haired doctor type, taking time from his busy day, probably feet propped up in surgical scrubs (Was he a surgeon? Did it matter? This was her fantasy.) as he typed away at his keyboard with an impish smirk on his face. He was probably picturing her to be a blond bimbo with big breasts that may or may not be real, complaining about her old lawyer husband. They were both fantasies, she decided. Even she was, in this case.

Roger: Let's get even badder, then. What are you wearing? (Lascivious leer)

She bit back a grin. It wasn't real, she reminded herself. "Oh, the usual. Little pink teddy that matches my nail polish. That's about it. You?"

Roger: Gets hot in Atlanta. I'm not wearing anything at all. :)

She gasped at that, then started laughing. "Sure. For all you know, I'm an eight hundred pound albino wearing that pink teddy."

Roger: Being naked and all, you'd see how I reacted to that last remark. Does the term "turtle" mean anything to you?

She laughed even harder. "Yuck! That's disgusting."

Roger: Says you, oh 800 lb Victoria Secret model.

She imagined the two of them in a room together, laughing like old friends. "I wish I could see you," she wrote back. "You seem so nice."

Roger: Wait a sec. I'll send a picture.

She almost told him no. Stop. She didn't want her fantasy to have a face. She didn't want him to seem more real. But she couldn't bring herself to, because she *was* curious. Maybe he was ugly. Or maybe he just wasn't her type. She was getting really drawn to this imaginary man she had created while her husband was off working. Maybe this was an antidote.

"You've got mail!"

She quickly clicked out of IM mode and looked in her mailbox. There it was…an e-mail from Roger's address, with an attachment. *Serve me right if my computer got a virus.* Wouldn't you know it, she thought as she clicked on the icon to reveal his picture. *I'd get a cybersexually transmitted disease.*

The picture slowly came into focus, to show a man with dark brown hair. He wasn't George Clooney, but his face was terribly appealing. She knew he was thirty-seven, but his age didn't really show. He looked as she suspected…impish.

And he had some nice pecs, she noticed as the picture continued to "develop." And…

Oh, my God.

From the looks of it, he was naked.

She stared in fascinated semihorror, waiting for the rest of the photo to load up. The chest was magnificent, lightly tanned. She could see why he was grinning so mischievously.

The Instant Message rang over the image.

Roger: Got it yet?

"Shut up. Still loading." She clicked it back and waited impatiently. It started to show the naked curve of his hips, and then…

A big, white block, with a sentence in a flourishing script font.

IF YOU LIKE THIS, YOU SHOULD SEE THE REAL THING.

She rocked her head back and laughed, louder than she could remember in a long time. The word bubble was placed strategically over his…well, over his nakedness. She quickly e-mailed him back. "You nut. I can't believe you had a picture made like that."

Roger: All these women were e-mailing me saying, "Send me your picture!" and I got tired of it. They were interested in sex and wanted to see if I was a candidate. I was joking with a friend, and she dared me to do this.

Judith felt a burst of ire. "So you've sent this photo to lots of women…" She stopped typing, hit the back-space key. "So you've sent this photo to lots of people, then?"

Roger: Too chicken! ;) You're the first.

The heated anger cooled into a very comfortable warmth between her breasts. "Oh. Well, it's cute."

Roger: You should see the real thing. Hypothetically speaking. :)

"I'm sure it's all it's cracked up to be and more," she answered.

"Judith?"

She spun. David was in the hallway.

"Honey, I've been yelling to you from downstairs. You've been laughing like a loon. What's so funny?"

He started to enter the office, and she quickly tried to shut things down. She hit the Instant Message, and his naked picture popped up, with its sly grin and saucy message. She gasped, trying to shut it down. "Oh, nothing. Sarah sent me some jokes."

He glanced at the picture, shaking his head and grinning ruefully. "Single people. How's she handling breaking up with The Benjamin?"

"Not so good."

She closed the picture file, but before she could shut down AOL, an instant message popped over:

Roger: You'd have to test it to find out. It feels even better than it looks…or so they tell me.

She almost unplugged the computer in her haste. The program signed off, and she turned to David, feeling a heated blush on her cheeks.

He wasn't even looking at her. He was rubbing his temples. "I had a really, really shitty day today. And I'm starving. Do we have any leftovers?"

She took a deep breath. "I…I haven't eaten." She shut down the computer, breathing thankfully as the screen went dark. "But I'm sure I could pull something together for you in no time. Why don't you change your clothes, come downstairs and tell me all about it?''

He smiled tiredly, kissing her on the cheek. ''Thanks, Judy. You're the best.''

Sarah called Martika's cell phone.

''Martika. And you are?''

''Tika, help.''

''Sarah?'' Sarah could barely make her out over the obvious club noise. ''What's wrong? Where the hell have you been?''

''I got fired.''

''Is that all?''

''And I slept with Benjamin.''

''Oh, fuck.'' Pause. ''I take it you didn't enjoy it?''

''It would've been better if I hadn't found out he was living with someone.''

''Double fuck.'' A long sigh, counterpointed by the beat in the background. ''What do you want to do? The boys and I can come get you in a second.''

''I want to go clubbing,'' Sarah said, looking over Martika's closet. ''I want to go *out*. Can I meet you?''

''Sure!'' Martika's voice sounded surprised and happy. ''Why not. We're over at Probe. It's eighties night. We'll get you drunk, and in a few hours it'll all seem like a bad dream.''

''My life is a bad dream.''

''Now, now. Save the maudlin till you get here. So much fun!'' Martika's voice turned matronly. ''Call a cab, sweetie. I don't want you driving, 'kay? You're too upset.''

"Okay, Martika," Sarah agreed. "Oh…can I borrow an outfit?"

Martika's laugh was loud enough to drown out the latent club noises. "Borrow an outfit? Honey, borrow any damned thing you want! Oh, I can tell this is going to be fun! I'll keep an eye out for you."

"Okay, Martika," Sarah repeated. "Bye."

"Byee."

Sarah hung up the phone, and surveyed Martika's crowded closet. She wasn't up for vinyl, but she felt…mean. Dangerous. She felt ready to kick the shit out of somebody.

She wound up going with the same short plaid skirt she'd been stuck in the first night she went out, and the black netting top over a black bra. She also pulled on a pair of Doc Martens boots that Martika had stuffed in the back of the closet. They were a little scuffed, and looked like they'd seen some action. She liked that. She went to the careful pile of makeup she'd gotten under Pink's tutelage—pale Christian Dior concealer to hide her tearstained eyes, Urban Decay over her lids and cheeks and "lip gunk" in the promising color called "Slash" across her mouth in a scowling pout. She dusted the whole thing with Lorac, and added a healthy rim of liquid eyeliner. She looked like a reject from the Sex Pistols, but the look was violent, and that was her statement for the night.

The Judith-angel-voice had gone conspicuously silent, she noted. The Martika-devil simply looked on approvingly.

She phoned for a cab, and spent the next forty-five

minutes, waiting and pacing (after stuffing the toes of the Doc Martens with toilet paper and adding a second pair of socks). She had her short blond hair sticking up like the fiery character in some old Claymation movie she'd seen. It was all she could do not to kick things—set things on fire.

She suspected the cabbie recognized this when she got in. He didn't look surprised or shocked—cabbies rarely did—but when she gave the address, he didn't try for any patter or flirting. Sarah was glad, and disappointed. She felt ready to roll, as Martika would say, with anyone...and not the sexual way, either.

He let her off in front of Probe, and she walked up to the bouncer. A huge man, shaved bald with a small goatee, glanced at her license. She grabbed it, then stalked past him, going in, paying her cover at the small window before entering the club itself.

It was different than the other club Martika had taken her to. It was smaller, more intimate, and unfortunately, more happy. Wham! was blaring out of the speakers, insisting that she wake somebody up before she go-go'd. *Or got out of the shower,* she thought, with that terrible rage.

It took another song (this time the more pleasing "One Night in Bangkok") before she finally found Tika, Taylor and Pink, huddled in a small balcony, smoking clove cigarettes. "Sarah!" Tika gave her a huge one-armed hug, holding the lit cigarette carefully away from Sarah's spiked hair. "Honey, how are you?"

"Shitty. I'd like to get hammered."

"And hammered you shall be," Martika said, putting out her cigarette with a flourish.

Taylor wrapped a companionable arm around the two of them. "All right, ladies, it's an early night for me…"

"No, it isn't."

Taylor looked at Martika imploringly over Sarah's head. "Tika, I've got a meeting in the morning…"

"I don't give a shit," Martika said, as they entered the club again, getting hit with Siouxsie and the Banshees' "Peekaboo." The kids in black clothes did as close to a Goth cheer as the impassive group could muster. Sarah didn't know what weird attraction eighties clubs had for Goth people anyway. "Our girl needs us!"

Taylor sighed, glancing at Sarah's face. "You really had a bad day, huh?"

Sarah nodded, as they walked over to the bar and promptly took up residence.

"What happened?"

"Where do I begin?" So Sarah began with the phone call from Temps Fugit. Then the *other* phone call.

"Ooh, that's a bad one," Pink commiserated, taking a shot of tequila and then continuing to talk like she'd just sipped water. "I can't tell you how many times things have gone shitty in my life and then suddenly, the phone is in your hand and you're asking information for a listing."

"I meant to yell at him, I swear to God, I meant to rip him a new ass," Sarah said. She was feeling the effects of her second shot like a slow burst of Novocaine. It was a preferable sensation. "And then he apologized…"

"Bastard!" Martika slurred.

"And then he asked me out to lunch…"

"Here we go," Taylor said. Martika leaned against him, and he patted her shoulder.

"And then he wanted to show me his house…" Sarah rubbed her face with her hands, doubtlessly smearing makeup but at this point not really caring.

"And you did the deed."

"And then found out that he was already *living* with someone. Living with someone! Named Jessica!"

She felt a tap on her shoulder, and she spun. *"Jessica!"* she yelled.

"Actually, it's Kit." Kit's face was, as usual, unperturbed. "But you were so close."

"Go way. I hate men."

Taylor glanced at her. "Ahem."

"Other than Taylor, I hate men."

Pink shot her a quick, appraising look, then shook her head, as if deciding not to even try. Sarah didn't know if she should feel relieved or insulted. She chose relieved.

"Hmm. I guess you wouldn't be interested in dancing, then."

Sarah glared at him.

"And a blowjob would be out of the question."

Sarah stared. Then, traitorously, a bubble of laughter emerged. She tried to clamp down on it, but it came out in a sputtering wave anyway. Pretty soon all of them were laughing.

"So that's the whole sordid tale," Sarah concluded with a wave.

"Well, you listen to me," Martika said, and she looked directly into Sarah's eyes like she was a hypnotist. "You've had enough of that bullshit, okay? You're only...how the fuck old *are* you, anyway?"

"Twenty-five."

"Right! You're just twenty-five. And you're in Los Angeles. You don't need to have all the answers. You don't need a man. You don't need a career path or a Palm Pilot or some fucking heathered oatmeal sweaters from Abercrombie and Fitch as you wait for your husband to give you fifteen precious minutes of his time to start two-point-five kids!"

"Diatribe, Martika," Taylor warned. Kit grinned.

Martika waved a hand. "Oh, you know what I mean. All I'm saying is, you're in a hell of a fun city, and if you play it my way, you can keep on having fun. Not worrying about what you're *supposed* to be doing. Just doing whatever you want."

"It sounds great," Sarah said, "but there's always a catch."

Martika shrugged. "Yeah. You have to not care what other people think about you...and you've got to make your own decisions." Even drunk, she shot Sarah the look of practiced, mischievous disdain. "Think you can do that?"

Sarah thought about it.

No more career paths and working late nights, paying her dues. No more waiting by the phone for a man's call that would inevitably be disappointing. *No more.*

"I'm willing to try," she said solemnly.

"Then come on," Martika said, dragging at her with both hands. "There's a whole lot of ass shaking to do before you're through *here* tonight!"

A couple of hours and many drinks later, Sarah was feeling no pain. This was better. Her ears were faintly ringing and had muffled the music to a nice, bouncy white noise, probably out of self-defense. Taylor was deliberately staying out, even though he had an early meeting, because he wanted to make her feel better. Well, she amended, because Martika told him he *had* to make her feel better, but nevertheless he didn't really have to stay. And Martika was continually telling her that she loved her and that everything would be all right. Now that she thought of it, she herself had been randomly telling people that she loved them since, oh, about her fourth shot.

She was pretty sure it was her fourth shot. It seemed so long ago.

"We're going home," Sarah finally said, as the club started to wind down.

"Let me give you a lift," Kit said.

"Gallantry!" Martika pronounced, lurching on to him.

Sarah's eyes narrowed. "Did you drink?"

He shrugged. "Two beers. I don't like drinking when I go out to a club. Too expensive."

Taylor laughed. "Tightwad!"

"Come on, let's go."

Since Martika had come with Taylor, she fell asleep in the back, sprawled indecorously. Sarah sat up front of the beat-up old Camaro, with Kit. The engine roared.

"Thanks for giving us a ride home," Sarah said dreamily, studying his face. It was like looking through frosted glass.

"No problem," he said, glancing at her. "You're pretty wasted, huh?"

She shrugged. "Let's just say there's been a lot of waste."

"Do me a favor?"

She tried to focus on him, but the effort was too much. She closed her eyes. "Sure."

"Take Martika with a grain of salt."

"Huh?"

"She's fantastic—she'll tell you so herself," he said, with his usual sardonic humor. "But think about what *you* want before you go in with any of her harebrained schemes, okay?"

"What are you saying?" Sarah's tongue was thick in her mouth—the words came out slow and stumbled over each other.

He sighed, pulling over to the curb in front of their building. "I'm saying, you don't have to be any particular *way,* to be okay. Understand?"

"No." Sarah smiled at him. "Thanks for the ride."

He smiled, then shocked her by lifting her netting shirt up.

"Hey," she protested slowly, but before she could

put her arms up, he'd tucked something into her bra and let the netting top drop.

"I understand you're looking for a job," he said. "He's a friend of mine, looking for a personal assistant. You might like him." His grin was quick. "I'll call you in the morning to remind you. I get the feeling you're not going to remember this at all."

I'm getting sick of interviewing.

Sarah scanned the streets. It was weird enough she was going to be working out of this guy's house, she thought, but the houses themselves—she'd never really had reason to make it into Bel Air, the richest area of Los Angeles. It made Beverly Hills look like a relative slum, from a housing standpoint. She felt sure a lot of the residents shopped in Beverly Hills. Or maybe they sent their maids out to shop for them.

Or their personal assistants.

She sighed again.

The houses she was looking at weren't really houses—they were mansions. One unlikely looking place had statues of Greek gods and goddesses, naked, flanking a long curving driveway. Others looked like they were imported from some lonely moor in Britain, sent stone by moss-covered stone. She finally got to the address: a large brick wall covered here and there with ivy tipped her off. She parked by the imposing iron gate and pushed the intercom button.

"Yes?"

"Sarah Walker to see Richard Peerson."

The voice that replied sounded haughty, and there

was a slight accent Sarah couldn't recognize. "And this would be regarding?"

She fought the urge to laugh. "I'm here to interview with him. For the assistant job."

There was a pause, then a reluctant "drive on up to the house" as the gate slid slowly open. She did as directed, seeing a brick mansion that looked...well, palatial. She stopped by a Silver Cloud Rolls-Royce that was parked at the edge of the driveway. She wasn't sure where the garage was. Somewhere else on the compound, she supposed.

Taking a deep breath and straightening her interview suit, she knocked on the door.

A minuscule Filipino woman answered the door. Scrutinizing her with squinted eyes, she nodded. "All right."

Sarah didn't know what test she passed, but was glad the woman didn't shut the door on her. She got the feeling that was definitely an option. "I'm Sarah Walker," she said, hoping to befriend this woman. "What's your..."

"You go up to the top of the stairs," the woman said, obviously not interested in exchanging pleasantries. "His office is third door on the right." With that, she turned and headed to the back of the house. To the...kitchen? To her room? Sarah watched her disappear down a hallway. Okay, this was just getting creepier by the minute.

She slowly walked up the curving staircase, her hand trailing on the silky wood banister. It's just a job. It would probably beat temping. And it certainly beat food service.

She knocked on the third door.

"Yes?"

She opened it, and gasped.

It was one of those old-fashioned libraries you always saw rich people owning in the movies or TV—a Batman-styled library, with books from floor to ceiling on every wall except one, which was dominated by a huge window. There was a large slab of desk in front of the window. At least, she assumed that was a desk. It was covered, every single square inch of it, with piles of papers. No...*drifts* of papers. Folders of every color peeked out through various pages. The chaos of it had taken over the desk, obviously, and—she took a quick peek around—it was making colonies on various chairs and a good portion of the floor.

"Hello there."

She turned her eyes toward the man sitting behind the desk.

"I'm Richard. Huh. Guess you knew that though, right? Ha ha."

Her eyes widened and a grin escaped. Yes, she could see this man being the creator of this mess. In fact, it made the mess seem more approachable.

He was in his fifties, possibly a very well-preserved sixty. He had a round face, that would have been jowly if it weren't for a distinguished silver beard that was slightly darker than his mane of silver hair that just brushed the back of his collar. He had blue-gray eyes that twinkled, and a perpetual grin. He was wearing an awful gray-and-burgundy running suit with an abundance of zippers, and he wore a I've-been-bad smile as he gestured to his desk and shrugged. "Oh, well, I'm sure I'll find that article eventually," he said on a sigh. "Let's clear you off a seat, shall we?" He wandered around the desk, and she saw that he wasn't that tall.... Maybe five-eight, with a chubby tummy that gave him a sort of Santa look. She bit her lip, fending off a giggle as he took a pile of papers off of a chair, glanced around for another place to put them, shrugged and dumped them on the floor near his desk. He trotted back to his "interviewing" spot while she sat in the chair he offered.

"So!" he said, with an *oof* as he sat down. "You're here for..."

She waited for him to finish the sentence, then realized that he was doing the same—waiting for her.

"An interview for the position of your assistant?" she said tentatively.

"Really?" He looked delighted. "Great! When can you start?"

She blinked. "Just like that?"

"Oh. Right. Can I, um, look at your résumé?"

She dutifully produced the sheet from her portfolio. He made a big show of looking it over. "What have you been doing lately? This last job ended a few months ago."

"I've been temping," she said.

"Why?"

She should have just taken the job, she thought with a wince. "I've been...this is going to sound lame," she prefaced, "but I've been trying to figure out what I want to do."

"And so you're trying out being an assistant?" He wasn't snotty, just genuinely puzzled.

She sighed. "No. I'm just trying to get a job where I can focus but I don't have to bring work home," she explained. "Would I have to bring work home here? Or work late?"

"Good heavens, no!" He looked appalled at the suggestion. "In fact, my old assistant, Ms. Honeywell, wanted to try to bring work home. She was...well, she was almost compulsively organized."

Sarah frowned. "I'd like to think that I'm pretty organized—not compulsive, I don't think I'm really that compulsive about anything."

"Oh, I'd hope not!" he said. He was getting more agitated. "I don't think I'm getting this across quite well. It...well, it *bothered* me."

"What did?"

"I'd go in, and she'd practically *pounce* on me with my schedule for the day. She had all these calendars and things *everywhere*." He sounded like a man who had been hunted down, Sarah thought with amusement. "You'd go in and there would be these yards of color-coded files."

"Sounds horrific," Sarah murmured.

"Oh, it was!" He shook himself, like a startled dog, shuddering. "Good grief. I had to type up a memo to get her to leave. I mean, firing her face-to-face was ghastly, and it didn't quite work anyway. Said she wanted something official." He looked at her, pleading. "Tell me. Do I strike you as an official sort of person?"

"Not remotely," Sarah said, before she could think the better of it.

He smiled. "Precisely!" He then looked at her warily. "So. What did you have in mind for this job?"

"Honestly?" This was *definitely* the weirdest job interview she'd ever been on. "I'll do a good job for you, but I have to say—I have no idea what I want to do with my future, I don't want to become the world's best secretary. I'll just do what you ask, and go home on time, and we'll figure the rest out as we go."

He smiled brightly, then reached over his desk. "You've got the job."

"Great," she said, shaking his hand in return. "Um…not to be too forward, but would it be all right if we talked salary?"

Chapter 10

Wishful Sinful

Judith was waiting for Sarah at Harry's Pub in Century City. She noticed she was chipping off nail polish, a nervous habit that was really beginning to up her manicure bill. She stopped, sipping her water instead.

She'd been trying to set up regular meetings—sort of "friend dates"—with Sarah, especially now that she'd broken up with Benjamin, a real source of stability in her life. She was still peeved about Sarah walking out of Salamanca, granted, but everybody knew Becky was no picnic, so it didn't reflect badly on her, Judith, that much. Besides, since she'd gotten married, she had very few friends, real, female friends, to speak with. She worked too hard, or spent the rest of her time with David.

She chipped at the cracking finish of her thumbnail. *Or on the Internet,* she corrected internally. She'd been spending quite a little bit of time there, lately.

She realized what she was doing, and left her nail polish alone. At any rate, she was going to talk to Sarah.

If the subject of Roger just happened to come up…

Stop it, Judith. There wasn't really anything to talk about there, anyway. She was there to give moral support to a friend—and if she happened to nudge her toward some career counseling, well, that was just the concern of a friend.

"Hey there."

Judith looked up. She still wasn't used to Sarah's "new look." The frosted blond waves, the new clothes. She sighed, getting up and giving Sarah a hug. "You look great. How are you feeling?"

"Like shit," Sarah said, sitting down and motioning to the waiter for a glass of water of her own. "But I've got a new job. That's something."

"That's good. Doing what?"

"You're looking at the personal assistant to Richard Peerson, author extraordinaire."

"An assistant…" Judith said, feeling worried. "This is just temporary, right?" Then she paused. "Wait a minute. Richard Peerson? The man who wrote *Being and Everythingness?*"

"Probably?"

"He's a multimillionaire bestseller," Judith explained.

Sarah shrugged. "Okay."

That was so like her. She's working for a millionaire, and all she can think of is she's a secretary.

Judith looked askance. "So. You're going to be an assistant." She decided not to pursue that line of questioning. "So. Have you spoken with Benjamin lately?" She put a hopeful tone in her voice. "I'm sure he misses you."

Judith watched as Sarah's face grew taut. "Oh, I'm sure he does."

"So you haven't talked with him?"

"Actually," Sarah said, sipping at her now-delivered drink, "I've slept with him."

Judith blinked at that, then smiled. "You're back together? Wonderful!"

"I didn't say we were back together."

Judith thought about it. "Oh. Well, they always say that rebound sex with your ex is better. And it's new yet…at least you've got the lines of communication open."

"Actually, the reason that we aren't back together is because I discovered he already had a live-in girlfriend, just after I slept with him."

Now Judith was aghast. "He did? He does?"

"I'm not getting back together with him." On this point Sarah sounded firm. "Ever. If there's one thing I can't stand, it's someone who would…would cheat on somebody else!"

Judith bit her lip, thinking back on her correspondence with Roger and the slightly risqué turn it had taken. "Well, it wasn't really cheating," she said, thoughtfully. "I mean, you guys weren't still together or anything, so it was more like he was seeing other people, and then decided to see you again."

"He wasn't cheating on me, he was cheating on what's-her-name. Jessica," Sarah said, her tone pained. "It doesn't matter who he cheated on, actually. He's just a big liar."

"Maybe he's confused…"

"Why are you defending him?" Sarah finally snapped.

Why *was* she defending him? "Sarah, I know you're hurting over this, but I can't help but think you brought some of this on yourself."

"What?"

"Well, that came out wrong. I mean, if you'd just been a little more…well, if you'd been able to deal more with your work down here, instead of quitting in such a flamboyant manner—if you'd have been more understanding of his career needs…"

"If I'd have been more understanding of his career needs, I'd have been *Benjamin's* secretary," Sarah spat out. "Judith, I can't believe you're taking his side!"

"I'm not taking sides, I'm being practical." Judith's voice could have frozen vodka. "You're the one who's being unreasonable. Sometimes, I feel like I don't know you anymore!"

"Maybe you don't." Sarah stood up. "Maybe you never did, Judith."

Judith stood up, too. "Sarah, please don't leave like this." She paused, looking around, feeling the stares of the other diners like little physical pokes. "You're causing a scene," she added, in a hissed whisper.

Sarah's eyes widened at that one. "You know what your problem is, Judith?"

"No, but I'm sure you'll keep me informed."

"You've never caused a scene. With anybody."

"It's not something I've aspired to, no." Judith sat back down. If Sarah was going to insist on acting like an ass, she wasn't going to participate as well. "Thanks for your input."

"I'm sorry your life is so sterile, Judith. If you can find a way over the wall you've put around your life, maybe I'll see you around."

Judith didn't even grace that with a reply, just watched as Sarah's frosted blond hair bobbed through the crowd and disappeared out onto the street.

"Why would I *want* to pick somebody up? Or get picked up?"

Martika, wearing a pair of low-slung, hip-hugging bell bottoms that showed off her new navel ring and a skimpy iridescent halter top that showed off her generous (but not new) boobs, eyed Sarah with an air of shock. "Why wouldn't you?"

Sarah looked around. There was one guy whose appearance made him seem straight out of *America's Most Wanted.* He eyed them as if they were appetizers. "Well, that man over there, for one."

Martika shook her head. "Contrary to popular belief, there *is* a certain discrimination here. You're not going for quantity.'' At Sarah's surprised glance, she huffed impatiently. ''Well, okay, you are going for quantity…but only because there's an expiration date on these things. Saying you're going through men like Kleenex is a lot more realistic than saying you're going to keep one Kleenex and treasure it for life.''

Sarah grinned, then gasped.

''What?''

Sarah checked as surreptitiously as she could. ''Sorry. Ever since that *Will and Grace* episode, I've been paranoid that this water bra thingy you had me buy might spring a leak.''

Martika laughed. ''Well, it gives you a chest. And men like chests. A lot. Don't let the models fool you…especially not in this city.'' She jiggled her rather ample figure. ''Men don't want to fuck a Popsicle stick, believe me.''

Sarah glanced down. ''That might pose a problem, when they realize this is mostly Frederick's of Hollywood and water.''

Martika waved a hand impatiently. ''You're jumping ahead. You're not sleeping with anybody—*yet*—'' and that last word was ominous ''—but you're going to have to learn the basics. Jesus. Didn't anybody sleep around in Fairfax?''

''Fairfield.'' Sarah shrugged. ''Sure. They just didn't have it down to a science.''

''If you're going to do something, do it right.'' Martika shrugged, obviously unoffended. She sat next to Sarah at the high table of the bar. Sarah forgot the

name of it. It was a step up from 5140, definitely more
of the chichi persuasion…but not that respectable. She
doubted Martika would have stood for it. "All right.
Let's pick a target."

Sarah glanced around the way Martika did, feeling
like a buyer at an auction. Considering *she* usually
felt like one being scrutinized for possible purchase,
it was a nice switch. "How about that one?" she said,
nodding at a clean-cut young man wearing a T-shirt
and a pair of long shorts.

"Don't make eye contact!"

Sarah quickly glanced away as the man was smiling
at her. "Why not?"

"He's got Westwood written all over him. College
boy. Probably just left a sports bar and can't find his
way back." Martika shook her head. "They're more
trouble than they're worth, believe me. And they're
usually *lousy* in bed."

"Oh. Right." Like she'd know the difference. She
wasn't quite ready to have that conversation with
Martika, though. "Okay, so what am I looking for?"

Martika smiled. "You want someone who screams
'sex' from every pore of his body and isn't overly
aware of it. You want someone who can make you
feel like the center of the universe—and it'll be *all
about you.* You want someone who isn't stuck on
himself, who can move his body, and who makes you
feel like wrapping your legs around him just by smiling at you. *That's* what you're looking for."

"And you keep finding that?" Sarah asked, incred-
ulous.

"Hell, no!" Martika shook her head at Sarah's naïveté. "But that's what you're looking for. What you hopefully wind up with is a guy who isn't stuck on himself, who isn't a one-minute egg, and who knows what to do with his hands. Or even better—" Martika grinned maliciously "—his tongue."

Sarah couldn't help it. She blushed.

"Man. You kill me," Martika said, noticing Sarah's pink cheeks. "Okay. There's a likely candidate."

The man was a dark-skinned Latino with eyes that reminded her of a Renaissance portrait. He glanced over at them once, bored, then looked away.

"Are you sure he's on our team?" Sarah asked, noticing that his casual clothes were definitely in the expensive range—black slacks, a tight black T-shirt.

Martika snorted. "Trust me. I attract more gay men than the Pride Parade, ask Taylor. If I went into a clothing store in East Nutless, Alaska, the only gay guy in a fifty-mile radius would come up to me and ask me what I thought of the shirt he was planning to buy, I swear to…there!"

Sarah looked around, startled. "There, what?"

"Our target." Martika's voice was smugly satisfied. "He did the relook."

"What?"

"He looks bored, but he glances back. He definitely notices us, and now he's sizing up his chances. He'd like it better if one of us was alone…less likelihood of him getting laughed at. But there's just two of us, so he might chance it."

Sarah hadn't really noticed any difference and wondered if maybe Martika were making it up. Then she saw it...the guy reached for his drink, laughing at whatever the guy next to him was saying—and he *looked directly at her,* his dark eyes almost swallowing her up in their intensity. He sent her the smallest smile, like he knew something she didn't.

Her heart pounded a little. This was like...like hunting or something. It was fun.

"Okay, now we've got a target. What next?" Sarah asked eagerly.

"Well, we let him come to us," Martika said. "If you weren't here, I'd probably be a little more blatant, or maybe go to him—guys do like that, and I hate waiting for shit, personally. But if we both go up...no. That's a little too high school for my tastes."

"Hmm. That doesn't sound too bad," Sarah said thoughtfully.

Martika quirked an eyebrow at her. "You want to give it a try?"

Sarah glanced at her, the fun leaving in a quick panic. "You mean now?"

"Sure. Why not?"

"I'm not ready."

"You just said it wouldn't be so bad," Martika wheedled, and her eyes were glinting. "Just make sure your hips shake a little, act like you're walking down a runway, make sure they notice you. Then ask him if you can buy him a drink. It should be pretty easy from there." She nudged Sarah. "Go on."

"I don't know..."

Martika sighed impatiently. "You don't have to take him *home,* for God's sake. You just have to buy the guy a drink."

"Um..."

"All right, just *say hello to the man,* all right?"

This did feel suspiciously like high school, Sarah decided as she started what seemed to be an interminable walk to the bar. He was sending more glances her way, she noted at least. She felt self-conscious about her walk. Until Martika had made a big deal about it, she hadn't thought about it, but now that she was thinking about it, every movement felt awkward and wooden. She successfully made it to the bar without tripping, at least, she thought. She'd work on sexy later.

Instead of walking straight up to him, she opted to be a little more subtle. She wasn't Martika—but he *had* made eye contact with her. She walked behind him, leaning on the bar.

"What'll it be?" the bartender asked.

Sarah turned, surprised. "Hmm. What do you recommend?" she asked, trying to maybe make her voice sound more like Lana Turner and less like Blossom from the Powerpuff Girls.

The bartender looked at her. *It's a bar,* his face said. *I recommend you order something or stop taking up space.*

She looked over the sign. "I'll...have a Blue Neon Fogcutter," she said ambitiously.

The bartender smirked at her. "Just one straw?"

"Um...okay."

He went to work, and she turned, wondering how she should start the conversation. He was talking to his friend about sports. About how badly the Dodgers sucked this year. *"Boy they sure do!"* No. She didn't know anything about sports, and it might be a New York sort of situation—New Yorkers could make fun of their city, but when a stranger did, it was a humongous insult. So what else could she comment on. *I like your clothes? What are you drinking? Don't I know you from somewhere?*

She sighed, impatient with herself. *Hey, mister. Nice shoes. Wanna fuck?*

This was turning into a disaster.

"Here you go. One Blue Neon Fogcutter. That'll be twelve dollars."

"Twelve..." She looked at the concoction he'd placed on the bar. It was in a martini glass—only the glass was the size of a small fishbowl. It was a shocking shade of blue and seemed to glow on its own in the black light over the bar. "Oh, my."

"Looks like you've got a busy night," the bartender said with a snigger. "Still want just one straw?"

She glanced down at the bowl o' alcohol in front of her...and suddenly it hit her. Her opening line.

She turned to her left. "I don't suppose you'd want to share it with me?"

Then she looked at who she was offering the invitation to, and gaped.

It was the cute Latino's distinctively less-cute friend. He was fuzzy all over, it seemed, and he didn't do the relook. He was all eyes, as if he were trying to stare at every part of her at once. His bushy eyebrows danced. "Love to," he said.

"I'm sorry. I thought you were…my friend," she said, feeling lame, and glancing back at Martika.

The guy was there. Her target was sitting on the chair she had only recently vacated, whispering something in Martika's ear. Martika simply gave him a Mona Lisa smile before sauntering over to the bar. Sarah noticed that every set of male eyes was riveted to her walk.

"Need help with that?" Martika said, throwing a twenty on the bar. She grabbed some change and left a tip, then took the drink and walked back with her sensual grace over to the table. Sarah followed her, feeling ridiculous.

"Sarah, I'd like you to meet Rinaldo." Martika's smile was like Martha bloody Stewart, for God's sake.

"Nice to meet you," Sarah muttered. Rinaldo nodded in response before turning his attention back to Martika.

"Rinaldo, this really is a girl's night," Martika said pointedly, looking at Sarah, then looking at his seat.

He got up, but then leaned over. "Can I call you sometime?"

Martika smiled. "Got a pen?"

Within minutes, Rinaldo was back at the bar with Fuzzy Guy, Martika's cell phone number in his pocket, no longer doing the bored relook but sending smoldering glances over at their table.

"How did you do that?" Sarah said, taking sips from the huge martini glass.

Martika shrugged, grabbing the straw and taking a sip herself. "This may take a little while. I've never had to train anybody. Although I will say two things. One, don't ever walk behind a guy, or try to be subtle. Men are like old computers. You want them to do *anything,* you've got to be painfully direct and relatively simple. Just trust me on this."

"Then why didn't you just say, 'Hi, whatever your name is...why don't we go back to my place and fuck?' instead of the whole brush-off thing?"

Martika smiled. "I have used something similar to good effect. But the main reason to avoid it is, men are funny. They like to think they're the hunters, that they made the move. Ridiculous, but there it is."

"So that was all about him doing the pursuit thing?"

"Don't make it sound so Mars-Venus," Martika said disparagingly. "I don't think men retreat to caves, and if they did I certainly wouldn't wait for them. I know what I want, I know how to get it. EOS."

"EOS?"

"End of Story." Martika grinned.

"So. What was the second piece of advice you had for me?" Sarah asked.

Martika took another sip of the drink, and gagged slightly. "Rule two—don't order one of these fucking things again. They're awful. It looks like 2000 Flushes."

* * *

Sarah had made a chain of two hundred and eighty-five paper clips before she realized with a certain horrid fascination that she was reaching clinical, perhaps certifiable, boredom.

She'd been at the job for a month now, and all she'd really done was exchange nervous greetings with her employer, Richard "call-me-Richard" Peerson. She'd spent the first week piecing together a calendar from his scraps of e-mails and letters and cocktail napkins, saying what he had to do on various dates. He had an inordinate fondness for Post-it notes in a variety of colors—they made up the bulk of her information. Then there was his handwriting. She'd found one piece of paper on which he'd scrawled and then written more legibly, apparently for whoever came before her. She was using it as a sort of Rosetta Stone, and now could cipher what he was trying to communicate. By week two, she'd been given the suspicious okay to buy an attractive leather organizer (he insisted on burgundy, since "plain black was so *blah*") and she'd managed to transcribe what she found into efficient to-do lists and monthly overviews. Richard had blanched just looking at it, so she simply told him each morning what he needed to do, while he handed her occasional scraps of paper where he'd jotted what it was he'd promised someone he *would* do, or letters from his publisher telling him when things *were* due.

That usually took about half an hour. She tried to make it longer by punctuating each little task with a sip of coffee or something.

Now, she was drinking whole cups between entering Post-it notes in the organizer, and she was still finished with her to-do list by nine-fifteen.

The "office" she was set up in was very attractive—heavy wood desk, modern PC with a nineteen-inch screen and a DVD-ROM (she supposed she could watch movies, but that seemed way too blatant), and a sleek black phone that looked like something out of a sci-fi movie. There were tall bookshelves on one side of the room, filled with varying volumes of fiction and reference material. There were matching file cabinets made of wood and a credenza—all empty, so far as she could tell. Richard had tossed all the previous assistant's disturbingly color-coded files in a box and stowed them in the cellar, apparently. A corkboard was set up on one wall, also denuded. The large window behind her showed his backyard and kidney-shaped, black-bottomed pool.

The other eye-catching piece of décor was a large circular mirror, framed in brushed bronze. She could watch herself as she methodically fed her caffeine habit, as she was now.

She stared at the mirror, looking at herself. Just like a cigarette ad: *You've come a long way, baby*. Her hair was now methodically kept up by Joey, her makeup was a tasteful blend of Lorac, Stila and Urban Decay, her clothes were the best she could afford from Fred Segal, Bebe and some funky boutiques Pink recommended. She looked great, not to be immodest. She felt sure it couldn't be that.

She grimaced at herself in the mirror, with her

"Gash" raspberry-colored lipstick, making a grotesque pout. Well, she was striking out in the male department, granted, but at least she was looking good while doing it. Even Martika couldn't find fault with that argument.

The thing was, she wasn't quite sure what she was doing wrong.

She tried an experimental come-on smile, watching her own reflection. "Hi there," she whispered. "My name's…no. I'm Sarah. *I'm* Sarah. No, no, that sounds stupid. Hmm…I'm *Sarah*. Sah-rah. S'rah."

She wished she didn't sound like a Powerpuff Girl.

She got up, standing in front of the mirror. It's not like Richard knew she was alive. She walked past him if she were going out to lunch, or if she was going home. Otherwise, she barely heard the clacking of his keyboard, and he wandered away often. Standing in front of the mirror, she got a look at her torso as well as her face. She crossed her arms, tilting her head.

"I'm Sarah. Come here often?" She listened to it out loud. *Way* too cheesy. "I'm Sarah." She smiled. Okay, *yawn.* "This is Sarah. And you are?" She laughed. She sounded like Martika on helium. This would never work!

She crossed her eyes. "Hi, my name is Sarah, and I am flirtatiously challenged. Would you like to give a donation to the RHF…the Romantically Handicapped Fund? Otherwise, you can volunteer to be a pal and take out someone like myself and make her drab but well-dressed life a little more exciting." She covered her face with her hands. "Oh, *blaeugh.* I must be losing my mind."

"But it's been entertaining."

That would be Richard's voice. Sarah peeked out behind her fingers, feeling the blush heating the palm of her hands. Slowly, she dropped her hands from her face.

"Um, hi," she muttered. "How long have you been there?"

He was staring at her like she had grown another head—but he had a small smile, nonetheless.

"Boy. Was that as embarrassing for you as it was for me?" Sarah said, with a weak half-laugh.

"Actually, I thought the last one was the best one. At the very least it hasn't been tried before. You might want to work on your pitch, though."

She wondered if jumping out the window might improve matters.

"You know," he said, "you *are* well dressed. And you're a pretty girl." He sent her a quick, startled look. "Not in any harassing way, of course."

"Of course," Sarah assured him.

"But you really *could* work on your presentation," he offered, almost shyly.

Sarah stared at him. *Because this job just can't get any weirder.* Well, she'd been trailing after Martika to no avail. Possibly her eccentric multimillionaire boss might have some pointers. "What would you suggest?"

He frowned, causing his snowy-white eyebrows to

knit together with concentration. "Well, for one thing, you might want to work on your voice."

Sarah groaned. "I know. I sound like a Disney character."

"The problem is, you sound like Minnie Mouse...only Minnie trying to do an impression of Tallulah Bankhead. Work with your strengths, dear."

"You mean, sound young?"

"I'm willing to bet that whoever it is that's giving you tips right now is a real freelance dominatrix-type."

Sarah thought of Martika. "That's pretty darned close."

"Well, that's not you. I don't mean that in a bad way, I just mean that you're not the type."

Sarah sighed. "So I should just be somebody's wife?"

"Good God, no!" Richard said, aghast. Sarah laughed at his vehemence. "No. I was thinking perhaps of going for innocence mixed with mischief— white to her black, as it were. With your hair, face and voice—well, I'm no expert, but I'd say you'll want to wear a lot more pastels."

Sarah frowned. "I like them, but thought maybe not. They make me look so young."

"That's a plus," Richard said, laughing. "Younger the better. I'd say border on schoolgirl. You can be like...oh, what's her name? Alicia Silverstone. Shorter hair, of course, but that sort of vixen-y... what's the word? Right. Womanchild."

Womanchild. All one word, Sarah thought, grimacing. Yuck.

He put his hands out in a conciliatory gesture. "Yes, I know, it puts feminism back into the Dark Ages." He made a little smirk. "But then, as I recall, so does hunting for men by practicing in front of a mirror."

Sarah couldn't help it. She scowled at him.

"You're a lot more fun than Ms. Honeywell," Richard commented. "Have you had lunch?"

Sarah glanced at her watch. "Um, it's ten in the morning."

"Oh." Richard blinked for a moment. "Then I'll take that as a no. How about brunch?"

Sarah found herself accepting a "bruncheon" date with her boss. Rather than the usual introductory meal with an employer—which normally involved minor dissing about the previous occupant of your position, a brief diagram of the politics in the office (who to avoid/who to suck up to) and some vaguely probing business questions ("where do you see yourself in five years?")—Richard went straight for the gusto. She found herself telling him about Benjamin and why she'd moved down to Los Angeles.

"Why, that absolute prick!" Richard said, shocking her into dropping some of her Juevos Rancheros on the tabletop.

"Funny how often that comes up," Sarah replied.

When they got back to the office, they'd managed to kill three hours by having a leisurely meal and by window-shopping on Third Street. He even stopped by Borders and bought her a few copies of his book. Sarah felt better than she had since she started this whole "assignment."

"I've got to write this afternoon," Richard said apologetically, as he walked her back to her desk.

"I'm sorry if I took up a lot of your time."

"No, no, not at all! This recharges my batteries," he said with a negligent wave of his hand. "Do I have anything else to do today?"

Sarah flipped open the organizer. "Um...nope."

"Great. Why don't you enjoy the rest of the afternoon?"

Sarah blinked. "Really?"

"Really! Get some of those clothes we talked about, take a bubble bath." He grinned. "Practice in front of your mirror at home."

She stuck her tongue out at him. She gauged him correctly—he laughed with delight. "All right then, I'm out of here. See you tomorrow, bright and early."

"Oh, no stress," he said with a laugh. "Come in whenever." He wandered back down the hallway.

Sarah gathered up her things, but before she could leave she heard the pounding of Richard's feet on the hallway floor. "Sarah! Wait a minute!"

She glanced over at him, puffing like a chimney. He'd run to catch up with her. "Yes?"

He handed her what looked like a club postcard-thing, an advertisment, but on closer inspection it was an invitation—and a swanky one at that, with gold foil and the whole nine yards. It said:

ANAIS.COM

"What's this?" Sarah asked.

Richard shrugged. "It's this…well, it's this magazine that's about sex. Very tasteful, of course," he assured her. "In fact, it's very intellectual. Covers all sorts of walks of life. Anyway, they're an offshoot of my publisher, and I got to know the editor over a piece they were doing on…well, it doesn't really matter now. But their parties are *legendary*. This is going to be someplace in Santa Monica, I think, or somewhere. You can bring your friends," he said.

Sarah looked at the card. "Well, I could certainly use a good party," she said. *Martika would approve of that.*

Richard beamed.

Chapter 11

Light My Fire

"This isn't a party," Sarah muttered as best she could in Martika's ear. "This is an *orgy*."

"Yeah, that's what I like about it," Martika replied.

The Anais.com party was being held in this store-front-type place with tinted windows, somewhere out in Venice, by a bunch of warehouses. The line to get in had been ridiculous, and people without invitations were being turned away. Sarah had brought the usual crew with her—Martika, Taylor, Luis, Pink, and even Kit. Everyone but Kit was dressed to kill. Martika was wearing an iridescent halter top and a minuscule black skirt with her traditional platforms. Pink was wearing a sixties-inspired A-line and white go-go boots. Taylor was wearing a metallic blue tight T-shirt and black pants. Luis reversed the combo, wearing a tight black T and blue pants. Sarah herself had taken both Richard and Pink's advice, and gone with a fragile baby-blue, baby-doll dress, and had clips in her hair and sparkles on, along with high stacked Mary Janes.

Kit…well, Kit was wearing jeans and a white short-sleeved shirt. Sarah fervently hoped that there wasn't a dress code.

As it turned out, she didn't have to worry about a dress code. From what she could see, people weren't wearing much of anything. There were two makeshift "bars" set up on either side of the room, both mobbed. The bartenders, all male for the most part, were wearing DKNY tidy-whities that left little if nothing to the imagination. The party was sponsored by Bacardi, so everything they mixed was a brilliant, milky neon color, and the smell of rum was pervasive. There were women wandering around in G-strings, high heels and bikini tops. There were also men and women dancing, scantily clad, on raised platforms and in a few cages.

"Hell of a party!" Taylor said, staring at a man who was wearing only a jockstrap, talking to a man looking disarmingly out of place in a three-piece suit…until you noticed that he'd opened his fly, and his penis was hanging out like an elephant's trunk. Okay, a little elephant. "I think I saw…that's Moby!"

"This is one of the coolest parties I've ever been

to,'' Pink said, with awe. ''Somebody just handed me a party pack, and it's a compact with some Ecstasy in it.''

Sarah blinked. She would pretend she didn't hear that.

''So…looking for a target, huh?'' Martika said with a smile.

Sarah let herself smile back just as devilishly. ''You know, I think I'm ready.''

''Ready for what?'' Kit asked.

Sarah frowned. ''Private conversation, Kit.''

He grinned. ''Then you shouldn't be yelling,'' he hollered over the DJ's frenetic mix.

She rolled her eyes, and leaned her head toward Martika, deliberately ignoring Kit. ''I think I'm going to take somebody home tonight,'' she said, taking a deep breath.

''That's my girl!'' Tika's smile was broad. ''Who?''

''Haven't decided yet,'' Sarah said, scanning the crowd. ''But I'll let you know.''

She ''circulated'' with Martika and Pink, while Taylor, Luis and Kit fought the crowd to get drinks. There were plenty of good-looking people in the crowd, although sexuality was frankly always a question. There were only what Martika would consider low-grade celebs here…that kid from a canceled sitcom, several B-list types. Pink thought she spotted some higher grade people, but they seemed to be in what worked as a ''private'' room. Even the hot parties had three degrees of separation, Sarah noted.

Everyone who was left was either frantically trying to have sex with each other (in some cases literally…there was an interesting tableau going on in one of the cages) or staring to see if they knew anyone— or were being recognized by anyone.

"I got hit on by a bartender," Taylor announced with enthusiasm. "Here are your drinks. Sarah, I have to hand it to you—this is a coup, for our little group."

Sarah smiled self-deprecatingly as Martika rolled her eyes. "I just got the invite from my boss…that's just knowing somebody, not doing anything."

"Girlie-girl, you're going to discover you know *quite* a few people," Taylor said expansively, almost spilling his drink on Martika. "And that's going to come in damned handy one of these days, you mark my…*oh my God.*"

Sarah noticed Martika's mouth dropping open, and Sarah turned to see what had caught their attention. And felt her eyes widen. She didn't want to blink and miss a fraction of a second of the vision before her.

He was six-two, and wearing a snug tank top that accentuated rather than covered his well-chiseled torso. His skin was a dark tanned color, and somehow glistening. His hair was a deep brown-black, softly curling. His dark eyes could have pierced Kevlar.

"Fuck me, that's *Raoul*," Taylor muttered to them. They had all leaned together, staring like schoolgirls.

"Raoul the underwear model?" Martika said, her gaze never swerving from his chest.

"Wow. I'm guessing he's famous."

"Are you kidding?" Martika said, giving Sarah a

quick half-hug. "The more important thing is, how can I get him to marry me and support me in the life I'd like to become accustomed to?"

Sarah looked at her. Martika actually looked nervous. Satan was putting on a sweater as they spoke, she felt sure. "So, go over and talk to him," Sarah encouraged, surprised at this little role reversal.

"I might." Martika looked around. "After another drink."

"After *several* drinks," Taylor corrected. "Come swim upstream with me for a minute."

"And get me a bottled water if they have any," Sarah called after them. Pink was busy dancing with a girl dressed up as a Fem-bot. Luis was sulking and making his way for the door. She didn't know where Kit was—and frankly, while looking at Raoul, she couldn't care less.

The guy looked absolutely godlike. He was the personification of a hot-fudge sundae and a sex junket in Cancún. Sinfully good-looking. She wondered what he tasted like.

This isn't like me!

She dragged herself out of her thoughts as she saw him, staring at her. He smiled. She felt her stomach twist in a nervous knot.

So. What was she supposed to do next?

He made it easier for her by slowly making his way across the floor, which made the knot of nervousness inside her tighten with each step that bridged the gap between them. Finally, he was just a few yards away.

Talk to him. Say something witty.

She forced her muscles to push herself away from the wall. She stood for a second, gathering her courage, and took one step forward.

''Hi!'' she heard a voice say brightly, and suddenly the man with the piercing eyes was flanked by the dynamic duo of Taylor and Martika. ''You must be Raoul.'' Tika shot him her best come-fuck-me smile. Taylor was running a close second—she wondered which Raoul would be susceptible to. Possibly both, she thought, dismayed. She ought to just sit her baby-doll butt right down on a nearby couch and pretend she'd just gotten up to stretch.

He was involved in conversation with them. Martika was doing a lot of smiling, and Taylor was doing more touching and leaning than was absolutely necessary...then she turned to Sarah and winked confidently.

Sarah frowned at herself. Why should she go run away? Sure, she wanted to get laid tonight...but it wasn't like she had to with the first guy she talked to. If, as she suspected, Tika wound up taking Raoul back to the apartment later, she'd simply have said hi and could possibly have polite conversation with him tomorrow morning over her grapefruit. Why not?

She walked over to him purposely. She put out a hand, and smiled. ''Hi. I'm Sarah.''

He leaned toward her ear. ''Sorry?''

''Sarah,'' she said in his ear. ''My name is Sarah.''

He smiled, and it seemed to be just for her. ''Sarah. That's nice. Homey.'' His accent made the words sound like drizzled honey. ''My name is *Raoul.*''

"So I've heard." She had to fight her natural instinct to do something ridiculous—kiss him, say, or swoon.

"Great party, isn't it?" he asked. His teeth were white enough to be dazzling, she noted. She wondered if he did toothpaste ads as well.

"Fantastic," she heard Martika say. "So how do you know Anais.com?"

Sarah frowned. Martika was gushing. Martika, to her knowledge, *never* gushed.

He shrugged. "They had me on the cover once. And a nude spread. No big deal."

Martika looked ready to drool on him. Sarah suspected Taylor already had.

"We know Richard Peerson," Sarah said. "He did a guest article."

"I'd have come to the party even if I didn't have a connection with them," Raoul said blandly. Okay, was he just staring at her, or was Sarah crazy? The way Martika was frowning suggested that she wasn't. How to handle this?

"Can we get you a drink?" Martika said, starting to steer him toward the crowded bar.

Taylor pulled away. "Have you seen Luis? I'd love him to meet Raoul!"

"I think he was headed for the door," Sarah volunteered.

"Great." Taylor frowned. "I sense drama. Dammit." And he vanished toward the exit.

"I thought you were *soooo* sexy in that Luis Vuitton ad,'' Martika gushed. ''Hopefully, this line won't be too long. What would you like?''

''Actually, I'm fine.'' In fact, Raoul looked somewhat overwhelmed. ''Why don't we sit down?'' He looked at Sarah as he said this.

Sarah started to follow them, then felt a brush at the small of her back, and spun. It was Kit.

''Have you seen Taylor and Luis?''

''I think they went outside,'' she said.

''What?''

She stood next to him, leaning up close to his ear. ''I said, I think they went outside!''

''Damn. They're my ride. I hope they're not fighting.'' He looked her over. ''If they bail, is it all right if I get a ride with you?''

She thought about her plan to bring someone home. ''Um…I'm not sure. I mean, I don't know what my plans are after this, you know?''

He nudged her back, studying her face. For no good reason, she felt guilty. She jutted her chin up. Not that she had any reason to. She felt sure Kit wasn't exactly a Boy Scout, either, and if some gorgeous supermodel was eyeing *him*, he'd be more than happy to get a ride home with her.

''You be careful,'' he said against her ear, his breath tickling her neck. ''Okay?''

She nodded. ''Of course.''

He stared at her a minute longer, then turned and stalked off.

Sarah went back to Martika and Raoul. Martika, she

noticed, looked edgy, just this side of nervous—but she was trying for bored, Sarah could tell. Raoul was staring directly at Sarah.

"Who's that?" he said, and his eyes were like prison floodlights, pointing straight at her. "Was that your boyfriend?"

"God, no," Sarah said, with a laugh. She saw Raoul motion to the couch next to him, where Taylor had been sitting. "Kit's just a friend."

"Like I said, it's a fantastic party."

He slung an arm casually over the couch back behind her shoulders. Now Tika looked aggressively bored, except for her eyes, which narrowed slightly.

Uh, oh. This isn't good.

"So, Raoul..." Tika said, leaning forward and showing a good amount of cleavage. "What are you doing later?"

Raoul took a glance, shrugged and turned back to Sarah. "Depends."

Sarah felt her cheeks warm, and smiled back at him, hoping the invitation was clear. This wasn't really her area. *But it's going to be.*

He turned to Tika, and Sarah felt momentarily bereft. But just for a moment.

"Would you excuse us?" he said to Tika, and turned back before he could see the look of shock on her face. He was too busy staring at her, Sarah. "Care to dance?"

She didn't see Tika's face anymore, only the dark luxury of his eyes. "I'd love to."

* * *

Would you excuse us?

Martika tossed back another Kamikaze. "One more for the floor," she told Taylor. He rolled his eyes, then went off to do as she requested.

The nerve. The fucking nerve.

She'd raised that ungrateful little slut. She'd taken her from a Fairfield farm girl to a bona fide club fiend, and this was the thanks she got? Sarah *knew* that she was interested. How often did Martika have to say "I want that guy" to make it clear? And there was just a protocol for this sort of thing. If your friend has a crush of some sort, it's poaching if you trounce her. Worse, it's *betrayal* if you waltz off with the guy right in front of her.

I taught her better than this!

It was the indignity of it. Martika had taught Sarah everything she knew about being sexy, about L.A. nightlife. For her to pretend that this was *her* party, that these were *her* friends, and that she was somehow a better lay because she was younger and she had her goddamn hair frosted and was wearing clothes that Martika herself couldn't fit into when she was that goddamn age anyway...

Martika stopped herself, midtirade.

Okay, that was scary.

Was that what was really bothering her?

Taylor walked up to her. "Have you seen Luis? I've been looking all over the damned place for him..."

"I don't give a shit," Martika answered.

"What's gotten into everybody?" Taylor said.

"Kit's vanished, Luis is probably off pouting some-where. Now, you're at one of the best parties we've *ever* been to, and you're sitting here looking like Joan Crawford meets the goddamn Grinch. What is going on with you?"

"I'm…Sarah is pissing me off. I almost had Raoul, and she dragged him off to the dance floor." Revi-sionist history, granted, but she didn't feel like going into the whole dirty epiphany. She gunned back the lime-green shot he'd handed to her, putting the glass down on the table in front of her with a loud slap. "But that's okay. I'll make up for lost time later."

She was feeling the buzz from the alcohol, so it took her a minute to realize that Taylor's face looked sheepish—which, for Taylor, was downright *wrong*.

"What? What?" She pinched him, making him wince. "Spill."

"Well, I think you'd better give up on the Raoul run tonight," he said, making a big show of straight-ening the glasses that were accumulated in front of them. "Because I think he just went home with Sarah."

"He went home with Sarah?" She blinked. This didn't compute. This totally didn't fucking compute. "What do you mean? He's driving her back or some-thing?"

Taylor coughed, delicately. "I don't think they just had driving in mind."

She now blinked at him. Raoul, the underwear model was going home with Sarah, the farm girl.

To have sex.

"That cunt!"

Taylor put a hand over her mouth, so the rest of her pithy sentence was muffled under his hand. Several people watched as she continued to curse and let out one final high-pitched wail.

When she was silent, just huffing quiet breaths of rage between clenched teeth, he let her go. "Tika, you would have done the same thing."

"I had dibs!"

He quirked an aristocratic eyebrow at her. "Oh. And your reputation will be ruined all over Sweet Valley High when school starts on Monday." He shook his head. "Get a grip, girlie-girl. I, for one, am proud that our little girl has moved up the food chain from boot-licking for bottom-feeders to free-fucking underwear models. We've instilled in her a sense of class, don't you think?"

"No, I don't think," Tika muttered. "I thought friendship meant more than that."

He clucked his tongue. "Sure. And the fact that a gorgeous, twenty-something underwear model picked our young frosted friend over you has nothing to do with it."

She glared at him.

"It's still all about you, sugar," he said and laughed.

She saw Luis stalking toward them, and thought of warning Taylor, but was currently way too pissed at him to give him any sort of advantage.

He turned just as Luis slapped him so hard he practically got whiplash. Some cruel part of Martika's heart actually lit up at that one.

"You slut!"

"What? What! What did I do?" Taylor said, yelling and protecting himself from the barrage of slaps that Luis was lighting on him.

"You've been fucking that DJ!"

Taylor looked up, scandalized. "No, I did not! I bought him a drink!"

"I'm through with you, Taylor. Completely!" And he promptly started castigating Taylor in Spanish and walked away. Taylor followed after him, Martika's problem obviously forgotten.

Martika gritted her teeth. While she was glad that Taylor was going to be punished for even *suggesting* that she was jealous of her little Tinkerbell protégé, she still felt poison rushing through her veins. She needed to blow it off, mellow out. The buzz was running through her, and it made everything else seem possible.

She needed a sports fuck the way junkies needed a fix. She wasn't going to find it here, obviously. She went to the valet, got her car and headed to Probe. Her club. Her turf.

She prowled out into the noisy, sweaty pulse of the first dance floor. People were moving frenetically, the trancelike pounding of the beat acting like a tribal aphrodisiac. She moved with it, feeling it through her, and she scanned the crowd for a likely candidate.

She found him, perversely, in a suit and tie, looking horribly out of place and, from the expression on his face, feeling horribly out of place. And on the make...she could gauge it from the hungry uneasiness that made him scan the crowd, much as she was. He was about twenty-seven, she guessed. Not as young as she would have liked, but still, she didn't need him for very long, and nobody really needed to know.

She danced up to him, very conscious of what a well-trained body could do with a set of boobs. He was hypnotized by the time she was within three feet of him.

She didn't even need to ask him if he wanted to dance…she walked up and put her body on his, gently guiding him to mesh against hers in an erotic way. She also made sure to lead, keep him on the beat. *The best way to see how a guy is in bed is to take him on the dance floor,* she'd told Sarah ages ago. Sarah had apparently been a good student if a somewhat piss-poor friend. She'd show Sarah how it's done.

He was breathing more heavily, and she could feel his prick all hard like a rod against her thigh. Good. He had some freight behind this package, she thought, as the rod stretched a little lower down her thigh. Time to try him out.

She leaned forward, brushing her cheek against his sweaty one, breathing in his ear, "Wanna go some-place private?"

He nodded, like a teenage boy, and followed when she took him out into the hallway. It was quieter there—although part of that could be the muffled deafness that came from being exposed to loud music. Club disease, she thought with a slow smile. The guy was pretty good-looking, and sort of dweebish. Like a virgin. She loved corrupting people. That same cruel part of her heart warmed.

"What did you want to talk about?" he said, his voice hoarse.

"This," she said, and leaned in for a slow, lingering kiss. What she did with her torso was nothing compared to what she could do with her tongue. He gasped, and suddenly was all over her, kissing her sloppily, hungrily, with a frantic, fumbling eagerness.

When he gripped one of her breasts, she let herself smile. Smoothing her hand over his chest from where she'd been caressing the back of his neck (and trying to keep him from going completely spastic in his desire for her), she reached down and grabbed his dick.

He yelped.

"Want someplace to put that, baby?"

He blinked. "This isn't going to, er, cost me, is it?"

She frowned. "Don't look a gift horse, kid."

"Here?" His voice rose to a higher pitch. He quickly lowered it, glancing back at the dance floor where they had came from. "Right now?"

"Well..." She debated going back to the house, but knowing that Sarah was going to be there with Raoul was a little too much. In her admittedly competitive nature, she'd probably fuck this poor guy to death. "Wait a second."

She took him by the hand again, leading him toward a back stairwell that Taylor had once shown her. It led up to an abandoned office, and to other various rooms...including the storage room. By luck, it was unlocked. "Manager's going to be pissed," she said, motioning him inside and shutting the door behind them.

Before the door was shut all the way, he reached for her. Within five minutes, her panties were off and her skirt was lifted up—what little there was of it. He practically ripped his zipper off in his enthusiasm.

"Condom?"

He reached—and she was sort of charmed by this—for his wallet, producing a foil packet. Wonder how long that's been in there? The little light there was, was not that great, and she could barely make out the heavy need on his face, and her frustration as he struggled with the packaging. She leaned back against some boxes and he stepped forward, toward her, fumbling to put it on. He pushed into her with a grimace and a loud groan, and she was right—he was plenty big.

He wasn't bad, either. He started to move, faster, and they were both pushing against each other, his pants around his ankles. A corner of a box dug into the small of her back, and she wrapped her legs around his waist, trying to leverage herself up.

"Unh…unh…" He was breathing in her ear, pressing so deep she thought he'd stab her heart.

"Yeah. Fuck me. Like that." She clawed at his oxford shirt, concentrating hard. She thought of Raoul, and grimaced, clenching tight enough to make him groan, part pleasure, part pain. She thought of the various guys that she'd fucked over the past…how many years? How many rooms, how many scenarios?

This wasn't helping.

She closed her eyes, and thought of her favorite fantasy—the gladiator/slave girl one. Thankfully, she came almost immediately, and bit his neck to stifle the scream.

"Ah... *AH*...." He pushed inside her. She pushed back against him, hard.

He pulled out and turned away from her, taking care of himself, putting the condom back in its foil packaging without really letting her see. Cute, she thought, pulling her skirt down and noticing she was pretty damned wet. She'd need to go to the washroom at this rate. Or go home and shower, then maybe go back out. She was tired, she realized, so maybe she'd just go home and stay there. *Oh, how far the mighty have fallen.* She pulled her panties on, hating that they would probably be damp for the rest of the night.

He turned to her. "So. Can I...did you want to give me your number?"

She laughed, suddenly feeling much, much better. "Why not?"

It was one in the morning, and Judith's back was starting to get sore from sitting at the computer for so long, ergonomic chair or no. "Roger, I really have to go," she typed.

Roger: Sleepy?

"Punch-drunk," Judith replied. "Usually, I don't stay up this late."

Roger: It's 4 a.m. here.

"Oh, my God. I'm sorry!" And she was. She'd been conversing with him for about…she frowned. Five hours. No, six. "I didn't mean to keep you up so late."

Roger: It's no problem. I got to talk to a pretty lady for a while…and correct me if I'm wrong, but you needed it.

Even though she knew he couldn't see it, Judith blushed a little. "It's been kind of bad these last few days," she agreed. Not that it had been any harder than any other week—she just seemed more *aware* of it now. "Also, I'm a little afraid." She thought about it. "Maybe not afraid. A little unnerved. I'm in the house alone."

Roger: You aren't used to it?

"You'd think I would be," Judith answered, not quite sure *why* she couldn't get to sleep tonight—why climbing into bed alone and closing her eyes seemed so daunting. "When David was on his internship with the circuit court, I barely saw him at all. It's just tonight that I feel weird."

Roger: A little lonely, maybe? (wiggling eyebrows)

Judith giggled, the sound echoing in the empty, late-night quiet. "Yeah, that's it."

Roger: I get it. Any port in a storm! :)

"Well, as you're three thousand miles away, you're hardly a handy port," Judith typed back, feeling strangely daring. It was really late, and she was alone. The conversation was hardly real. It was more like an extension of a dream.

Roger: Ah, but I could be...even from here. (SERIOUS eyebrow wiggling!)

Now Judith laughed. "I'm not afraid of you."

Roger: That's because you've never kissed me. I'm told I'm quite good.

"Oh, there's a threat," she shot back. This was just silly. Little kid silly. "What, you're some kind of Don Juan, is that it?"

Roger: Put it this way. Remember Bull Durham, when he talks about believing in slow, deep, soft, wet kisses that last three days?

Judith felt a very teeny tingle at the words. She'd always loved that part. "Yeah, so?"

Roger: I'm not that hasty.

Judith was still laughing, but she felt a little warmer...and the laughter was just a bit more breathless. "So you believe in slow kisses. I've had slow kisses."

Roger: And not just on your mouth.

Judith wasn't sure she was reading that correctly at first. Then, as she put what he was saying together, the blush intensified. "You're bad," she typed back, albeit a little unsteadily. She was getting tired. She ought to wrap this up…

Roger: I just believe in being thorough. There's a lot a man can do with two lips and a tongue, believe me.

She suddenly got an image…God, she couldn't… she'd never. But for some reason, alone in her house, typing to a stranger, it sounded good. Hell. Sounded *great.* "Yeah, yeah," she replied, trying to get the light tone back and not let on how unsettling she was finding his messages. "All men think they're hell on wheels. For all I know, you've had a lot of women who were really good at faking it! :)"

Roger: Wouldn't know till you tried, huh?

Judith was very, very warm. She shifted her weight nervously in the seat. She was getting a little—oh, hell. She was getting *really* turned on, which defined ridiculous. "Well, again, you're three thousand miles away," she typed in. *And even if you weren't…*

Roger: Well, I could walk you through it. :)

It was just the Internet, she reasoned. It wasn't real. *No one would know.*

"Give me an example," she typed. She was almost shivering now, staring at the screen.

Roger: First of all, kissing is really important. Say, about an hour of kissing. Deep, slow kissing. I'd start taking your clothes off, and you'd start taking my clothes off, but the kissing would be the important part. That, and touching. I'd learn every inch of you. I mean EVERY inch.

Judith couldn't believe she was reading this. Still, she didn't want him to stop, either. *When was the last time I kissed David for longer than the ten minutes it took to get him hard?* And when had taking off her clothes been anything other than a means to an end? His touch had stopped doing anything for her for longer than she could remember. She just hadn't really thought about it until just now, as a stranger typed sweet, graphic nothings on her screen.

Roger: Then, when you're naked and I'm naked, I'd put you on the bed. And then I'd move the kissing lower. Your breasts—they'd deserve attention, but I'd definitely take my cues from you. Would you like me to pay attention to them?

Judith hadn't thought about it. "Yes…but not too long," she answered back.

She was playing along.

There was a pause, and Judith wondered if she'd shocked him—or if he were really just joking. Or if he'd fallen asleep.

Before she could think about what she was doing, or be embarrassed, the message came across:

Roger: Am I shocking you? Because if I'm not, there might be something you might want to try.

Was he shocking her? No. She felt an ache in the pit of her stomach. She was horny, ridiculously so. She wanted sex, *really* wanted it. And good sex, at that. "What did you have in mind?"

Roger: If you're feeling…if you want, I think I can make you feel a whole lot better. You're going to have to help me out, though.

"How? What do you want me to do?"

Roger: Use your hands the way I'm describing. Pretend they're my mouth, my lips.

She felt warm, shockingly so. She glanced around, as if somebody could see. The window shade was drawn, the house was empty. Feeling the tiniest bit guilty—and excited—she slowly pulled her nightgown up, and put her left hand inside her panties. It felt strange. Naughty, she supposed. She tickled herself. "Now what?" she typed awkwardly with just her right hand.

Roger: If I were with you, I'd put you down on the bed, stroking your thighs…your inner thighs. Press kisses on you, until I got to your sex. Then I'd slowly open you, just a little, and dip my tongue in, tracing around…

Judith felt like she was in a trance. Both hands down her panties, one leg up on the desk, she did as instructed, reading the messages hypnotically through half-lidded eyes. Her fingers traced, dipped, caressed. Then they started pushing, getting faster. Her breathing shallowed. His words kept coming, faster, and she was arching her back off the ergonomic chair. She couldn't get enough of herself.

"Oh…oh… *OH*," she yelled, as she hadn't with David in years…not for real. The orgasm hit her like a fist, almost causing her to fall to the floor.

When she came to—no pun intended—she didn't know how long the messages had been going—nor did she realize when they'd stopped.

Oh, my God.

She wasn't sure what she had let happen. She felt light-headed. Guilty.

She wanted…

"What else would you do to me?"

Sarah walked into the darkened apartment with Raoul just behind her. They'd danced close there at the party, the DJ's mix wrapping around them like chain mail, drawing them roughly closer, giving them a beat to grind to. He wanted her…she could feel that much. She wanted him—wanted what he represented. He was gorgeous, she didn't know him, barely knew his name. With any luck, he was a dim bulb who barely knew his own name. He represented everything she now stood for—style rather than substance, enjoying the now rather than wondering if they had a future.

How would Martika put it?

She wanted to fuck the daylights out of Raoul, the Underwear Model. *Tonight.*

Martika. She felt a teeny bit guilty, but somehow felt that Tika would probably be proud of her initiative tonight. She'd harangued her enough about her obsession with Benjamin and "picket fence syndrome," chastising her for her Fairfield Farm Girl values. Well, now she was Sarah in the City, as it were. She could do this.

It would help if she didn't feel so nervous.

She'd dated Benjamin for about six months before she'd finally slept with him, after having several dates, after knowing him in social circles for approximately a year. Her first boyfriend had been her high school sweetheart, someone she'd lost her virginity to. This was going to be…

Nerve-racking. She took a deep breath as she locked the door behind them.

"Nice apartment," he said. She wondered if he felt nervous at all. Did guys get nervous? she wondered.

"Thanks." She cleared her throat. "My room is over there." She pointed. "My *bedroom,* I mean."

He smiled, and it seemed like a knowing smile. Of

course it was knowing. They'd been on the dance floor, and she'd asked him if he wanted to see her apartment. She'd basically meant to say "Would you sleep with me?" but didn't know how she would get the words past her lips. Then, like now, she didn't need to. He knew what was going on.

He led the way. She prayed her room wasn't too much of a mess. Maybe it wouldn't have made a difference to him—after all, he was getting sex out of this—but it would have definitely added to the edge she was already enduring. Thankfully, the room was fairly tidy. At least the dirty clothes were piled semineatly on her wing chair. She threw a sheet over them, then looked at him nervously.

He led the way again, reaching for her, kissing her. She kissed him back, feeling the first twinges of arousal battling back the nerves. Pretty soon they were both breathing heavily. She tugged at his shirt. He pulled it over his head.

Suddenly, things were happening. She tried kicking off her platforms, but that wasn't working. She tore at her shoes, falling onto her pile of dirty clothes. He kicked off his shoes successfully, reaching for the fly of his slacks and stripping down to his, well, trademark underwear. He stood there for a moment, staring at her, a small smile.

Wow. I've got a living, breathing underwear ad in my bedroom.

Then he took off the underwear, and she stopped tugging off her boots to stare. "Well, okay," she breathed.

He started to reach for her. She still had panties and her strapless bra thingy on. She kissed him, felt him reach around and unclasp the top, disengaging long enough to gently tug the thing away from her. So now there was just panties between them.

He started to guide her to the bed, totally in control. *Problem,* she thought. "Do you have a condom?"

He frowned. "Well, no."

She blinked at that. "You weren't expecting to have sex without one, were you?"

"Do you have one?" he answered instead.

She frowned. "Honestly. You could be carrying all sorts of…you could risk exposure to all sorts of diseases without one!"

He sighed, leaning back on the bed, his body looking like a statue…his erection looking very much like a flesh-colored flagpole. "I thought we were here for sex, not a service announcement." He paused. "Sometimes passion affects me this way."

Dim Bulb, she thought disparagingly, feeling the flame of her passion douse a bit.

He reached for her, tugging her down, kissing her neck, her breasts. She was taken aback by the suddenness of it. To her surprise, her breathing sped up again. She could feel his dick pushing at her.

"Wait a second. Wait a second." She managed to tear herself away from him, and made a naked dash for Martika's room, praying she wasn't there. The room was a mess—bed unmade, clothes strewn around, bra on a lampshade…she wasn't even going to question how that got there. She went to one of the bedside tables and opened the drawer. She was greeted with what looked like a diary and what looked like a vibrator. Okay it *was* a vibrator. She winced, closing the drawer, then went to the other table.

Paydirt. She grabbed a couple of condoms—the drawer was full of them.

She rushed back to her room and almost slammed the door. Okay, the flagpole was still there, ready to go. She handed him a condom. He gave her a sweet, patronizing sort of smile, then ripped into the foil, grumbling slightly as the thing managed to negotiate his size.

Sarah was really feeling pretty proud of herself as she pulled her panties off, leaving them on the floor by her bed. "Um, did you want the light on or off?"

He thought about it. "Doesn't matter. Whichever you like."

"Under the covers, I suppose?"

"Sure."

She bit her lip, pulling back the blankets and reaching to shut off the light. "You didn't want music, did you? I could put on some…*mmmrph.*"

He'd silenced her with kisses. He seemed to have grown three extra sets of hands. He was touching her all over. His kisses left a trail all over her face, neck, torso. He was everywhere at once. She wasn't being made love to—she was somehow being assimilated.

"Erp." She tried to protest, but there was suddenly tongue, and not hers, in her mouth. She concentrated on kissing and breathing so she wouldn't pass out and miss anything.

She felt sort of turned on, she supposed. It would be easier to tell if she could figure out where her body ended and his started....

Fwoomp. He entered her suddenly, and she gasped. Something that big slides into you when you're not expecting it, and it's no joke. She threw her head back, trying to angle a little better so she'd get friction where she needed it. She was used to accommodating herself with Benjamin—this wasn't as tough as she thought it would be.

He was going a little quicker than she would have liked, though, and he was breathing hard. She reached up, putting a hand on his shoulder. "Could..."

"Oh, yeah. Ohhhh..."

He pushed against her hard enough to think one of her ovaries had been dislodged. Then he shivered and almost crushed her.

Oh, you've got to be kidding.

She tapped on his shoulder, twice, like a high school wrestler acknowledging a pin. "Raoul?"

He groaned, then rolled off her, taking forever it seemed to pull out. He removed the condom, taking a tissue from her bedside table to wrap it up and throw it out. Then he just lay there, still.

She was lying there too, stunned. O-kay. Now what?

She waited for him to initiate conversation. Or maybe he'd get dressed and go home. Or something.

He started to snore.

She blinked. Okay, this could *not* be happening. Just couldn't.

She waited a little longer, then nudged him. Then nudged a little harder.

He rolled over, taking a lot of the blanket with him.

Oh, for the love of Pete.

She got up, an easy feat considering she wasn't hampered by covers, she thought with a grimace. She pulled on a pair of boxers and a T-shirt, and went out to get herself a drink.

She heard the shower running. Martika was home?

She thought about what she was going to say about all of this when she got out of the shower. She poured herself a glass of orange juice, debated about putting vodka in it, but decided to stick to the straight stuff. Then she sat at the table and waited.

Martika came out, a towel wrapped around her head and a slinky nightgown on. Her glance at Sarah was full of unmitigated surprise. She glanced at the shut door to Sarah's bedroom. "You're done?"

"Yup." Sarah frowned. "Correction. He's done. I've been done but am not done. Does that make sense?"

Martika's finely sculpted eyebrows jumped so high they were hidden by the towel, and then she started to laugh.

"It is funny," Sarah admitted, chuckling a little herself. "Tika, I'm sorry. I knew you were interested in him..."

"Don't worry about it," Martika said expansively, going and getting herself a glass of water and a handful of vitamins. "I mean, I *was* pissed initially, but after all, I *did* train you. Your first time out, your first one-night stand, and you hit a home run. How could I not be thrilled by it, right?''

Sarah smiled. This was the Martika she knew—the den mother of Hollywood Boulevard. ''Thanks, Tika. I owe you.''

''Yes, you do, although the full story of Raoul's bed prowess ought to do.'' She laughed, then stopped abruptly. ''Wait a sec. He's still here? Shouldn't you be...'' She paused. ''Don't tell me. Is he in there sleeping?''

''Snores and all.''

Martika threw back her head and let out one of her full, leonine laughs. ''This just gets better and better! Did he have a little dick?''

''Certainly not,'' Sarah said, still remembering that last jarring push. ''But he was a little haphazard with it, if you know what I mean.''

''We'll have to rename him Lightning and the Wrecking Balls. Oh, I can't wait to tell Taylor.''

''You'd tell Taylor?'' Sarah said, scandalized.

''Of course,'' Tika said, with a wave of her glass. She downed the pills. ''You'll understand tomorrow, believe me.''

''One thing,'' Sarah said. ''Now that I've, er, slept with him...how do I get rid of him?''

Martika's eyes widened, and her grin turned evil. ''Ooh. If you really want to make it up to me...can I throw him out?''

Sarah smirked, pointing to the door. ''Have a good time.''

Chapter 12

Hello, I Love You

Sarah stood in the "Love & Relationships" section of Waldenbooks on her usual two-hour lunch break. She was feeling…well, probably the best way to describe it was worked up. She was feeling too adventurous to just brush it off, but too particular to be indiscriminately horny. That was what she supposed she'd felt with Raoul.

And look what a disaster that turned out to be.

Not this time, she thought, picking up *The Kama Sutra* and looking at the diagrams, trying to steel herself against any curious bystanders' gazes. She wasn't going to charge into a one-night stand. She was going to test—and plan—and next time, she was going to find a guy who could truly make her sexually happy.

As Missy Elliot said, she wasn't lookin' for some one-minute man.

If she could manage another guy with Raoul's looks, that would be great. But she was willing to trade drop-dead glam for a little staying power. No, make that a *lot* of staying power. And he had to have skill, and be open-minded. She'd had Ozzie and Harriet. Now she was looking for Henry and June.

Now, where am I going to find a guy like that?

"Sarah?"

Sarah looked up, shutting the book with a snap.

It was Jeremy. Cute Jeremy, from her Temps Fugit assignment. The one she'd made labels for.

Hmm.

She smiled. "Jeremy. It's nice to see you."

He stepped up to her, looking yummy as usual in a white oxford shirt, dress pants and a crimson tie. His smile was slightly crooked, and his stare piercing, just like she'd remembered. She stood straight, all but pushing her breasts at him, and smiled coyly. *Now, all that practice comes into effect.* He didn't have a wedding ring, and she thought she'd heard around the office that he was a player of some sort.

Oh, he'd do *very* nicely.

"I've been trying to get a hold of you," he said.

"You were?"

"I was so disappointed to hear about what happened to you," he said, his gaze only briefly dipping to her chest before he managed to make eye contact again. She smiled. "I mean, the accusations…they didn't seem like you at all. You seemed like such a *nice* girl."

Sarah frowned, not sure if this was going to help her eventual case or not.

"I couldn't believe that you were working for somebody else and had deliberately deleted financial files. I mean, corporate espionage…it was just inconceivable."

Sarah chuckled. "Oh, yeah, that's me—the Mata Hari of the secretarial pool." She batted her eyes at him. *Mata Hari. Sexual dynamo. Get it?*

"So I did some research."

She paused, momentarily shaken from her seductive path. "What?"

"Yeah, and guess what? Janice had us fifteen million over budget, the budget she was responsible for, and she didn't even know what was happening. She deleted those files *and* the backups, and then tried to pin it on you to buy herself some time. When there was no way she could salvage it when the numbers reappeared, she tried to blame a bunch of other people. It brought down an audit, and it turned out that not only had she badly bungled managing the money, but she'd spent about fifty grand on stuff for herself."

"No way!" Sarah was flabbergasted. "On what?"

"The usual—charging massages and hotel rooms and whatever to the corporate account, saying they were for various clients when they were really for her."

"Oh, my God."

"I put in a call to Temps Fugit, explaining what had happened and trying to clear your name." Sarah was thrilled to see his smile turn a little wicked. "And they didn't even have the decency to give you my phone number."

She was about to thank him, when she realized that his interest wasn't purely that of a Good Samaritan. She licked her lips. "Well. What in the world can I do to thank you?" she said, her eyes going wide.

His grin grew a little more wolfish. "I really can't imagine."

"Dinner might be a good start," she said slowly, studying his expression. To her chagrin, it grew a little bored.

"Well, maybe we could improve on it."

"Dancing," Sarah said. "I'd have to insist on dancing."

His eyebrows rose at that one, but he was still smiling when he asked, "Why dancing, in particular?"

Go for the gusto, Walker! Sarah took a deep breath. "Because everybody knows the best way to evaluate how somebody is in bed is to see how they are on the dance floor."

She prayed she wasn't blushing.

She'd succeeded in shocking him, if only for a moment, but his answering smile was pure, sinful *sex*. He leaned close to her...she could feel the heat from his body.

"I see," he whispered. "Am I being evaluated?"

She looked up at him, barely moving when he brushed a quick kiss across her lips, now shocking *her*. "You're going through tryouts," she said cava-lierly, unable to stop herself from glancing around to see if anybody noticed. Man, he smelled good.

"I see. And dancing is the next step?"

She nodded, her breathing became more shallow.

His voice went even lower, his breath tickled her ear. "What's after that?"

She smiled. "Oh," she said, deliberately putting the book down with its cover showing. "I'm sure I can think of something."

He glanced at the book, then made a low, almost feral sound.

"I think I like you," he said simply, although his eyes were lit like bonfires. "Tell me you're giving me your number."

Martika was sitting on her customary couch at Pointless Party, her club du jour. She'd been frequent-ing the Hollywood club for the past two months—she didn't think it was going to last too long. She hadn't picked anybody up in about two weeks—in fact, the last guy she'd tried to pick up had...

She frowned, pushing at her stomach. Damn. She needed to stop eating at the roach coach that cruised by her design studio for lunch. She sipped at a Coke, hoping it would settle her down.

Not that the guy wouldn't have fucked me. It was just I wasn't interested.

At least, that's how she remembered it playing out. The bottom line was, her sex life was beginning to suck (although not literally, for a change)...and the social scene in L.A. *swallowed,* not to put too fine a point on it.

She wasn't interested in partying too much tonight, anyway. She had a mission: making Taylor feel better. His latest breakup with Luis finally stuck—the repulsive little lizard-boy hadn't shown up for *weeks.* She thought she'd seen him with someone else at Beer Bust, anyway. She wasn't going to that as much, either—while she loved being a girl in Boystown, the gay-guy scene had begun to pall on her. If she wanted that much drama, she'd just hang with Taylor.

"Can I get you another drink, sweetie?" she asked. He wasn't even dressed up—for Christ's sake, he looked like Kit had put together his ensemble. She couldn't remember the last time she saw him in wrinkled jeans and a regular T-shirt. He shrugged. A bad sign.

She scooted over the vinyl seat until she was leaning against him. She put an arm around his shoulders, squeezing it for comfort. "I've said it before...you're better off without him."

"Yeah, but I *knew* him. I was used to him. Even his pissy qualities were familiar."

"That's enough of that," Martika said briskly. "Just because he was easy doesn't mean he was right. You deserve better."

Taylor's eyes were red-rimmed, and his normally sardonic face held a look of—what the hell was that? Sorrow? Or...contempt?

"Martika, you're not helping."

She frowned. "Well, I'm trying to. I mean it, sweetie, you deserve the best."

"How would you know what's best for me, Tika?"

She smiled, leaning back a little. "Because I know what's best for everybody."

"Then what's best for you?"

She shrugged. "This. Hanging out, enjoying myself, and comforting my very best friend in the whole world."

"Don't take this the wrong way," he said slowly, and she wondered if his couple of drinks were making him lethargic, "but have you considered getting a life?"

His tone was so comfortable and familiar that it took her a minute to register what he'd just said. "What the fuck...?" Her voice went up an octave, and she pulled away from him, eyes narrowed.

He held up his hands protectively, motioning her to settle down. *Like hell,* she thought. "Tika, it's not that I don't appreciate your efforts. I do. But you never really understood about Luis. You don't understand about loving somebody like that—where you'd do anything for them."

"Oh, that is such bullshit," she snapped back. "Look at everything I do for you! Hell, I even take care of Sarah...okay, so I don't have a committed *relationship.* But fuck, who needs one?"

He sighed. "I'm not saying you need to find somebody to be happy."

"Damn right."

"I'm saying," he said, and his voice was heartbreakingly gentle, "that you're *not* happy. And you're hardly in a position to tell *me* how to be happy."

She blinked. If he'd gotten up and slapped her, she wouldn't have been more surprised.

"How long have we known each other?"

She shifted gears, trying to move away from his words. "Since I was sixteen."

"Since you ran away from home," he said. "I've known you since you changed your name. And you know what the weird thing is? Other than growing out a little, you haven't changed a bit."

She smiled. "Thanks."

"That wasn't exactly what I meant."

"Listen, I know I've made some dumb choices, but I've lived with them. Remember when I got married?"

He rolled his eyes. "Oh, Christ. I'd blacked that out."

"Well, it was stupid, but I made a go of it until he divorced me." She frowned. "I gave it my all for a year and a half. You helped me pick up the pieces… Don't tell me I don't know about loving somebody. I just choose not to waste it on men I fuck, that's all."

He shook his head. "Tika. What am I going to do with you?"

She shrugged. "It's my life. I play, I pay."

"And that," he said, "is my point. To you."

She frowned.

"I'll be fine, Martika. Just…let me do this on my own, okay?"

She thought about it, but her stomach hurt too much.

"Nope," she said, finally. "Like it or not, you're getting taken care of. Now what do you want to drink?"

Judith looked out over the lawn party being held at the dean's house for the relatively small (*but just as good as USC,* her husband often remarked) law school. It was certainly trying to be as opulent as USC, she gave them that much. It looked like something out of a forties movie—men in dinner jackets and black ties, women in cocktail dresses. She herself wore a pale pink silk dress, cut like something you see madams wearing in Chinese whorehouses in films of the Old West. David liked her to emphasize her heritage. The fact that she didn't speak it, wasn't pure Chinese, and hadn't been to the country meant relatively little. Her mother would have found the whole thing funny, actually.

She looked out over the lawn, with the milling crowds of people, and looked into the windows. She could see the dean's library, his home office setup. He had a computer, she thought.

No. You're not checking e-mail now.

She'd tried to put the previous experience out of her mind, and she hadn't read Roger's e-mails since…and there had been more of them. But she'd thought about him, and his words. Even after David got home. He was a little shocked when she wanted sex on his return, and she participated more whole-heartedly than she had in a year.

She had done more than that, though. In the tub, by herself, remembering Roger and that flow of description, his words, her hands. She felt vaguely guilty, even now.

She smiled at someone passing by. "Hello..." *Michael? Daniel?* "Eric. So nice to see you again."

Eric introduced his date, Phyllis. He then went on to describe the weather ("unreasonably cold!"), his new job with David's firm ("so happy!") and the latest film project that Phyllis was working with ("she's an intern!"). Judith smiled politely through it all.

David came up, and the shift of conversation and everything else went to him. She felt relieved. The dean came over to join their knot of socializing. She noticed Eric got flustered and dragged Phyllis off to the bar. The dean motioned to his wife to join them.

"What is this, six years now, David? And you still keep coming. I'm so glad you've stayed loyal to the school."

David smiled and sipped at his Scotch, making that little clicking noise with his tongue after the sip. "I loved going to school here. It made me who I am."

The dean's wife floated over in a pale yellow dress that she shouldn't have been wearing. It made her look sallow, Judith noticed. She linked her arm with her husband. "And you're a fantastic lawyer, David dear. But you really might want to think about being a teacher someday."

"Someday."

Judith and David had thought it over. Were thinking it over to a certain degree now. But there were plans, timelines, goals.

"Well, I know I'm thinking of it more lately." David smiled broadly. "I figured, being a teacher might be better when we have kids."

Judith choked on her drink.

"Are you all right, dear?" The dean's wife asked kindly, but the dean moved on after a cursory glance in her direction.

"Kids…you're past thirty, David, it's about time you started thinking of it. I'm sure Judith has, isn't that right, Judith?"

"Of course we have," David answered instead, which gave Judith the option not to answer. Or took the option, depending on how you looked at it. "But the time isn't quite right yet. I'd like to make partner first, lock that in, put in some time."

"You don't want to be sixty-five when you watch your son ace through law school, Dave," the dean said, with an all too knowing laugh, motioning to his own son, trying to look surreptitious as he copiously drank margaritas from the free-flowing pitchers. "You definitely don't want to be in your dotage when they surpass you."

"Then I want to give him a damned awful high bar to jump over, Barry," David said. They did the secret-handshake-wink thing that apparently only lawyers understood. She wondered if maybe they taught it to you after you passed the bar. Maybe included it in an instruction booklet with your test scores.

"Can I get you another drink, dear?"

She looked at Marta. Marta, Barry's wife of God knows how many years. She was unusual, fancied herself a writer apparently. To the best of her knowledge, the extent of her writing was a series of voluminous letters to friends and families over the Christmas holidays and doing some sort of children's books for her son, the same said son who was currently "acing through law school." Their law school, not surprisingly. She had always seen Marta as pressed, polished, rather like one of the other furniture pieces. She'd overheard one of the law students (who had also indulged rather plentifully from the margarita pitcher) call her Marta Stewart. She'd laughed and felt ashamed, both of laughing and of agreeing.

"No, I'm fine." If it got really bad, Judith supposed she could sneak a sip of margarita if the good son hadn't gone through it all.

Roger would find this funny.

"So, Judy," Dean Matthews turned his focus on her, finally and uncomfortably for her. "How is it at that little job of yours?"

To lawyers, it seemed like all other jobs were little jobs. "I'm a production supervisor over at Salamanca advertising…one of the youngest in their history, actually," Judith said, hoping she hit the tone just right: just this side of bragging, emphasizing being important and accomplished enough to be David's wife but to never have delusions of outstripping or outshining him. Like that was somehow possible.

She was getting bitter. Better that she not drink, she realized.

"Well! That's got to be keeping you busy, especially with David working so many late hours. I know him—he was like that in school."

"Yes, yes." A Merchant-Ivory sort of grin of understanding—understated, speaking volumes. "I try to do what I can."

"Of course, you'll be giving that up when the baby comes," Marta said.

The matter-of-factness in her tone surprised Judith. "Well, we hadn't really discussed it. Maybe for the first couple of years…"

The three of them burst into laughter. More surprise, this time more discomfort. "Kids are a full-time endeavor. Believe me, I know." Marta fluffed her hair, then nodded at Jeffrey, their soon-to-be-blotto son. "Once they're out of the house, you feel like you've suddenly got more air to breathe." When she noticed that the men had stopped laughing, she smiled, one as practiced and smooth as Judith's own. "So you've got more time to devote to your loving, harried husbands, of course." That got them laughing again, even though it wasn't close to funny.

The look in Marta's eyes wasn't close to funny, either. More like a clerk at a convenience store, trying to somehow communicate that there was a man with a gun behind the counter.

Help me, it said.

Get out, while you can.

"I was wondering, Dean Matthews…"

"Barry, please!" He clapped Judith on the shoulder, a little too hard. "After all these years, you can definitely call me Barry."

"Well, then, Barry, I've got a hot project that's going on at work, and I need to check in," she said smoothly, linking her arm in his and gently leading him back toward the house. "Not to seem like too much of a workaholic, but could I jump online on your computer for just a quick minute?"

Sarah stood, dressed in a chic little white dress that left little to the imagination. The club was Moomba, which Martika had roundly denounced as "bougy" and a "chichi starfucker rattrap." Of course, as Taylor pointed out, Martika had made no such comments when it was the Love Lounge, hosting clubs like Cherry and Club 1980s. "She's old school," Taylor had murmured, putting slight emphasis on the *old*. Martika had ignored him for the rest of the night.

She sipped at a drink while Jeremy, her date and "tryout," was in the men's room. She couldn't help but wonder who was being tested here. She wished that Taylor, Pink or Kit were in the crowd somewhere, for moral support. Even Martika, even though she'd been snippy and hard to be around lately.

The crowd was rich, well-dressed…preening. It sort of reminded her of the Anais.com party.

For his part, Jeremy turned out to be a good dancer. They'd done a few slow bump and grinds, starting out about a foot apart and, before he'd gone off to the rest room, making it to, say, a millimeter apart. If that.

Unless he carried pepper spray in a front pocket, the guy gave Raoul a run for his money.

Sarah took a sip of her Cosmopolitan. Thankfully Jeremy was buying drinks—they were hellishly expensive in here.

He'd been saying things to her all evening—teasing her for being some kind of temp, asking her if she did absolutely everything.

"Whatever the job requires," she'd replied, surprised at her own licentious streak. She'd brushed up against him, suggestively. It gave her a little charge, taking the initiative like this. She definitely had the reins, here.

"Having a good time?"

She jumped, then mentally cursed herself. Of course, she'd look a lot more in control if she'd just *get comfortable.* Just because this place wasn't Probe or the World Club, or even Velvet...

"You okay?" Jeremy's voice was a little more emphatic now.

"Sorry," she said, thinking to explain. "I...this isn't a club I'm used to."

"Where do you normally go?" he asked, amused.

She told him. His eyes widened, and he laughed.

"Oh. More of the trashy circuit," he said dismissively, causing Sarah to cross her arms in a defensive posture. "Nothing wrong with that. Hell, if you're broke, it's the way to go."

Now Sarah *definitely* didn't like his tone. "My friends hang out there," she said firmly.

"Don't pout. Much as I like the baby-girl look on you, pouting is rarely attractive."

She exaggerated the pout, then flashed a smile at him. "You could make it up to me," she said.

His eyes went low-lidded. "You don't say."

She took a deep breath. Ignore his attitude—focus on the body and what he could do with it. She didn't have to keep him. "You could always…"

The shrill beeping of a cell phone interrupted his request. He glanced at the number flashing on its faceplate, and muttered something. "I've got to take this. Let's go outside—I think this place is pretty much done."

She negotiated the steep steps that led out of the club while he yelled "Hello? Hello?" with his cell phone to one ear and his hand to the other. She stood at the base of the steps, watching as he wandered around the corner of the building, just before he disappeared down toward the end of the block.

Just when I was going to go for round two of the tryouts, she thought. Probably not sex—she was going to insist on foreplay, and plenty of it.

Sarah was deep enough in her own thoughts that she didn't notice who had approached her. The grumbling, however, tipped her off almost immediately.

"I don't see why we have to go to this club," a male voice groused. "We could have just gone to Islands, then rented a movie."

"Honey," a female voice wheedled, "we *never* go out."

Sarah turned…and was face-to-face with Benjamin.

"Hello, Sarah." He was wearing a suit—it looked lame, out of place in this very trendy nightspot. He looked like he was a Jehovah's Witness, come to save some sinners. He also looked uncomfortable. He was really more of a sports bar type. Moomba was going to be a poor choice for him.

Sarah's gaze moved slowly to Benjamin's companion. Tall, impossibly thin. She could probably hold a wallet in the side of her pelvic bone, Sarah thought uncharitably, thinking of the pounds she herself had put on through indulging in drinks and restaurants. The woman had straight chocolate-brown hair that curled at the ends in a slight pageboy. She wasn't smiling at Sarah.

If I were her, Sarah thought, I wouldn't smile, either.

He stood there for a second, awkwardly, with his— date? lover? girlfriend?—standing off to one side. "How've you been?" he finally asked.

Since I ran out of your house because you slept with me in the bed you slept in every night with your…Jessica?

She shot a quick glance toward Jeremy. He was still down the street, engrossed in conversation. She shrugged. "I've been fine. You?"

"Business is doing really well. They're talking promotion, but I don't know. I get a little sick of this city," he said. "I might look for something else, something back up North. Without the smog and the weirdos."

Sarah couldn't help but notice that his companion

didn't really look pleased at this announcement, the frown making her attractive face look suddenly older. Sarah wondered how old the woman actually was.

"Have you got a job yet?" He actually managed to sound concerned. Hell, he probably *was* concerned. Walking away from a job that had career advancement to be a temp/secretary/whatever was probably tantamount to death to so-called normal people. *Was* death, she thought, or at least that's what she'd been raised to believe.

"I have a job now."

"Oh. Something with a future, I hope?"

Sarah shrugged. "I'm not really looking for something with a future."

"Just something to get yourself some space? That's probably a good idea—you've been so stressed." Of course, *now* he was understanding. How convenient. Of course, he was now with someone else. As if just remembering that himself, he turned and said, "Have I introduced Jessica?"

So it *was* Jessica. And he'd managed to just ace her in one fell swoop, throwing Jessica into the mix with a broad and faintly smug smile.

Jessica smiled. It was probably supposed to be warm, but there was a shade of wariness there.

"No, you hadn't introduced Jessica, but of course I figured, who else could it be? Hi, Jessica," she said, gritting her teeth and holding out a hand. "I'm Sarah. I used to be engaged to Benjamin."

The woman shot a pained look at Benjamin. Obviously, she didn't know that bit of information. Instead of looking older, Jessica suddenly looked younger, and vulnerable. In that moment, Sarah hated Benjamin. She hated him enough for the two of them.

"Actually, I like my new job a lot," she added carelessly. She could have mentioned their last time together, but wouldn't. The woman would find out what Benjamin was like, soon enough. Chances were, she wouldn't have cared. If Jessica had found out, what would she have done? Sarah didn't want to think about it. "You could call what I do being a secretary if you wanted, I suppose. I'm a personal assistant. To Richard Peerson."

His grin seemed indulgent. "Am I supposed to know him?"

She shrugged. "He won the Pulitzer for fiction and is a multimillionaire bestselling author. But you're right—I guess not everybody would know that."

She'd hit a sore spot, and she felt glad…and somewhat dirty that she felt giddy about his discomfort. She ignored that part.

"So, you get his coffee and change his toner," he said, with a grin to Jessica that she returned uncertainly. "Movin' on up, Sarah."

"Sarah! I'm sorry, I couldn't get him off the line. Why can't some idiots leave their work at work?" Jeremy was slightly out of breath. He'd done a business-jog over to stand by her side, and the little motion had ruffled his hair slightly. He looked sophisticated in his casual but expensive ensemble, especially compared to Benjamin's obvious conservative tastes.

Jessica all but goggled, and again, Sarah felt that guilty little thrill of pleasure. "Am I interrupting?"

"No. This is my ex-fiancé, Benjamin, and his…um. Jessica," she said. She wasn't quite sure *what* Jessica was to Benjamin. Judging by Jessica's frown at Benjamin after the introduction, Sarah guessed that the woman was feeling the same way.

Sarah sidled up to Jeremy, leaning close to his ear. "So. Still up for more…tryouts?" She tried to whisper it to him, but got the feeling Benjamin overheard.

"Unfortunately, I can't." To his credit, he looked genuinely disappointed. "I have to drive on back and go over some numbers."

"So," she said, ignoring Benjamin's glare and now sending over a deliberately sexy smile. "Guess you're one of those idiots, huh?"

Jeremy blinked, then laughed. "Guess I am. But trust me, we are doing this again." He leaned down and kissed her, to her surprise, right on the lips, lingering slightly. "I'll call you later. I'm really, *really* sorry to be rushing off like this. Are you going to be okay?"

"Of course," she said easily. "Don't worry…my car is just over there."

He walked off toward where his car was parked, but not before shooting a sexy smile at her and winking. She felt warm, and happy.

She turned back to Benjamin and Jessica. Jessica had a satisfied smile on her face, until she noticed Benjamin smoldering, and then the smile quickly turned into a tight blank expression. Sarah got the feeling this was something Jessica had been practicing, probably for a long time.

"I've got to go. I'm going to catch up with some friends," she said, her voice light. "But it's been…" What? She fumbled for a proper description. Interesting? Vindicating? Unnerving? "I'm glad you're doing well," she finally said. "Anyway, I've really got to go."

"I'd hate to keep you," he said, and his tone was frosty.

"Don't worry," she said, and she couldn't resist. "You couldn't."

Chapter 13

We Could Be So Good Together

Sarah had gotten used to the routine. She would get in, have breakfast with Richard in the kitchen, then leave him alone to type until he ambled in asking if she felt like lunch or she left for her extended break, around eleven-thirty or twelve. Then, in the afternoon, it was extended Internet research. Usually Sephora.com, looking at the new makeup offerings Pink had mentioned, or possibly Amazon, checking Richard's sales ranking with a casual boredom. Not that she'd share what she found—numbers, as Richard always said, made him nervous. Then she'd jet out at four. The process repeated itself.

If somebody would throw in "a naked guy to pleasure her whenever she rang a small bell," as Martika would say, it would be the most perfect job ever created.

The phone rang. "Sarah Walker," she answered, in her best *I'm important* tone.

"You sound so much like a grown-up, it's eerie."

She smiled. "Kit."

"If you've got the time for us peons, I was wondering if maybe we could do lunch—Taylor's rounding the crew up, I mean. And then, of course, I'd drop you back to your fabulously important job, to talk to people who are far more interesting and socially acceptable than myself."

"It's not like that," she protested. "My job isn't *that...*"

The phone beeped—call waiting. This could be Oprah, she thought with a laugh, wouldn't Kit think it was a hoot? "Could you hold on for a second?"

"No."

She grinned. "Thanks," and clicked over. "This is Sarah Walker."

"This is Jeremy."

The voice was too damned sexy. "This is a surprise."

"Want to go out, have a little fun?" Was it just her imagination, or did he put a sort of Shakespearean emphasis on the word *fun?*

"I'm sort of busy, Jeremy." No need to let him think she was panting for him—she sort of felt that was her other mistake with Raoul, actually.

"You're always sort of busy. All work and no play, etcetera."

"I play."

"Do you, now?" Sinfully sexy. Ridiculously sexy. Sarah felt flushed, for pity's sake. "I wonder. I'd like to play with you, Sarah."

"I'm sure you would," she said, thinking of Kit on the other line. He didn't sound like that at all, not this total seductive, complete *player* voice. Kit was just a friend. He was a relatively good-looking, relatively funny guy. She might like to try someone like him sometime—later. When the poison she was feeling toward relationships was out. Jeremy, on the other hand, was imminently fuckable and, conversely, easy to walk away from. And so damned *sexy!* "I'm not ready to play just yet."

"Well, you've got my number," he said. "I'll keep calling you until you are ready, though. Bye, darling Sarah."

She loved the way he said her name. "Sah-rah," two long "ah's." It sounded exotic…less like bread-and-butter quilts.

She clicked back over to Kit. "Sorry about that."

He paused. "That was a guy, wasn't it."

It wasn't a question.

She felt her chin go up. "Maybe. What makes you say that?"

"Because I don't think you get that breathless talking to reporters." She thought she heard a snicker. "Unless you're more dedicated to your job than I thought, anyway."

Strangely, she felt a teeny, almost imperceptible pang of—guilt? *Like hell.* ''I'm sorry,'' she said, mimicking Martika—so sweet, you almost didn't feel the smack. Almost. ''You know, of course, that they're all just appetizers until I get to you.''

''Naturally,'' he said, not missing a beat. ''Unlikely I'll get action, though. I'm a nice guy. In my experience, you've got to be a bit more of an asshole to get any in this town.''

''When was the last time you got some, then, Kit?''

''That's sort of a personal question, isn't it?''

She shrugged. ''You don't have to answer it.''

''Yes,'' he said. ''I know.''

There was a pause.

''Okay, that was weird,'' Sarah said.

''What?''

''That whole conversation.''

Kit paused again. She knew he understood what she was talking about. ''But it *was* a guy, right?''

''Does it matter?''

She could hear the shrug, she swore to God. Like the phone shifted. ''I'm just curious.''

''Why?''

''You're a friend of Tika's. I'm a friend of Tika's. We both know what she's like with men. They're the center of her world—briefly, and regularly.''

Okay, now she *really* didn't like the direction this conversation was taking. ''So, what?''

''So you've been taking a lot of cues from her lately,'' Kit pointed out. Then, in a quiet voice, lower than his usual mumble, she made out the phrase: "I've been a little worried."

"Worried about what? That I'm going to sleep my way across town? Is that all you guys think about?"

"You're right. A guy thinking about sex. How unusual."

"Yes, I've been screwing every guy that crosses my path," she said, rolling her eyes, leaning back in the chair. "I've been taking extra yoga classes for when the Third Fleet's scheduled to come in. I'm giving out frequent user cards—after every tenth session, I buy the guy a sandwich." She huffed impatiently. "Honestly."

He paused. "Hmm. I'm always in the market for a good sandwich."

"Screw you, Kit."

"Among others, eh?"

She squealed in annoyance, then hung up. When it rang, she answered it. "Yes?"

"Hi, I'm your local navy recruiter, and I wanted to let you know the Third Fleet's in…."

She promptly hung up on him again. She started laughing. Kit was—like the kid brother she never had. Or the guy in third grade who always threw rocks at her, little ones. He was easy to talk to, probably easy to cry on, and definitely harmless.

In short, Kit was a nice guy.

He was right. She didn't want to sleep with a nice guy, either.

"I think I'm dying."

Taylor leaned back on a chair at the Bar Marmount,

watching Martika look at her drink. "Excuse me," he said, gesturing to an invisible three-foot circle surrounding his seat. "This is a drama-free zone."

"I'm not being drama," she protested, sprawling back in her own chair disconsolately. "I feel it. I feel sick. I can feel it in my chest, in my stomach, in my head...everywhere."

Taylor sighed the sigh of the much beleaguered. "Sure you do. So what does it feel like?"

"Like I'm going to throw up," she said nervously, feeling nauseous just thinking about it.

"Girlie-girl, you've got a history of stress-stomach. Did they ever confirm those were ulcers?"

She frowned at him. "That was when I was working at the design house, Taylor."

"You can't say you're not stressed out now, Tika. Sarah's starting to turn into a little diva with the Raoul incident, the fact that you're rooming with a woman period, the fact that your design job is stepping up a notch, the fact that you're turning thirty..."

She hissed at him, glancing around.

He rolled his eyes. "All sorts of stress lately. You're not the only one."

She knew he was referring to their discussion after Luis dumped him. She had tried to respect his need for space, or whatever. It had been short-lived. They had spent a few days apart, then they were back to normal. Normal for them.

"Well, and I've been having headaches. And I've been way bloated."

"Tell me about it," he said, glancing over her all-black pantsuit ensemble. "Time to go back to the gym, honey. That's not water weight, that's fat."

"Don't be bitchy to distract me," Tika said, swirling her soda around. She sipped at her Pellegrino. She would've loved to have gotten drunk, but the last time she'd tried…ugh. She reminded herself of Sarah's regurgitational ballet, that first night on Stoli. "I'm really worried."

"Obviously. So why don't you go to a doctor?"

"Because I don't want to hear that I'm dying."

Taylor sighed, then stood up and opened his arms. "Come here."

"Taylor, what are you…"

"Don't argue with me, woman," he said, in his best butch-straight-guy voice.

She got up. He enveloped her in his arms, something only a man of his height could do. "You are *not* dying."

"You don't know that," she said, muffled against his shirt.

"Shh. You are not dying, because it's *all about you*. You are simply too fabulous to die. If you die, not only will the sorrow be too much for the world to bear, it would be pointless because the world would cease to exist if you weren't dutifully standing at the center of it, giving us purpose, telling us what to do. Giving us something to dream about. *You cannot die.*"

She felt tears welling in her eyes, and she hugged him a little tighter. They must've been a sight—standing like big hugging giants in the middle of a trendy bar in Los Angeles, looking like refugees from the death of disco, with an Amazonian club queen crying like an actor in some really bad drag dinner theater. She laughed at the image of herself, even as she cried, knowing she was going to look like a raccoon when this was all over. She felt Taylor's broad hand smoothing down her shoulder in comforting strokes.

She thought of her father, inexplicably—how long it'd been since she'd spoken to him. Back then, she was still a giant, gangly fifteen-year-old. She ran away a little under a year later.

"Feel better?"

"Are you kidding? After that speech? I felt like you ought to have been playing the theme from *Patton* in the background." She sniffled, sitting down in her chair. She mopped at her eyes, pouting at the thick black that came off onto the cocktail napkin. "Boy, I'll bet I look gorgeous. But I will say this—my stomach feels a little better."

"Damn," Taylor drawled. "If you really do die, can I get your car?"

"Bitch. You drive like an old woman."

"You drive like some ugly NASCAR driver," he said, shrugging. "We balance. You know what you need?"

Her phone rang, playing a tinkling electronic version of "Animal" by Nine Inch Nails. "What do I need?" she said, glancing at the number that flashed in the display. She didn't recognize it.

"Another trip to Pointless Party," Taylor said, all

but rubbing his hands together in glee. "We're due, don't you think?"

"Okay, I suppose. But no drinking…I'll explain later. This is me, and you are?" she finally said, answering the phone.

"Martika?"

She didn't recognize the voice. It sounded high for a guy, sort of, and…well, vaguely familiar. Which narrowed it down to, oh, about five hundred men. Conservatively. "Yes? Who's this?"

"This is Ray."

Still no bells. "Ray…"

"From Pointless Party. From…" He lowered his voice, as if in uncertain company. "You know. The storeroom."

The…oh. "Right! It's been a while." A few weeks, anyway. She shouldn't have to remember everybody she'd screwed in the past few weeks. Actually, what with dealing with Taylor and enduring new diva-Sarah, she'd been off her game. Maybe she hadn't slept with anybody since then. Maybe not. He was pretty good. "Strangely enough, I was just talking about going back there. Wanna come?"

Taylor was mouthing "Who?" to her, and she made a pantomime of closing a door, then moving her hips as if getting laid. He laughed, even as she noticed other patrons staring at her. She smiled sweetly at them. Ray still hadn't spoken. "Can you talk?" he said, instead.

She frowned. "Of course I can talk. You're hearing me, aren't you?"

"I mean…well, this isn't easy to say."

She rolled her eyes. His story, as they say, was getting tiresome. "Try just spitting it out. Or try not saying it."

"You remember that night?"

"Vaguely," she said, just to be bitchy.

"Well," he said, "I have a confession to make. I'm, well, married."

She smacked the heel of her hand on her forehead. "I see." She gestured to her ring finger on her left hand. Taylor started laughing even harder. "Well. Mistakes were made, consider yourself uninvited, and it was…well, uninspiring, to be perfectly honest. Have a nice life."

"Don't hang up!"

She sighed, throwing her head back in exasperation and staring at the ceiling. "You mean there's *more?* What, are you married to a *man* or something?"

"No! No. Nothing like that. We've been married for a year, and I've been wondering if maybe I made a mistake. When you came on to me…" Tika winced at that part. "I wanted you. I wanted to see if I could have sex with someone other than April."

"Fantastic. So glad I provided a useful service."

"Well, the thing is, I was very upset, I was sort of plastered. I wasn't myself. I had trouble with the condom."

"I think I remember that," she said. "I was fairly plastered myself."

"Well, it broke, but I wanted you so much that I…"

"Wait a second," she said, feeling her body go cold. "What do you mean, it *broke?*"

"I said I was drunk, right? I was clumsy, and impatient, and stupid…"

"Are you saying you had sex without it?" Now the cold radiated from her stomach to her throat. That nauseous feeling was now clenching at her chest, like fire. Oh, the ulcer was in overdrive, who was she kidding?

"I told everything to April, naturally. I realized afterward that I wanted to be with her for the rest of my life, that I'd made a dreadful mistake…"

"Oh, fuck you," she said sharply. "Why the hell are you calling me? What have you *done,* you dickless little twerp?"

"She wants you to get a blood test. She wants to know what you may have given me." He sighed.

Martika's eyes almost exploded with the shock. "What?"

"It takes six months for an HIV test to be absolutely certain," he said, his tone high and mournful, like a teenager who'd been pulled over by a cop. "She doesn't want to wait six months to figure out what's going to happen to me, if she should stay or not. She thinks you ought to get tested…"

"Well, you tell your little wife that she can just wait it out and deal with you," Martika said in a low voice. "Besides, how do I know that you haven't slept with anybody else? Idiot!"

"Now see here," he said, and the righteousness of his voice made her frenzied, "I don't make a practice of sleeping with total strangers. There may have—oh, okay, there was *one* other time, but really…''

"If I had you here now, I'd string you up by your balls," she hissed.

He sighed. "My wife…"

"This is none of her goddamn business! This is all your fault!"

"You were…"

"Shut up, shut up. You can't make me take those blood tests."

"She might," he said thoughtfully. "She's a lawyer."

Tika hung up, then shut off her cell phone.

Taylor's eyes were wide, nervous. "What just happened?"

"I'm going in for a blood test," she said. "Oh, and I might just be dying, after all. Or killing someone. That *asshole!*"

Judith was sitting at her desk at work. Her ordinarily clean office had developed a bad case of clutter—there was a cold cup of coffee growing fungus by her penholder, and behind her on the credenza her schedules were strewn like dropped playing cards. Her organizer still had the previous month in it—she hadn't bothered to refill it, much less write down her daily tasks.

She stared at the screen…waiting.

Roger: Judith? I need to talk to you.

Judith heard the ping of the message, then got up, trying not to look flustered, and shut the door to her office…and then closed the vertical blinds.

"Roger." She could feel her cheeks heating with a blush. "I missed you," she typed, feeling stupid but saying it anyway. She didn't message him all weekend—David had used the computer most of the time, ham-handedly fumbling at briefs. "I tried to message you at two in the morning on Saturday, but you weren't there."

Roger: It was 5 a.m. I got your e-mail, though. I'm sorry I wasn't there to talk to you.

Judith felt her heart beating heavily in her chest. It was ridiculous, this.

She'd woken up in the middle of the night this weekend, feeling the bulk of David's boxer-covered body pressing against her side, and she'd felt…revulsion. The need to write to Roger had been tangible, driving. She had assumed he wouldn't be online—but she hoped. Not finding him, she'd contented herself with rereading e-mails from him. And she'd written one herself, pouring out her heart. And obviously, he'd read it.

Roger: I've been thinking about you. Every day.

"I've thought about you, too," she wrote back, wondering how he took the e-mail she sent. What he thought of what she'd written.

She'd started e-mailing him the night of the law school party. He'd apologized if he'd offended her. On the contrary, she said that it wasn't anything, they were just friends, it was just the Internet. They were just having fun.

And continued to have fun—the next time David had to go out of town, once when he was at a soccer game with some interns. She'd managed it various times, waiting for the beep. And had been indulging in baths almost every evening—thinking of Roger every time.

Roger: Judith, what you said in the e-mail...

Judith felt her stomach contract. "Which part?"

Roger: The part about you thinking you might be in love with me.

"Oh. That part."

Roger: And then the part where you said you knew that was stupid.

Now she was definitely blushing. "It *is* stupid," she typed. "I mean, I don't know you, I'm *married*, for pity's sake..."

Roger: You're not happy there.

"That's no excuse!" She was typing hard enough for the keyboard to clack in protest. "I made a commitment. I mean, sure, it's not the way I thought it would be. But what is?''

Roger: You deserve to be in love.

"That doesn't change anything.'' She felt like crying. She couldn't—she was at *work,* for God's sake!—but she wanted to put her head down on her desk and weep.

Roger: I love you, too, Judith. And I don't think that's stupid.

Judith blinked, then reread the sentence again. And one more time. Then blinked away tears.

That changed everything, somehow. She didn't know what she'd do next, but...he loved her, she thought. They loved each other, somehow.

Roger: I wanted to tell you when I saw you in person, but I think you needed to hear it now.

"Oh, Roger,'' she whispered, typing in: "So now what do we do?''

Roger: I don't know. I've never been in this situation before.

Judith wiped the tears away, then yanked a compact out of her top drawer and repaired any makeup damage. Her eyes looked a little smaller, but she doubted anyone would notice.

"At any rate, it's nice to know you're there," she typed. "It's nice to know somebody out there loves me."

It was sweetly unfulfilling. She was loved. She was in love. It would be enough. Like one of those fourteenth-century chivalrous things. Unless you counted that virtual sex thing—which, frankly, Judith wasn't even really admitting to herself.

Judith, you must be losing your mind. What next? Clandestine adventures in B&B's that have an Internet connection? A "quickie" behind a closed office door—by yourself? Have you lost your mind?

She didn't care. She was happy for the moment. That was enough.

Roger: I think I need to come out to L.A. and see you.

Judith read the line, and all the happiness and emotion that had whirled through her at his first proclamation of love went cold, still and clammy. "You WHAT?" she typed.

Roger: I'll fly to L.A. We need to see each other. We need to talk about this.

"But…why?"

There was a long pause between instant messages.

Roger: Because that's what people in love DO, Judith. You can't expect us to keep going on this way.

Judith held the sides of the computer, as if for balance…or maybe as if she could shake some sense into him, long distance. "You can't. My husband! My family! What will they think?"

Roger: I'm not in love with them. What difference does it make? Don't you want to see me?

He couldn't possibly be serious. They only had a cyberaffair, for pity's sake! This wasn't…

This was real. Strange, more than likely pathetic, but very, very real.

She'd spent most of her life catering to other people—being the perfect daughter, perfect girlfriend seguing into the perfect wife. She was a model employee. She didn't even litter, for the love of God. She rarely even speeded.

Her mind raced. She took a few deep breaths, trying desperately to remember what her meditation coach had taught her about stressful situations. When was the last time she'd seen him?

Roger: I don't want to hurt you more…but I want to see you, feel you, more than anything.

Could she do it? Could she move from a virtual affair to a real one? Did she want to?

Did she want more than an affair?

Roger: Judith—if you don't want me to, I won't. It's all up to you.

She typed, slowly and methodically, then stared at the send button for a second. Biting her lip, she clicked on it, seeing her own message come over as if someone else had typed it:

Judith: When?

Chapter 14

When the Music's Over

"Richard?" Sarah knocked on the door, lightly. "I was hoping I could leave early today. I've got a date."

She almost walked out with just that, but Richard's voice stopped her. "Actually, it's good that you're here. I...well, I was hoping I could talk to you a minute."

Sarah walked into his office, wondering what was up. Maybe he had a press junket coming up—no, she couldn't remember anything like that on his schedule. Hell. Maybe his publicist Emily had called him directly while she was out at lunch, and he'd answered the phone. Those calls always upset him.

She snuck a quick glance at her watch before plunking down in the seat opposite his desk. "Are you all right?" she asked, concerned. She was in a hurry, but she genuinely liked Richard.

"What? Yes. Well, no. Well…" He was wringing his hands slightly.

Now Sarah was really concerned. Wringing hands meant serious worry. "This doesn't look good."

"It's not bad!" he assured her…then frowned, causing her to move from concern to worry. "Well, actually, it is bad."

"Just say it fast," Sarah said. "We'll figure it out."

He looked downright mournful at those words. "God. I mean…Sarah, we can't go on like this."

Sarah frowned. "Go on like what?"

"We eat lunch together every day, we hang out and go shopping…we have all this *fun* together."

"And that's a problem?"

"Unfortunately, yes," he said in dire tones. "I'm…well, remember that deadline that's coming up?"

"In three weeks? The redemption book?"

He looked down at the desk. "Remember how I said it was pretty much in the bag?"

"Yesss…."

"Well, I fibbed."

Her eyes narrowed. "So how done are you?"

"I've almost got a rough," he said, with an upbeat tone.

"A rough?" She was aghast. "You can't just turn in a partial rough! You said you were just tweaking!"

"Tweaking the plot, to be precise," he said.

She sighed. "Well, this *is* a problem. Do you want me to call Madeline?" Madeline was his editor. She'd already fielded a few calls from Madeline. "I mean, if I'm distracting you, then I can help you out. I'll tell her that you're sick—or that something's come up. Or…"

"Sarah, I have to fire you."

Sarah stopped in mid-helpful-monologue. "What?"

"I don't like it either!" he wailed. "But I talked with Madeline today already, and I told her…well, she sort of *wormed* the problem out of me. And they're really upset, Sarah. You have no idea!"

You sold me out? It was probably wrong of her to think that, but he was sitting there, telling her she was unemployed *yet again,* and that because she'd become his friend, it was somehow her fault. That made no sense to her. No sense at all.

"I'll write you a really good letter of recommendation," he said. "And a month…a month's severance."

She looked at him. The betrayal must have shone across her face like a floodlight.

"Two months," he amended. "And we can still go to parties, huh?"

"Oh, Richard," she said, with a long sigh. Two months' severance, especially from this job, was more than fair—it was insane.

Can't I do anything right?

"I'll do whatever I can to make it up to you?"

Sarah gripped the handle of her purse. "Well," she said, slowly, "I guess I can get out early today, huh?"

Martika sat in the Ob-Gyn's office. She'd had blood taken for tests a few days before, and had been sweating it out, almost calling Taylor every hour on the hour. She'd considered talking to Sarah about it, but lately she'd been so full of it, with her clothes and her dates and her giggling, that it was all Martika could do not to give her a stepladder and tell her to get over herself.

"Ms. Adell?"

She looked at him. Dr. Powell. Sounded respectable. Frankly, sounded like someone older. He reminded her of Niles on *Frasier*—he was finicky and precise, and looked at her only fleetingly. "Yes. So, give me the bad news. Am I dying?"

He looked at her then, shaking his head. "If you mean do you have any diseases—no. At least, not showing up at this time. As you know, it takes six months to be truly sure with HIV, but within three months, you'll be eight-five percent positive, and so forth…"

"And everything else?" Not that she *wanted* to die. But she was feeling a little drama. "Am I in danger of anything else?"

He shook his head. "No, you've got a clean bill of health. I would still warn against unsafe sexual practices, however."

He sounded like her grandmother. Man, Taylor was going to have a field day with her. Still, her stomach felt better than it had in weeks. She got up. "Well. I'm glad that's over with. It's been..."

"You'll want to sit down, Ms. Adell," he said, and she stared at him. "The pregnancy test came up positive, so we'll want to talk about that."

"Whoa. Wait." She sat down with a *thump*. "What was that?"

The young doctor winced, his blond hair covering his blue eyes for a second. He nervously brushed his bangs out of the way. "I am correct in assuming this is something you didn't plan for, then?"

She blinked at him. Could the man have gone through however many years of med school to have come out this much of an asshole?

"I don't know, Sherlock. I came in here for V.D. screenings. What do you think? Sound like I have a happy little domestic life?"

"It's L.A." He shrugged.

She blinked at him. Okay, that was a good answer. "So. Pregnant. Baby." This was too *Twilight Zone* for words. "How...far along am I?"

"Just a month or so, from the looks of it."

"Just a month." She took a deep breath. She wasn't all that late, she realized, but she'd been sort of stressed and that made her irregular.

Now she had even more to be stressed about. And that wouldn't be the reason she wasn't getting a period. Baby. About a month along.

"Well, what can I do about it?" The question was almost rhetorical. Martika felt numb, like she was in some kind of dream state. Rather like being on some really good weed.

"Ms. Adell, are you asking me about terminating your pregnancy?" His voice was awfully calm, she noted. He was so professional about this. Wondered if they taught him that in med school, as well.

"Um. Yes." Of course, yes. She wasn't ready for a baby, was she?

Keeping the baby. The thought wouldn't have crossed her mind.

"Well, we'll have you meet with a counselor first. Then we'll schedule the procedure." Like scheduling a haircut or something, she thought. Numb, numb. "The day before, I'll put a piece of seaweed in your uterus, to encourage dilation, then I'll go ahead…"

She'd started to blank out his words. He's got really thin lips, she thought inanely. Like he had no upper lip. Like his even white teeth—the kind that must have had braces at some point—were just waiting to jut out if he so much as parted his slash of a mouth…

"Ms. Adell?"

She blinked.

"Shall I give you the paperwork?"

She started to say yes.

It came out "Can I think about it?"

It was just a job—a stupid job at that. I've got more important things to worry about tonight.

Sarah knocked on Jeremy's door, noticing that her palms were sweating slightly. She fanned them by her sides for a second, not wanting sweat marks on her clothes. She heard his heavy footstep, and took a deep breath.

Tryouts were over, she told herself with gritted teeth. She wasn't going to keep testing. Jeremy was one hell of a kisser, and he could use his hands, from what she could tell. She had high hopes for the rest of his body. This wasn't a repeat of Raoul, this wasn't even one of Martika's one-night-sex-a-thons. This was going to be epic.

Sure, she was still stinging over getting fired. But it was all about attitude. After tonight, she felt sure she wouldn't feel stressed about *anything.* She smiled at that thought.

The door opened. Jeremy was standing there, looking like a model as usual. His eyes widened slightly. "Sarah. I'm so glad you could make it. I've been looking forward to tonight."

"Oh, so have I." She stepped in. "Beautiful house." Good grief. She sounded like Eddie Haskell.

He smiled. "You should see the bedroom."

And they were starting off with a bang, she noted. He seemed as impatient as she was—but he was handling it better. She followed him through the foyer. The house was *huge,* she noted. Not a mansion like Richard's Bel Air affair, but it definitely made Benjamin's house look like a starter home and her own apartment look like the projects. The furniture was expensive. There were Japanese prints on the walls. She squinted, realizing that the ugly-looking samurai and the lady with the kimono falling off were...

She glanced away, quickly. *Eyew.*

Jeremy laughed. "You're so cute." He stopped in front of the pornographic print. "This is a classic painting, actually. The Japanese are so much more graphic than Westerners about some things. You should see their animation."

"I have," Sarah countered, staring studiously at a safe-looking vase. She knew it was stupid to be embarrassed, but... "They project hentai anime over at Perversion sometimes."

"I keep forgetting how worldly a life you have, Sarah," he said, his voice low and gravelly.

Sarah felt a pleasant frisson of heat tickle up her spine. This was the right idea. This would be fine. She'd just been thrown off her stride a little, that's all.

"I wonder...how much do you want to play, really?"

She knew her chin was jutting up defensively, but somehow she couldn't help it. She should have expected that this wouldn't be wine and roses. That was romance. This was hard-core sex...it was bound to have some unsavory edges to it.

"Listen, I'm just in this for a good time," she assured him. He still had that laughter on his face. She was actually getting angry. "Listen, I'm as much of an adventurer as...:" She stopped herself before she could say *as Martika*. "As anybody," she finished lamely.

He laughed. "Well then. We'll have to see how we can accommodate our young adventurer."

The chill she felt was less pleasant than the previous thrill. This was a tough business, this sex-for-fun thing. And he certainly wasn't helping anything.

"So, can I get my young Robinson Crusoe a drink?"

"Um…sure." She thought about it. A drink would take the edge off. It wasn't like she was going to go anywhere for a few hours. At least, she'd better not.

"What would you like?"

"What have you got?"

"Dear, we've got everything here."

"Oh. Well…how about a Stoli and cranberry?"

His little smile seemed to mock her. Maybe she was being hypersensitive. It had happened before. "Sure thing. One Stoli and cranberry, coming right up."

He wandered off, and she sat, feeling awkward. Maybe she should just jump him? She certainly didn't want to listen to him talk for much longer. She wanted to get down to it. She wanted to have *Wild Orchid* sex. She wanted something more tender than porn and a helluva lot more time-intensive than Raoul the Underwear Model.

She felt like she was at point A, that was point B, and she had no idea how to draw a line between them.

"Just make yourself comfortable," Jeremy called from the kitchen.

She took a deep breath, and quickly pulled her top over her head. *Okay, Sarah, you're trying for seduction here. Can you handle this?*

She reached around awkwardly. Trust her to choose her most complicated bra to wear when she's trying to seduce someone. She got the hooks free with a flourish, and gingerly took the thing off. She was too busy glancing out the window to see if anybody was watching, but she heard footsteps before she'd fully disrobed.

Okay, Sarah. Go for it.

"I thought we could..." she said, then stopped abruptly.

The woman had glossy red hair, that fell with unforgiving heavy straightness down her back. She had large green eyes that were staring at Sarah curiously. "We could what?"

Sarah let out a little, muffled "eep" and almost ripped her ears off yanking her shirt back on. She heard the woman laughing even as she blindly dressed.

Jeremy stepped back. "Oh. Hi, Mindy."

"Mindy?" Sarah glared at him, getting to her feet and banging her shin on the coffee table. The bruise would be nothing compared to her current painful humiliation. "Don't tell me...I seem to be playing this role a lot. Girlfriend?"

Mindy grinned, holding up her left hand. The diamond there glittered mockingly at Sarah. "So close."

"You're married?" What was it with men? Was there not one fucking decent, committed man in all of Los Angeles County? Hell, in the *world?*

"Well, yes. But that's not the point here, is it?"

"I should fucking think so!"

Mindy laughed, and Jeremy stroked her shoulder. "You're right, Jeremy. She's cute."

"You...you told her about me?"

Jeremy nodded, walking over to stand closer to Sarah. Sarah flinched as he stroked her shoulder the same way. "Of course. Mindy and I have no secrets from each other."

"Listen, obviously you two are into this whole 'open marriage' thing, but I wasn't really..."

"Sarah, you said you wanted a sexual adventure." Jeremy's voice was gentle, but held a slight edge of impatience. "What were you expecting?"

"Not this." She tugged away from him, backing away like a cornered animal.

"It's really all right," Mindy said in an equally soothing voice. "Really. Nobody's going to hurt you."

"All right? *All right?* So you don't care what he does or who with? What, would you be okay with *watching* us, too?" Sarah said sarcastically. "Or doesn't your 'openness' extend to that?"

"I certainly would not be all right with watching," Mindy said, and she looked vaguely affronted.

Sarah nodded, glaring at Jeremy. "See?"

"I would naturally insist on participating."

Sarah turned her head back to Mindy so fast, her neck cracked. *"WHAT?"*

Mindy smiled, and stroked Sarah's cheek. "This is the real adventure. I'm so glad Jeremy found you. You look like a high school freshman...and this whole surprised indignant thing is delicious." She leaned in, and Sarah felt Mindy's breath on her neck. "You might like it. If you're looking for an adventure..."

Sarah bolted past her toward the door. She didn't stop running until she was down the block, holding her side, wincing against the stitch there. She leaned against her car, setting off the alarm. She hit two of the wrong buttons before finally shutting the damned thing off.

Oh, God. Oh, God.

It was then she realized she'd forgotten her bra, and the reality of the situation hit her. She clambered into her car, locked all the doors, leaned her head on the steering wheel and started to cry.

Chapter 15

Crystal Ship

Judith sat at the food court in the Century City Mall, right across from the AMC movie theater. She knew what he looked like. He knew what *she* looked like. If that wasn't enough, she was wearing a very cliché red rosebud on her jacket. To the best of her knowledge, there were no other Chinese women in the Century City Mall food court wearing a red rosebud, so the likelihood of Roger going off with one of them seemed fairly slim.

Oh, God, what am I doing?

She was hyperventilating, was what she was doing.

She should have talked to somebody about this, she thought hastily.

Talked to who? Sarah, whose idea of love is having sex with carefully selected strangers?

Face it, the only person she'd even gotten close to in the past few months was Roger—the caring "voice" on the other side of her computer screen. Only in the twenty-first century, she thought bitterly, where infidelity crossed state lines without any physical contact.

She sighed. It'd be funny, if it were happening to somebody else.

But the things he'd said to her, the way he'd made her feel...that wasn't a joke. She hadn't felt that way with David in a long time.

She frowned. Maybe ever.

"Judith?"

She looked up, then clamped down on a gasp of horror.

"Dean Matthews?" She looked around wildly, hoping she was wrong, but there he was, pompous tweeds and all. "What are you doing here?"

He gave her a strange look. Her tone *had* been a trifle accusatory, so she tried for a casual smile, the way the question *should* have been asked. He smiled tentatively in return. "Oh, you know, Marta and I are just doing a little bit of shopping. I left her in the Disney store. She loves that stuff."

He was waiting for her to strike up some conversation, while *she* was waiting for her illicit not-quite-in-the-flesh lover to show up. *Perfect. Now all I need is David here and have him witness Roger doing a striptease for me in front of Dean Matthews.*

"So…how is Marta?" Judith asked.

"Doing fine. I've been staying home a bit more—trying out retirement, as it were—and I think it's a nice change for both of us. Marriage suffers when there's too much work, you know?"

She nodded. *This is God laughing at me.*

"You know, when I was in my first year of law school…"

Oh, no, he's going into lecture mode!

"I had this professor…God, what was his name? Anyway, he said something I'll never forget." He grinned, putting up a finger like some historical figure pontificating. "He said 'Students, look to your right, then look to your left. I promise, only one in three of you will still be with whoever you're in a relationship with before your law school career is over. Married or not. Life here is too hard.'" Dean Matthews shook his head. "God. And the numbers only got more grim once you graduated. I hit lucky with Marta. She's stayed by me all this time, through everything… impossibly long hours, well, you know what it's like."

Judith kept nodding. She felt like one of those bobblehead dolls that people put in cars. She didn't trust herself to say anything.

"Just like David's hit it lucky with you! Eh? Eh?" He winked at her, then glanced at his watch. "Well, I'm sure Marta's cleaned the place out. Better go find her before she goes wandering. Tell David I said hello?"

"Um, sure." *And explain what I'm doing at the Century City Mall on a weeknight? Oh, certainly. That could happen.* She let Dean Matthews give her a polite half-hug. Then he stopped, glancing at the lapel of her almost-new black blazer.

"That's a very pretty rosebud."

"Thanks." Judith was surprised at how cool she kept her voice. "I'm trying to spruce up the old image."

She didn't know if he bought her explanation as he walked away. What if he told David? What if he told Marta, and she told everyone else, and David found out? What if...

"Judith?"

A nasal twang jolted her out of her thoughts. She turned.

Roger.

He was just as amazingly handsome as he appeared in his picture. He had a rose in one hand. The flower was exotic looking—orange with scarlet at the edges. His tiny grin was impossibly sexy.

"Roger?" she whispered.

"In the flesh, as it were."

She winced.

That can't be his real voice.

And yet it seemed to be. It kept going, relentlessly. "I waited until you were finished talking to that gentleman...didn't want to walk into anything, y'know."

"Gentleman" came out sounding like *gintlemihn.*

Worse, it had a painfully high pitch…almost girlish, with a slight whine.

She stared at his face instead—that strong, chiseled jaw, those deep, intelligent eyes.

"Did you, er, want some food?"

Don't speak. Please, please don't speak.

She shook her head, staring at him. "No, I'm not talking…I mean, I'm not hungry."

"Oh. Okay." He gestured to a table. Numb, she sat down.

They sat there for a moment, blessedly silent. Then he cleared his throat.

"It's so good to see you." His gaze was soulful. "I've been wondering what you'd be like, you know, in the flesh."

"Uh-huh." If only there were some way to *type* this to him!

"I'm a little nervous."

"I'm a little married," she said, a little more curtly than she'd intended. "This is hardly a meditation session for me."

He was silent then, and she felt guilty about it.

"I'm sorry," she said, finally. "This is…I don't know. I don't know how I thought this was going to pan out. Maybe like in the movies—something like *The English Patient,* where the lovers just can't help being in love. Deep, tortured looks."

A more manly voice, she thought uncharitably.

"Well, I don't know about that, but I know that this isn't quite the way I pictured it, either." He took a deep breath.

She frowned. "It isn't?"

"Well…it's just *different* over the Net, that's all. I don't…I mean, I can't…" He ran his fingers through his hair, looking for all the world like a Guess model. She could overlook the voice for a face like that.

But could she overlook *marriage?*

"Different how?" she said instead.

"I don't know. You were just so lost and unhappy when you started writing to me, and I thought…hell, I still think I could help you. I don't know. Save you, or something."

"*Save* me?" Judith didn't know why she bristled at that, but she did.

"I don't know," he said. "I guess I thought I'd come here, and we'd kiss, and then I'd sweep you home to Atlanta with me. But from the look of you, that's not a workable plan." He took a deep breath. "And from talking to you…"

There was a long, painful pause. "You've only talked to me for a minute, Roger," she pointed out. He couldn't possibly have a problem with her voice, could he? God, the irony here was thick enough to cut with a knife. "What's the problem?"

"You're—well, *cold.*"

Her eyes flew wide-open at the blunt words. To further her shock, he actually blushed.

"I don't mean to be rude," he drawled in his squeaky voice. "Honest. It's just—you're so much more *vulnerable*…on Instant Message."

She blinked. She seemed more *vulnerable* through

baud rate and bandwidth? "And how do I strike you now?"

"Like if I get too close to you, you'll hit me."

She sighed.

"This isn't working, is it?" she said sadly.

He shook his head. "We could try taking it easy. I'm here for a week…on a little vacation. I've got a friend out here that I'm staying with. We could just talk on the phone…maybe jumping from the Internet straight to a face-to-face conversation was more than we could handle…"

"No, I don't think that would work." Okay, she *knew* that a few hours' conversation with that voice would not work. His voice, God help her, already grated on her nerves like a rasp. "Maybe…maybe we should stick to the Internet."

"Maybe." He scooted his chair closer to her. "I really thought I loved you, Judith. After all those things you told me, I thought we loved each other." He stroked her face, and before she could help it she shied away. "I don't really know you, do I? Not the real you."

She shook her head slowly. "If it's any comfort, neither did I."

He sighed, and the sadness of it would have broken her heart if it hadn't sounded as if it had come from Minnie Mouse. "Well. Maybe we shouldn't talk for a while, then."

She shrugged, but she felt a pang. He was her closest friend at this point—she wasn't sure if she was ready to lose that.

"I won't vanish," he assured her, in off-key tones. "But...this is weird. I'll just need a little space."

She nodded.

"I think I'd better get going."

She nodded again.

To her surprise, he leaned in, kissing her softly, full on the lips. It made her tingle, ever so slightly.

"It really is a shame," he said, close to her ear, making her spine twitch more uncomfortably, like nails on a chalkboard.

"You have no idea," she murmured.

She watched him walk away...watched other women give him appreciative glances. Watched him disappear into the crowd.

So what was this really all about?

She thought she'd found a grand passion—the *English Patient* variety. What she'd wound up with was a complete farce. Something funny, ironic, ridiculous.

She'd wanted romance, and gotten none.

She still did, she realized. She wanted more from her life.

This wasn't about Roger, she realized.

This was about David.

She stood up, taking her rosebud off of her lapel and leaving it on the cold metal table.

More importantly, this was about her.

Martika sat on the couch with her hand absently on her stomach. Her belly was slightly poochy, she noticed. Of course, it had *been* slightly poochy. To be honest, it had hardly been a washboard since she'd turned twenty-four or so. She was now thirty, so the bump of her stomach was probably fat, not baby— yet. She had no right to be sitting here on the couch, watching TV, patting her stomach like some bad TV-movie-of-the-week expectant mother.

But you are an expectant mother.

She'd told Taylor, naturally, and he was aghast, just as she supposed she should have been. Hell, *she* was. She prided herself on being unflappable, but this—she was completely flapped. She credited her hormones for the roller coaster of emotions raging inside her— she really ought to go though with the abortion, and chalk it up to a really, really bad experience. And naturally, she'd be more careful in the future. No more random fucks, for one thing. That was hardly a sacrifice. She'd be more careful. She'd have a relationship. Maybe she'd even find "the one."

But her hand continued to rest where it was.

Wonder if it's a boy or a girl? By this point, there would be no way to tell. But it was weird. She'd only thought of babies in relative terms—other people's, to be specific. Kids hardly fit into a clubbing lifestyle, frankly, and her life as it was now was her own. Kids represented responsibilities. Permanence. PTA meetings and day care. Getting no sleep. There was also that weird thing they did when they were two and turned into little monsters. She'd seen enough of them on TV to know.

But it still didn't stop her from wondering. This wasn't just a kid. This was *her* kid. She could feel its presence in her body like some alien taking up residence, but not in the bad, X-files sort of way. She thought that all that stuff in movies about "feeling" the baby, especially in this early stage, was just bullshit, but the beginning tenderness in her breasts and the nausea were all accumulating with amazing rapidity.

As much as she loved him, Taylor didn't understand about this. She needed to talk to a woman about this.

That meant Sarah.

She hadn't been exactly cordial to Sarah, but still, this was an emergency. She felt sure Sarah would understand.

She heard Sarah's key in the dead bolt, and her hand twitched reflexively. She supposed she looked like Al Bundy, sitting on the couch with her hand on her stomach. She moved it to the couch, fighting the urge to put it back on her abdomen.

"Hi, Sarah," she called before Sarah even walked down the hallway. "Got a minute?"

"Today has been from hell," Sarah said. "I've just been fired. And, worse, the guy I was planning on sleeping with turned out to be a complete asshole. Don't even get me started on his wife." She groaned and plunked down in the love seat. "I want to go out to a club and get drunk until I don't remember my own name or how I got home."

This wasn't exactly how Martika had planned on sharing her story. Obviously, Sarah needed to vent a little. She hoped it wouldn't be too long—she really didn't have the perspective for this.

"So, I guess you'll be looking for another job, then?"

Sarah glared at her. "You think?"

"No need to get bitchy." Martika's voice was sharp. She *definitely* didn't need to hear this twenty-five-year-old's woes when she was sitting here pregnant. "I just had a problem that I wanted to talk about, that's all."

Sarah's eyebrows jumped to her hairline. "Oh, for...of course, Martika. *Tell* me about *your* problems."

Martika's eyebrow quirked at her. *Oh, nuh-uh.* "Excuse me. Tone."

"Don't you get sick of the mother bit?"

Martika made a little gasp-noise, genuinely shocked. "What?"

"You put the mother in smother, I think is the term. You do it with me and Taylor and anybody else you get close to—for as long as they *can* stay close to you. I swear! You tell me not to pay attention to my job, to get a fuck-a-thon-life, and I do, and here's where I wind up! I'm miserable!"

"And that's somehow *my* fault?" Martika yelled. She was pissed off. She *definitely* did not need this. "Because you've got some strange mother obsession and you think I'm *smothering* you?"

"You do!" Sarah jumped up and started pacing, her Prada mules making dents in the carpet with her hard stomps. "God. It's always about you. *You* know what's right. You always know what's right! And you're always telling *me* what's right and what I ought to do! And when it doesn't work out, you won't let me complain about it! Why? Because your problems are *so* much more important than mine. Because it's all about *you!*"

"In this case, listening to a twenty-five-year-old whine because she doesn't have the perfect life really doesn't sound all that fatal to me," Martika said coldly. "When I met you, you were so whipped by that prick you called a fiancé, you practically rolled over when he fucking whistled. You did the same thing with your jobs, Sarah…everything but 'fetch!' Jesus, you should *thank* me."

"Thank you? *Thank you?*" Sarah's eyes blazed.

Martika hadn't seen her like this before.

"Why should I? Everything I had before made sense! I knew what I wanted!"

"You wanted to be some little *wife,* with no life of your own, just because it was something to do," Martika spat out. "You want to hear about problems? Let me *tell* you about…"

"No, you won't," Sarah said, surprising Martika again with the vehemence in her voice. "You'll listen to me. You're not as cool as you think you are. You're not hip, you're not edgy, and you're *not in your twenties.*"

That, Martika wasn't expecting. "What the fuck are you saying?"

"I'm saying, there's nothing wrong with being thirty," Sarah said, deliberately using a sweet tone. "Unless you're trying to be eighteen. Then, it's fucking *tragic.*"

The shot hit Martika right in the chest, and she felt tears well up. She'd taught Sarah how to do that, was all she could think. She'd taught her to be this bitchy, to get a spine, and it had up and bit her on the ass.

And I think I want a kid?

The pain redoubled.

"Martika, you're a relic. You took a hick girl from Fairfield and took her to some B- and C-list clubs and told her that fucking was fun and jobs were stupid, and she believed you. Well, I see the way you really are now. You're just an insecure, prematurely middle-aged woman who hates herself so virulently that she's got something to prove to everyone she comes into contact with. You're not the woman you think you are, Martika."

"Jesus." Martika said hollowly. "I had to talk to you. I thought of you as a friend. But if I'm going to get told off in my own living room..."

"It's in my name," Sarah said coldly.

Martika got up, grabbed her purse, cell phone and bag. "Keep the goddamn apartment. I'll be out of here in a week."

Sarah's eyes widened at that. She took a few deep breaths. "We're both... I'm sorry, Martika. It's just been a really shitty day, and I just...I guess I've been a little pissed off..."

"No, you said what's really on your mind," Martika said coldly. "So it's time I said what's on mine. Maybe I am a thirty-year-old woman who's an Oprah victim, who needs to learn to love herself and get a bunch of therapy and stop fucking every guy she comes into contact with. Maybe I've got issues. But if you *honestly* think that you had it made before you met me, then you're deluding yourself. You don't want to figure out how to live your life! You want somebody to tell you how to do it, since you obviously don't trust yourself to do it right!''

"Well,'' Sarah said softly, ''I've decided it's not going to be you anymore.''

Martika looked at her, feeling the crying jag starting and biting her lip hard. ''Fuck you, Sarah.'' Then she turned on her heel and walked out.

"This is one of the worst days of my life,'' Sarah said disconsolately.

"Where's your mentor?'' Taylor asked, sitting on the opposite couch, next to Pink. Pink wasn't paying attention. Rather, she was paying attention to a cute guy on the dance floor.

"That's part of the problem. We got in this huge fight.''

Taylor chuckled. ''Don't worry. Her mads last maybe forty-eight hours.''

"This has been building up.'' Sarah put her drink down on the table next to her. ''I mean, she's been pissy ever since I got that invitation to the big publishing party.''

Taylor's eyes narrowed, and he leaned over. Pink used the opportunity to approach the guy on the dance floor. ''So what exactly did you argue about?''

"Well, she was telling me that I shouldn't worry about losing my job, *again*, that I'd find another one, and that I just had to get drunk and party and forget about it.''

Taylor's eyebrow curved up. ''And you said?''

Sarah sighed, glancing away for a second. The place seemed as it always was, with its flashing lights, and music pounding hard enough to shake the seats they were sitting on. She'd been using this spot for months as a sort of installment-piece art therapy. Hopefully it'd work tonight, too. ''I said…well, I said that it hadn't seemed to help her any.''

Taylor let out a short, barking laugh. ''Shit. Bet that went over like a house on fire.''

''And I sort of told her she was smothering me.''

Taylor's eyes widened. ''You didn't.''

''Well, she's this compulsive mother to all of us,'' Sarah muttered, taking another sip of her drink. They were making the gin and tonics strong tonight— Tommy had to be out. He normally monitored that sort of thing. ''You've got to admit she chafes on you sometimes, too…''

''Well, of course, but I don't admit that to *her!*'' Taylor let out another snort of amusement. ''Sarah, we are Martika's family. Instead of going crazy like we do, or breaking down, she spends her energy telling us how to live our lives. That's just the way she is. She is uber-mom of Santa Monica Boulevard.'' He shook his head. ''So what happened then?''

''She stormed out. I didn't feel like apologizing, so I came here.''

Taylor sighed, then glanced up. ''Hell-oo. Cute guy at the bar.''

Sarah turned, listlessly. She noticed she had a buzz going. Early. That probably wasn't good. The club wasn't too far from home, but if she got really hammered she could always call a cab, she reasoned. So she finished the rest of her drink in a swallow.

Taylor straightened up, and was staring at her. "Oh my. He's checking *me* out," he said, very much like a high school girl trying to play it cool. "I think it's time for me to get a drink. Do you need a refill?"

She glanced down. "Um, better not. Without Martika here..." She clamped down on the words. She didn't need a keeper, dammit! "Sure. Why don't you get me another?"

"Right-oh."

She watched as he casually sauntered up to the bar, ordering the drinks, and then striking up a conversation with the guy who was scoping him with an almost careless glance. She didn't know how Tayler did it, but every time she was impressed by his acting skills—like he hadn't been squeaking with excitement about that same guy, not two minutes ago.

To her surprise, Kit sat down next to her. "You okay?"

She suddenly hated that he could read her moods, especially when he only seemed to have one mood. A one-mood-fits-all sort of guy. Or maybe just an extra-large mood. She giggled at the thought. Yes, she was definitely getting her drink on good this Friday night.

He frowned. "I said, you okay?"

"Well, don't I look okay?"

There was a slight flicker in his sardonic eyes. "Is that you fishing for a compliment?"

"Fuck off, Kit."

Taylor walked over with a drink in each hand and his new crush practically panting by his side. "Here you go, Sarah, my dear," Tayler said expansively, putting her drink down. "Oh! I see Kit's here. Well, you're in good hands. I think we're going off to another club now. You'll be all right, right?"

Sarah rolled her eyes. Another club? Ha! Not from the gleam in Taylor's eyes. "Sure, sure. I'll be fine here."

"Great. See you!" He went off at a gallop, she noticed.

She glanced over. Kit's frown was even more pronounced. "What does he mean, you're in good hands?"

She shrugged. "Beats me."

"Where's Tika?"

Sarah scowled at him. "I don't need a keeper, Kit."

"Obviously. What, did you get in a fight with the resident Glamazon, or is she off getting laid as well?"

Sarah shrugged. "Probably. I don't know."

"Sarah, why are you here by yourself?"

She turned on him. "I don't need you here taking care of me! I don't need anyone here taking care of me! I am a grown woman. Granted, I'm a grown woman who is currently unemployed and relation-shipless, but I *take care of myself!*"

He nodded, like one placating an insane person. "I see. Unemployed and relationshipless."

She sighed. "Trust a man to put it in the worst light."

"Well, did you like the job you lost?"

"It's not about liking my job!" She noticed that she must have roared that last bit, because people were staring at her. She toned it down a bit, so that he was leaning toward her to listen. "I mean, it's about enjoying my life the way it is. I have—*had*—a job that paid the bills, you know? I wasn't leaping along a career path."

"There's nothing wrong with a career path."

She blinked at him. "I know that!"

"Inside voice, please."

She could have bit him, she felt that riled. She turned her head to focus entirely on him—the buzz was kicking in but strong. "I thought I finally had it. I'd tried to have a career path, and five-year goals, and work on my circle of influence, and that went to shit. Now, I try to have fun and just be a slacker, and I fuck *that* up. How can you fuck up having no direction?"

He grinned. "Some people have extraordinary talent."

"Well, I'm sick of it. I give up."

"You're going back to goal setting?"

To her embarrassment, she felt tears in her eyes. "I don't know what I'm going to do, Kit. I just don't know."

She looked down at her lap, then at her drink.

He put an awkward arm around her shoulders, and she shrugged it off, clumsily.

"Listen, Sarah, I'm sorry…"

"Don't tell me you're sorry," she hissed. "I don't want to fucking hear that anybody's sorry. Everybody's sorry. You don't have to say it."

She sat there, silent, and he did the same. She felt a strange sensation…her heart beating a little faster. She glanced at Kit, like she'd seen him for the first time—and under a microscope. "You know, you've got these funny eyes," she pointed out. She couldn't seem to help pointing it out.

He had that amused half smile on his face. She noticed that he also had a little scar on the left-hand side of his mouth. "Do I?" The words seemed to come out in slow motion.

"Uh-huh," she said, gripping her drink. She drank about half of it, then realized she was getting some on her shirt. She put it back down with a loud clank. "Your eyes are these sort of greeny-brown, with yellow. Like…like a cat. Or maybe a lizard."

"So nice of you to notice," he said, and she felt him stroke the back of her hair. That was weird, she thought. "Sarah, baby, how much have you drank?"

"That's the thing," she said, thinking about it. Very hard. "This is only my second…I think."

She turned her head to study the glass, and abruptly stopped.

The dance floor seemed to be going in slow motion, too. That is, the lights, the dancers, all were in this reel of suspended animation—a few frames a second, as it were. She stared in rapt fascination, studying it as if under investigation.

The women, in the semidarkness, were wearing microminis and halter tops and all looked to be about twenty or so—and then she noticed those who obviously weren't. The men were staring at the halter tops or the minihems and all but salivating—but there was an edge of desperation, of vulnerability...no. Of *fear* in their eyes. Why hadn't she noticed that before, she thought? The women hid it better, she noticed, but there it was—that hungry searching to connect, physically, emotionally, however they possibly could. The desperation hung in the air like a fog of pheromones. She felt like holding her breath.

"Sssss...."

She barely noticed the sound. She was too busy staring at the room in front of her. It was as if she could see *between* the lights, all of a sudden. In one flash of a strobe, she seemed to see the club, as if in daylight.

There were exposed beams, a high ceiling. It was a warehouse. It was like finding out that Kubla Khan's Pleasuredome was actually a Costco. And the floor...between the naked legs and stiletto heels, she could make out the sticky black surface, covered forever in a thin layer of Permaslime from the spilled drinks and dripping sweat. She fought back a retching sound. The "stage" was a series of cratelike boxes, spray painted black.

The images were hitting her harder now, faster. The bartenders, with their looks of studied indifference. The bouncers, with their molded masks of menace. The dancers, with their calculated sex appeal.

It was a horror zone. A nightmare.

She finally turned to see Kit. No longer sardonic—his face was worried, she noticed, and for a moment, she could see more of a soul in his eyes, rather than his practiced disdain. It's something about this city, she realized. The need to seek, the need to protect, all in one bizarre capsule…

Capsule…

"Kit," she said, and the words were thick like loam. "I think…somebody put something…."

"I know, baby, I know," he said, and the words sounded distant and hollow, like he was using a paper towel tube as a megaphone. "I'm taking you home."

Chapter 16

Love Her Madly

Martika stood in front of the beige stucco building, her stomach dancing, whether from the joys of pregnant nausea or the stress of being back at her parents' house for the first time in... God, was it twelve years already?

Her stomach heaved again. Okay, it was both pregnancy *and* stress, but stress was definitely at the forefront.

The house hadn't changed all that much—there'd been a new paint job, but her mother's rosebushes still stood sentinel at the edge of the sod-green lawn. She wondered inanely if they'd bought a new car, or if her father still drove the off-white Volvo station wagon in which she'd lost her virginity. Not that her dad knew—at least, she hoped not.

God, she was nervous.

She hadn't been here since she'd left home. She'd gone to community college by herself and gotten a job, had earned her own money and made her own way, and she didn't need their shit anymore. She'd changed her name, first for friends, then legally. She'd deliberately left this place, and all the ugliness she had connected with it. Now she was back...back, and pregnant.

Why? Did she want to throw it in their faces? What was she doing?

She walked up the concrete pathway that led to the front door, and stared, and pushed the doorbell, hearing the muted chimes inside. Her stomach muscles were clenched like a fist—she was suddenly glad she hadn't eaten breakfast. Her heart was beating in fight-or-flight response, just like she'd seen in caged animals on the Discovery Channel. To be honest, flight seemed like the wiser fucking idea at this....

The door swung open. The woman in front of her seemed impossibly short at five-two or so. Had her mother always been this short?

Her mother started to greet her, something innocuous that held a tinge of "What-do-you-want-from-me?", but the words never came. She studied Martika's face. "Eleanor? Is that you?"

Martika winced. "Hi, Mom."

Her mother went pale and silent.

Martika felt tired. This was a stupid idea. She'd been right the first time. She shouldn't have come back to this house. What was she expecting? What did she think was going to happen?

She made as if to turn, sighing a little, and her mother's voice stopped her. "My, you're tall."

It was the perfect statement. Martika gestured to the heels she was wearing. "Steve Madden," she said, turning her ankle and watching the light reflect off the rhinestones on the straps. "They take a little getting used to, but…"

She let the sentence peter off as she realized her mother couldn't make sense of any of that sentence. Or, for that matter, her daughter. She just continued to stare. Then she said, "Well. They're lovely. Why don't you come inside, sit down for a while?" The question was extremely tentative…like someone trying to persuade a gunman to turn himself in, but not wanting to be pushy about it.

Martika followed her in anyway, her heels clicking on the Spanish tile. That was new. When she'd lived there, it was carpeting. She glanced around. The house had been redecorated in a Southwestern style. It was…. Well, boring, to be honest. But it was different. Right now, that was something she appreciated.

She stopped as they passed the living room.

There were pictures, she remembered that much, but she saw pictures of herself, back when she was a teenager, back before she'd run away. She had no pictures of them, no pictures of the house in her apartment. Didn't even think she really owned any.

Her with braces. Her, dressed for the Little Miss Pasadena contest, looking scared. Her in a spelling bee.

One last photo. Her, with her parents and brother. Dressed all in black with enough kohl around her eyes to rival Robert Smith of the Cure. Sulking at the camera, at the people she was forced to pose with. She'd left shortly after that she recalled.

Her mother saw the photo, as well, and looked at Martika with a sense of apprehension, but then ushered her into the dining nook off the kitchen, to a new glass-topped table that hadn't been there before she'd left.

"Can I get you anything?"

Martika thought about it. "Tea?"

Her mother's eyes widened at that. Her mother loved tea. Martika had hated it for that very reason. As she'd hated so many things. This was ridiculous, she thought, as her mother showed her an assortment of herbal teas and black teas. She chose Raspberry Zinger, and wondered if it would be giving too much away to ask for dry crackers. She'd see how she fared with the tea.

Her mother set the kettle boiling, and they stared at each other, waiting.

"So. How have you been?" Her mother's voice was polite, as if she'd just come upon a neighbor she hadn't seen in years.

"I've been…" She stopped. "You know I'm not okay, Mom."

Her mother's eyes showed concern. It was hard not

to instinctively hate her for it—and Martika realized that was why she was here, suddenly. "You wouldn't be here if you were okay, Eleanor."

"Martika. I go by Martika now." Just as reflexively, she felt a stab of pleasure at the hurt in her mother's eyes. *No, I don't answer to the name you gave me.* Still, the hurt vanished and only the helpful concern remained. That much had not changed, no matter what cosmetic changes had occurred to the house.

"Unusual name." The kettle whistled, and her mother turned from her, pouring the two cups of tea. "Martika. So why are you here...Martika?"

Martika took a sip of the tea, pausing, so she wouldn't have to answer right away. How to plunge into it? "It's been...what, ten years?"

Her mother's face turned unexpectedly shrewd. "Twelve. To be precise."

"Twelve years."

"And now you're back. It's a pity you didn't come later, your father would have loved...loved to have seen you." Her mother's voice cracked, and she pressed at her lips, as if to stop a cry. When she got it together, she didn't look at Martika, just looked at her cup. "Maybe you could stay for supper. If you wanted." Again, that pleading-not-pushing.

Martika sighed. "Mom, I wanted to talk to you about why I ran away."

Her mother's eyes shot to her now, flashing. "I worried. Do you know how long I worried? Even after you called me and said you wanted nothing more to do with me, with us. I never understood that, Martika. What did I do to make you hate me like that?''

Martika sighed again. God, this sucked. ''It wasn't…I just couldn't live here anymore, Mom. I couldn't deal with the expectations of being here.''

''I never pressured you!'' Her mother's voice raised a little bit. It wasn't a full-blown yell, but definitely something more than her normal cultured tone. ''Not when I knew you were having sex way too young with those awful young men—oh, yes, I knew,'' she said, when Martika's jaw dropped at her words. ''Not when you were smoking in the house, cigarettes and God knows what else. Not ever! I just loved you, like the little girl I'd always…''

''*I was never the little girl you always thought I was!*'' Martika roared. ''Dammit, *that's* why I left. You always had all these good ideas of things for me to do, and you made such a show of *accepting me,* accepting all my lousy, slutty ways. You didn't ever tell me to stop doing something, you never hated me as much as I…hated…you…'' She stopped.

That sounded so fucking Oprah. *Girls who hate mothers who love them too much.* Jesus, that was so unforgivably trite. Taylor would be laughing at her.

Her mother was biting her lip now, hard. ''*Why* did you hate me?'' she repeated.

''I don't know. It seems stupid, now. I just—you never understood me. You never loved me. You either loved this girl in your head, or you made a big show of loving this evil little changeling that replaced the perfect girl you thought you had. You either loved

Eleanor or were being some good forgiving type for hating Martika, get it?''

Her mother pursed her lips tightly, then spoke. ''What brought all this on? What, it's taken you twelve years to come to this conclusion? To see that I was some big hypocrite? And *that's* what's brought you here...''

''I'm pregnant.''

Her mother stared at her. Then she started to laugh, a mirthless, low laugh. ''I see,'' she said. ''Strangely, I think I was expecting this conversation about eleven years ago or so. I was so angry with you—so convinced that you were going to screw up your life, become an addict or homeless or pregnant.'' She shot Martika a sly glance. ''I can't help but notice—no wedding ring?''

''I've got a fairly good idea who the father is,'' Martika said brazenly, ''and I don't really give a shit.''

Her mother sighed. ''I definitely expected this conversation earlier. Are you planning on—'' as if she couldn't even really bring herself to say it ''—keeping the baby?''

Why do people keep assuming I won't?

Martika gritted her teeth. ''Yes. As a matter of fact, I am.'' And was pleased to see the look of surprise on her mother's face. ''At least, I think I am.''

''Well, you can't be coming here for my blessing—that much is obvious. What is it? Do you need a place to stay? Frankly, I don't know that you'd like living here.'' But something of that appealed to her mother, she could tell. "You could stay in the guest house, over the garage, but don't expect me to watch the baby while you go gallivanting off with God knows who…"

"Mom," she said, interrupting her plans and tirades, "I've just got one question."

Her mother looked at her expectantly.

Martika pushed the cup of cold tea around the tabletop for a second.

"Mom…what if it hates me?"

Her mother blinked.

"I don't think I could do it," Martika said, despising the quaver in her voice. "Don't think I could deal with that."

Not if she hates me like I hated you.

Her mother got up and sat next to her. "You're right, in a way," she said, and to Martika's surprise, she took her hand. "I wanted to be perfect. I wanted you to be the perfect daughter. And when you weren't, I tried to make up for it—tried to show that by loving you I was still doing the right thing, even if you weren't. It was all about me. With your kids, it can't be all about you." She sighed. "And for that, I'm sorry. I'm more sorry than you'll ever realize. Took me years to figure it out."

Martika saw the sincerity in her eyes, along with the stubborn tilt of her chin that she, herself, possessed. She knew how hard the words were.

Reluctantly, she leaned in. Her mother hugged her at the halfway point. Suddenly, things seemed better, if only for a moment.

* * *

Sarah woke up slowly, hearing a deep, rough, growling sort of panting. She felt warm…too warm. And uncomfortable. She was lying on something hard and lumpy.

She turned, and a pair of brown eyes surveyed her with an implacable calm.

"Woof."

Sarah yelped, and promptly fell off the couch and onto the floor, narrowly avoiding hitting her head on the nearby coffee table. She glanced around, wildly.

I don't know this room! Where the hell am I?

The room was painted Navajo white, much like her own walls—except you could barely *see* these walls. There were movie posters everywhere. Humphrey Bogart scowled at her from a poster over the couch, advertising the *Maltese Falcon.* Dustin Hoffman looked nervously out of a poster of *The Graduate,* and Kim Bassinger's blond hair fell in a graceful wave as she surveyed the room from *L.A. Confidental.* There was a huge black wooden entertainment unit with a big screen TV and a bookcase full of DVDs and videotapes.

She glanced back at the couch. This was a real dog, not a movie poster. Sarah wasn't a dog person, so she didn't know what breed it was, but it had gently curling hair and spots and a big, pink, lolling tongue. It also looked like it owned the couch and was confident enough in that knowledge not to make an issue of it. It stared at her placidly.

"Um." Sarah rubbed at her butt, sore from where she fell. "Well. This is different."

"How are we feeling?"

She spun, her back protesting the sudden movement. Kit was leaning against the door frame of what she guessed was the teeny kitchen in this…

She was in Kit's apartment.

She suddenly felt very, very aware of the fact that she was wearing only underwear and a T-shirt. She supposed she ought to be thankful for that much coverage.

"What are…dumb question. What am *I* doing here?"

"Sleeping it off. I see Sophie asserted herself." He gestured at the dog.

"Sophie?"

The dog lifted her ears, then chuffed softly and settled more deeply into the quilt that Sarah herself had been buried under. "My dog. She usually sleeps in with me, but she isn't used to company, so I guess she decided to let you know who the real woman of the house is."

She glanced around. It was a starkly male sort of place…

"Wait a second. Why don't I remember coming here?"

"Somebody slipped you X last night at the club." At this, Kit frowned, unfolding himself from his relaxed slump against the door frame. He was wearing a tank top. She was surprised at the cut of his muscles.

Okay, now is not the time to be noticing Kit's body. She yanked her T-shirt over her knees, covering all but her feet.

"What were you doing out by yourself, anyway?" His frown was deep, and though his voice was its customary laid-back semidrawl, his gray-green eyes snapped with energy, surprising her again. "Taylor and Tika should've known better."

"I don't need a keeper."

He glanced at her, and she felt it run over her body very pointedly. She also felt the heat of her blush. He quirked an eyebrow, nodding at the couch. "Obviously."

Sarah padded after him, the hardwood floor feeling cold under her bare feet. "What are you saying? That I tried to get high? That I made the mistake of going off by myself and clubbing without a chaperone? Do you think I wanted this to happen?" She crossed her arms in front of her chest. "Well, excuse me, Mr. Clint-Eastwood-Substitute, I didn't realize a little woman like myself couldn't venture out in the big world without someone's protection! I suppose I brought this on myself! How very antifeminist of me!"

The look he shot her might as well have had a subtitle. *Grow up*. He pulled out a box of tea. "Can I get you a mug?"

She felt infuriated, frustrated that he wouldn't rise to the bait—that he didn't really seem to care at all if she were being an insecure, childish twit. Which she was, and she knew it. But she didn't want to know it.

"You really shouldn't go clubbing by yourself."

She sighed. "I was waiting for that. I know that, I guess." But she didn't.

"Why did you do it, anyway?"

"Rebellion thing?" She laughed, and sat at the ugly Formica table in his kitchen. He put a heavy white mug in front of her. The tea smelled really good...tasted good, she noted as she took a sip. "I don't know. Martika was doing some drama thing—she wouldn't tell me what was wrong, she just wanted me to worm it out of her. And I've just gotten fired from my personal assistant gig. And...I don't know. Things just sucked. I really, really wanted things to work out, but..."

"Sarah, what are you so afraid of?"

She blinked at him. "What do you mean?"

"When I first met you, I thought you were the most afraid person I'd ever seen in my life. Pretty, but desperately scared."

The "pretty" registered briefly, but the rest of the sentence drowned it out quickly. "Scared of what?"

"I don't know. It's like you're constantly trying to get it right, have an answer, have a plan."

"Well, I like paying my rent, for one thing," she said. "Homeless doesn't seem like an especially fun way to live."

He sighed. "Yeah, but you're going to make rent. You might not like what you're doing, but you won't starve and you won't live on the street."

She frowned. "I haven't been all that worried about anything for the past few months. Ever since Benjamin and I really broke up."

He sat down next to her, with his own mug. His eyes were misty—dreamy, she noticed. He seemed much less a skater-skank, she thought, then almost blushed at the uncharitable turn of her thoughts. So he wasn't her dream man. He wasn't as smoothly charming as Benjamin, as sensual as Jeremy, or as devastatingly handsome as Raoul.

Those might not be bad things.

"You've been trying to become Martika, for God's sake. You've done everything but dye your hair red."

"I have not!"

"Let's not bullshit here. You go out to clubs because she does...you were trying to prove that you could take care of yourself just like she can."

"I can!" Sarah said, then bit her lip. There it was again—teenage girl. Where the hell did that keep coming from?

"Again, obviously." He shook his head. "Martika and I might not see eye to eye on most points, but I'll give her this—the woman's got killer survival instincts. You seem to be wearing a sign that says Rape Or Murder Me Please."

Sarah grimaced at him. "I see. So I'm an idiot."

"I'm not saying that." To her surprise, he took her hand. His hand felt firm and warm. "I'm saying you're trying too hard. You want to show that you're this tough chick that just parties and doesn't care about anything else, and that's not you."

She yanked her hand away, disconcerted, and got up. "I see. And your time behind a counter at the Coffee Shop has made you a pop psychologist now, I see?"

"Lashing out at me isn't going to help you, Sarah."

"Stop analyzing me!"

"Dammit, Sarah!" He stood up too, surprising her with his flash of anger. "I had to drag you over here last night—the way you were acting, I didn't want to leave you alone and I couldn't get a hold of Martika."

Sarah stalked to the living room, and swept down on the couch by Sophie the Dog. The dog looked at her, barely budging an inch. Sarah rubbed at her temples. She was upset. She was ashamed. She didn't want to be here.

"I'm sorry I inconvenienced you," Sarah said stiffly. She looked around the room. Her club clothes—a little sundress, her big boots—were piled on the floor by the door. She started to walk toward them.

He put a gentle hand on her shoulder. She didn't want to be so ill-mannered as to shrug him off again. Going with his insistent tug, she turned to face him.

"Dammit, you're stubborn."

She reluctantly looked up into his eyes.

"I wasn't inconvenienced. I was *worried.*"

"I don't want you to be worried," Sarah protested.

He stroked her cheek with his fingertips. Her body was starting to react. Jesus, had it been that long? Was she getting that depraved…

"Then don't make me worried. Why don't you stop trying to figure out what your life needs, and just go with it for a while?" He chucked her under her chin, gently. "Then I'll stop worrying."

"That's so easy for you to say." Any attraction Sarah might have been succumbing to disappeared in a flash of anger. "I mean, what do you do? You pay for rent on an apartment with your dog. You've got no relationships, no career path. You live day to day. *I want more than that.*" Her voice was all but shaking with it. "How can you live like that...with no focus?"

He was very quiet—it was a physical sort of quiet, as if all the molecules that made him up suddenly went still for a second. "Hmm. So that's how you see me." He took a little sighing breath. "Well, here's a question—what sort of focus are you looking for, and why do you need to know what you're going to do?"

"Why do I need..." She was flabbergasted. "Well, let's see. How about because I can't imagine just punching in and punching out of a job I hate, and knowing that I'll be doing it until I retire, if I can even afford to retire. Or maybe because I don't want to be alone when I'm old—or now, for that matter. I'm sure that seems shallow to you, but when I was with Benjamin, no matter how shitty he was to me, or how selfish, or how demanding, at least I knew what I was supposed to do. To be honest, all the jobs I've had have been pretty much the same. I haven't cared about any of them. Then I met Martika, and it made sense. The only focus I had was having fun, living for the moment. But even that didn't work for me. So here I am—right back where I started. *And I hate it!*" To her surprise, she started crying, fat drops that crawled down her cheeks. She tried hard to prevent them. When she got more of a grip, she took a breath and said with a quavering voice, "Shit. Sometimes I feel like if somebody would just tell me what the fuck I'm supposed to do with my life, even if it sucked, I'd feel better because at least then I'd *know*."

She avoided looking at his face. She didn't know what she'd see there. Pity? Possibly. He was very compassionate. More likely it'd be his usual disdain. Obviously, if any of these things were important to him, he wouldn't be living like this, now, would he?

She turned, heading for her dress...and there it was again, the gentle, relentless grip. She finally looked at him.

"Everybody feels like that."

"Sorry?"

His look was one of patient blankness. "*Everybody* feels that way. Haven't you noticed?"

She blinked at him.

"Martika is doing her club thing because it gives her a sense of purpose—sort of antipurpose, if you want. Your friend Judith tries to please everybody in sight—that's her sense of purpose. Everybody thinks they've got the answer. If you don't have any sense of purpose, if there's no reason for you to get up in the morning, sooner or later you'll find a way to stop getting up in the morning."

She snuffled, to her embarrassment. "So...what's your reason for waking up?"

He smiled, and it made his lean face attractive. "Writing."

"Writing?" she asked blankly.

He nodded. "I was like you, once. I was going to graduate school—going for my doctorate in psychology, fiddled around with writing just for fun, on the side. Nobody I knew made it all that successfully as a writer, anyway. But I found myself fiddling with the stories more and more, and concentrating on the psychology less and less. I got my master's and then I quit."

"You've got a master's in psychology?"

"Does it matter?" He shrugged, and walked over to the couch, obviously the embarrassed one now. "I moved to L.A. because I was doing a research study, and it just amazed and appalled me. I'm from San Diego—life is different down there. Anyway, it's not important." He sighed. "I got a shitty little apartment—not this one. I was sharing with three other guys. It was ridiculous, but it was cheap. And I started to write. Didn't quite pay the bills—I got the Coffee Shop job to make ends meet. And I swear to God, I've never been happier in my life."

"And that's it?" She was envious...bitterly so. He sounded so happy—so *directed*. "You found what you wanted to do in life?"

"I think part of me always knew what I wanted to do in life. I was going full bore on a path that was wrong for me, and somehow, everything nudged me back to writing."

He started scratching Sophie behind the ears. Sarah sat on the arm of the couch beside him—like he was a religious entity. Somebody from Gen X who had figured it out.

"Nothing's nudging me."

"Maybe it's because you haven't been listening,"

he suggested gently. "Maybe you need to stop looking, and let it find you."

She frowned at him. "You sound awfully New Age."

He laughed. "Sorry. It's a habit."

She tucked her feet into the T-shirt again—this would be why Kit often looked baggy. The thing was voluminous. "So. Do you think you'll ever be published?"

He laughed again. "Actually, I am."

"You are?" She felt like hugging him, an emotion that momentarily covered the envy—even though part of it was magnified. "Anything I would have read?"

"Probably not." He gestured to a corner of the room. There was a desk with papers scattered across it, a corkboard with clippings and notes pinned to it in an artistic scrawl. Nearby there was a bookshelf. "The bottom row there is what I've written. Only three so far, but..."

She hopped up, went over and scanned the titles. Two looked like science fiction/fantasy novels. The third was a hardback—*Shaman in a Cadillac*.

"That hardback is my latest." He sounded proud and embarrassed at the same time. "It's about when I first came to L.A., and when I was studying."

"Can I read it?"

He got up, plucking it off the shelf. "It's yours."

"Really?"

"Really."

"So...you must've made some pretty good money on it. Do you have to still work at the coffeeshop?"

She had her suspicions, but she wanted him to confirm it.

"We'll see when the next royalty check comes in. But I'm doing pretty okay. Besides, I only work part-time, I like the owner...and it keeps me grounded."

"That's like winning the lottery and still working," she said.

He put his hands in his pockets. "Well, I don't think I'll do it forever, but the routine helps, strangely enough."

Sarah sighed. "I wish I had something like that. Something I loved to do." She bit her lip. "I think the thing I'm afraid of is there isn't anything I love to do. Maybe take care of my boyfriend. That's a stupid, codependent thing to be good at, isn't it?"

He shrugged. Obviously, he wasn't saying anything more.

She looked at the book in her hands...heavy, important. Obviously, a labor of love. "I mean, what if I wait for something to find me, and it never comes?"

"Then, hopefully," he said gently, "you won't have wasted all your time stressing about it, right?"

She huffed. "Thanks for nothi..."

He kissed her.

She wasn't...well, she supposed at some level, she *was* expecting it. But she hadn't expected it to be like this.

It was just his lips first, gentle, almost tentative. She didn't move. In fact, she barely breathed. But after a few minutes, he leaned forward, putting one hand up gently, cupping the side of her face.

Oh, my God.

She didn't know how it got this way. Maybe in all her lame attempts at sexual adventures, she'd forgotten how purely stimulating—and comforting—a kiss could be. But he kissed her like they did in the movies, leaning her against the nearest wall as he gave her his complete and utter attention. She found herself clutching at his back, and he was threading his fist in the hair at her nape and stroking at the underside of one of her breasts and *oh my God,* she couldn't believe anything could feel like this, hadn't felt this way in such a long time.

It's not love, she thought absently.

She started tugging at his clothes, yanking at his shirt but growling impatiently when he pulled away so she could tug it over his head. His eyes were anything but lazy now. He was tugging her somewhere— she realized it was his bedroom. She had no idea what it looked like, barely registered the bed coming up to meet her when she tripped and brought him down on the mattress with her. He laughed, breathless, and so did she. Then he tugged *her* shirt off, and next thing she knew they were both naked, kissing, holding each other like life preservers. And laughing when they came up for air.

He paid more attention to her than any man had, ever, in her life. He kissed her *stomach,* for pity's sake. He lavished attention on her earlobes. She felt like the drugs from last night hadn't completely worn off—everything was magnified, but in a good way this time. She did some nibbling and kissing of her own.

When he finally put a condom on, she was still giggling, still nuzzling at him. When he got on top of her, he stopped, smiling down at her, his expression saying: *Well, shit. Isn't this something?*

She smiled back, then closed her eyes when he entered her, slow, just the way she liked it. *Isn't that something,* she thought, silently agreeing with his unspoken question. She was having sex, and enjoying it. It was something indeed.

It was late afternoon by the time she stirred from his bed. They'd been at it for the better part of four hours—not just having sex all the time. Sometimes they talked, little snippets of nothing. He'd napped for a little bit, and she'd held him as he breathed, feeling closer to him than she had to pretty much anybody in a long time.

This feels right, she thought. *This feels* totally *right.*

She felt that way now—like she'd stayed at his place forever. She looked around. More movie posters. *The Princess Bride. Sunset Boulevard. The Doors.* A window looked out to the street beyond.

She curled into his pillows a little more. Maybe they'd go out for dinner, she thought. She didn't know if he was working at the coffeeshop or what, but she felt sure she'd see more of him now. That was—she smiled. Incredible wasn't the word for it. It was somewhere between phenomenal and really, really comfy.

Which was why she wasn't expecting him to come out of the bathroom, baseball cap perched backward on his head, T-shirt and torn jeans already on. He'd even slipped on a pair of shoes.

"I've got to go," he said, without preamble.

She blinked, and like every other insecure movie female, she tugged the sheet up, as if this would somehow preserve her dignity. "Okay," she said, not wanting to say *"right now?"* and complete the stereotype.

He nodded, and grabbed a dog leash off of a low table. Then he started out the door.

"Kit!" she yelped, unable to stop herself.

He stopped, turned, leash in hand. "Mmm?"

She narrowed her eyes. "Am I...will I see you later?" *Dammit.* She still dipped into stereotype—and a weak one, at that.

He shrugged. "I guess. I think Taylor said something about later."

She stared at him, waiting for him to clarify. He didn't.

She stood up, not caring if he saw her naked. "Wait a second. I'll go grab my clothes and I'll be out of here in a minute."

He frowned. Finally, a little stronger emotion. "You don't have to."

"Actually, yes I do," she said. "Unless you're giving me a reason to stay here?"

He was now staring at her, bewildered. "Well...what did you have in mind?" He glanced at his wall, and smirked. "Dexter's Laboratory is on at four."

She huffed impatiently, pulling on clothes haphazardly, not caring that her hair probably stuck out in all sorts of improbable angles. ''Gee. Let me hold my breath.''

He stood in front of her, nudged her chin up. ''What do you think is going on here, Sarah?''

It would have been better, Sarah thought, if he weren't smiling. No. If he weren't *smirking*.

''Did you enjoy yourself?'' he asked. ''I mean, that's what all this was about, wasn't it?''

Like a slap. Like a fucking *slap*.

She wasn't doing this again. She contuinued to put her clothes back on with an almost zenlike calm. Then she put on her shoes, growled at his dog and looked at him.

''I did enjoy myself,'' she said, her voice low. ''Thanks. I'll call you if I need to *enjoy* myself again.''

He sighed, and stepped in front of her. ''Sarah, I think you're making a mistake.''

''Do you love me?'' she said, point-blank.

If there were ever a question to make a man blanch, it was that one. He blinked at her. ''Ah…I hadn't really thought about it,'' he said slowly.

''Then I guess I already made one.'' With that, she walked past him.

''I accept you, Sarah,'' he called down the hallway at her. ''Isn't that good enough for now?''

''I don't want good enough *for now*,'' she called back, yanking the strap of her purse onto her shoulder. ''And I don't want *you!*''

Chapter 17

Unhappy Girl (Dance Remix)

"Cigarette?" Taylor said, offering Martika one as she got into the car.

She waved it away with a shake of her head, then looked out the window, rolling it down and letting the fresh air hit her in the face.

She wasn't sure how he was going to take it. He'd been her best friend since—well, since forever. He knew her better than anybody, and she knew him better than anybody, and she had no fucking clue how he was going to react to this news.

"You okay, princess?" Taylor said. "You're going

to love Arthur. He's so yum, it's ridiculous. And he'll *love* you.''

''You sure?'' Martika said weakly, her conversation with her mother still fresh in her mind. She hadn't decided if she was going to move back yet—that was *completely* up in the air, and she wasn't going to ambush Taylor with those sordid details. Not yet, anyway.

''Of course he'll love you,'' Taylor said, scoffing. ''He'd *better* love you. If he doesn't, he's hitting the road.''

She turned to him, genuinely surprised. ''Really? You mean that?''

He turned to her, smiling indulgently. ''Sweetie, you know I do. I mean, an incredible fuck is an incredible fuck—but when you come right down to it, who do you want to grow old with? Your best friend, or some fuck?''

She beamed. ''This is why I love you.''

''Ha.'' He rolled his eyes, then winked at her. ''I thought it was because…''

''I'm keeping the baby.''

He stopped. ''I'm sorry?''

She took a deep breath. ''I'm keeping the baby. I decided to keep the baby.''

There was a pause, and she felt like sinking into the seats, covering her face. Not that she thought it was a bad decision, or the wrong decision. Frankly, there wasn't any other decision for her.

''I see.'' He seemed at a loss for words—a really un-Taylor-like state of affairs.

She waited for a minute longer, then said, "You think it's a really stupid idea, don't you?"

He didn't respond. He just kept driving.

She felt herself get angry—knew it was a defense mechanism, but hey, if she didn't need defense on this subject, she'd hate to see what she *did* need the god-damn mechanism for. "I think I'll be a stellar mother."

"Is that why you're doing this?"

Martika looked at him, wanting to see if he were getting pissy and self-righteous again. But he wasn't. His face was as impassive as that man's expression-filled face could get. She growled.

"I've got a ton of good reasons for doing this." She took a deep breath. "I'm sure it seems like a stupid idea, *to you* I mean, but it...I mean...I've got a ton of good reasons for this. A *ton*."

"Name one, Tika," he said.

"Okay," she said, sharply, then paused.

Because I've always wanted to be a mother. No, too whiny.

Because I couldn't stand the idea of losing it. Because I've finally got a chance to love somebody without worrying about what they think of me. Because I've finally found someone who might actually love me. Because the rest of my life didn't make sense until this happened.

She took a deep breath.

"Because it's not about me," she said, softly. "This time, it's all about her."

He took that quietly, then to her surprise, he pulled the car over, turning off the engine.

When he looked at her he smiled. "This sort of news needs proper hugs," he said, and to her shock, he clambered over the stick shift and hugged her thoroughly.

"You're going to be her godfather, you know," she said, against his shoulder.

"I'd like to see you try to nominate somebody else."

Two days later, Sarah sat at a couch at the Barnes and Noble in the West Side Pavilion, sunk in the green-and-white upholstery, wishing she could disappear from the earth. Martika had been AWOL, probably sleeping at Taylor's or prepping her next live-in lover—she felt sure that Martika's foray into platonic same-sex boarding was a short-lived experiment at best. She'd called Temps Fugit, but couldn't bring herself to work this week…too many memories, especially when they tried to place her back at Jeremy's office. And she hadn't talked with Kit…

No. She wasn't even going to think about that little bit of stupidity. She sipped disconsolately at her Starbucks Mocha.

Back to the beginning. No roommate, no way to pay the bills, no job worth mentioning, very few friends, no fucking direction whatsoever.

How pathetic could one girl get in L.A., right? She glanced at the books she'd picked up. She didn't want any of them, ought to be watching her money anyway.

She stared out the windows and at the other customers instead.

No bloody good. She thought she'd had the answer—thought that she'd finally figured out what she was going to do. Sure, it wasn't a brilliant plan, but it didn't seem to make any difference. Now, the future was hitting her smack in the face.

What are you going to do?

She wished she hadn't had that fight with Tika. She wished she hadn't been fired. She wished…

"Sarah?"

She looked up.

She *really* wished this wasn't Benjamin speaking to her.

Benjamin looked his usual self. His clothes had not improved tremendously, she noticed with catty satisfaction as she straightened her pink Fred Segal T-shirt. "Benjamin. I didn't see you."

"I noticed. You looked…" He paused and took a deep breath. "What's wrong, sunshine?"

Oh, don't you dare *fucking go there.* She smiled, a perfect, Martika inspired disdain-and-disinterest special. "I'm fine. I've just been so busy lately."

"How's it going with the roommate?"

"Couldn't be better."

"And the job? Still with that Peerson guy?"

"Oh, I'm still surveying my options." It came out breezy. Perfectly casual.

"Still checking out your options on the relationship front, or are you still with that sharp guy from the club?"

"Jeremy's just one of many." She shrugged, trying to make it believable. "I don't like to be tied down."

He sat down on the couch next to her. His voice lowered. "Then why do you look like your life has turned to shit?"

Her heart rate shot up. "What do you mean?"

"You never were any good at lying to me, Sarah. It was one of the things I appreciated about you. So don't lie now." He sounded reproving. "I'm worried…"

"Worried about what, Benjamin? Worried that I might be having a good time without being in your august presence? Worried that I might be boning some guy?"

"Worried that you're obviously self-destructing."

As he wasn't far from the truth, she bit her lip. When she felt she was more in control of herself, she shrugged. "As you can see…I'm fine."

"I can see that you're upset." He was using that salesman voice. She was too tired to put up any defenses. "I've missed you, Sarah."

"Oh, eat me."

He blinked, then laughed. "God, I like what L.A.'s done for you. You used to be such a retiring, spineless little thing, but now…now you can stand up to me." He smiled a little more suggestively. "I really like that, Sarah."

"I don't care." She tried to turn her back on him, but he gently nudged at her arm.

"I'm sorry. That came out wrong. What I'm trying to say is, I really do miss you. We were a great team."

She looked at him. Puppies didn't have eyes that sadly coaxing.

"Remember…when I was in business school, and you were still at Sac State, when you'd type up my papers? Huh?"

She nodded. She hadn't minded—it was painful to see how slow he typed, she told herself.

"Or the way you used to stay at my house, and you'd cook for me because you knew I had a final? You'd make sure I had food stocked, you helped me with laundry…"

"Are you just trying to rub it in about what a schmuck I was, Benjamin?"

"You weren't! You were helping me out. And now, I'd like to help you out."

"Oh, really." She grimaced at him. "Well, you suck at typing, and unless you've been taking some cordon bleu class I'm not aware of, I'll pass on your cooking, too."

"Sarah, I want you back."

She stood up. "Okay. We're done here." Ignoring startled looks and frowns of people trying to concentrate on their reading, she stalked out of the store to the patio level outside, where café tables were placed. Before she could get to the escalator, he stopped her.

"Please hear me out."

"Why? Jessica not listening to you enough?"

"I broke up with Jessica," he said with a voice that wasn't the wheedling salesman but the irritated boyfriend. Strangely, she trusted this voice more. "She was so intense, she just… It's hard to say. Ba-

sically, she wasn't you." He sighed. "She'd just sit there with these big cow eyes and stare at me. You've got more fire than that, Sarah. You always had a plan. I need that now, more than ever."

"Why?"

"I'm going to take a new job. Back North," he said in a fervent tone. "Neither of us were cut out to live in L.A., Sarah. This place is a toilet."

She shrugged. "I'm used to it."

"You can't tell me you wouldn't rather be back in a community. What about all those things we talked about? Kids, a nice place to live? Can you honestly tell me you can see doing all that here?"

She didn't answer.

"And what about your plans, Sarah?" His voice was pitched lower now, as he eased her over toward a café table, away from pedestrian traffic. "Is this honestly how you saw your life turning out? No relationship, no job...now trouble with your housing? Is this what you'd rather stay here for?"

She bit her lip. Then she said, in as calm a voice as she could manage, "So what are you offering me here, Benjamin? Huh? A chance to live *near* you, somewhere in the sticks in Northern Cal? A chance to wait while you get your life in order, without a job, without..."

"No. This is about me making your life easier. You helped me, remember?" His smile was as wide as the sun. "You wouldn't have to get a job. You wouldn't have to do anything. You'd live with me." He took a deep breath. "Marry me, Sarah."

"What?"

"Marry me." He held her hands. She was too stunned to pull them away. "I know this isn't the most romantic thing in the world, but I'm packed up, I'm leaving soon. I was really upset when Jessica and I…well, not that she was gone, but that I'd made such a bad mistake. I was going to Northern Cal to start over. I wanted to call you. Then when I saw you…it's like a sign, corny as that is."

"You want me to marry you?" she repeated. "As in, soon?"

"As soon as possible. I don't make the same mistake twice."

It was so sudden. Of course, it wasn't *that* sudden—they'd been engaged for years, before their little…

Wait a minute. Am I seriously considering this?

"Why should I, Benjamin?" She pulled her hands away, crossing her arms, surveying him like a judge. "Give me one good reason."

He paused, weighing his answer carefully. Then he gave her a calculated, challenging grin.

"Sarah, I love you and want to take care of you. You can start over. What have you got to lose?"

She thought about it.

No roommate, no job, no focus, no hope, and now…a guy who finally says he loves me and wants to help me.

"It's not a good one," she said finally, letting him pull her into his arms, her mind was still churning. "But it's a reason."

* * *

When the phone rang, Judith jumped six inches, her heart beating like a war drum. She answered it sharply. "Hello?"

"Judith, it's Sarah."

"Sarah." Of all the times to call. Judith opened the oven, poked at the roast viciously. "What is it?"

"You sound busy," Sarah said. "Am I calling at a bad time?"

I'm about to disclose the details of a cyberaffair to my husband. Yes, Judith supposed this was inconvenient.

"I'm making dinner," Judith said instead. "What...are you all right?"

"I'm...well, I guess I'm fine," Sarah said. Her voice sounded weird. "I just wanted to, er, invite you to something."

She wasn't in the mood for being social. "I...this isn't a great time...listen, can I call you next week? Maybe we can do lunch, talk some things over." Judith felt sure she'd need to by then. *If I can just survive this dinner!*

"Oh. Well, actually, this sort of couldn't wait."

Judith glanced up at the ceiling, as if God could somehow grant her more patience. "Oh?"

"You see, I'm getting married Friday, in Las Vegas. I was wondering if you'd be my maid of honor."

"You're getting married?" To Judith, the words were completely alien. "To who?"

"To Benjamin, actually."

Judith gaped. "*What? Why?*"

Sarah paused on the other end of the line. "Because

he loves me. Because he…I don't know. He makes sense.''

Judith clutched the phone. ''When did all this happen?''

''Well, he asked me about a week ago, and we decided, since we'd been engaged for five years, it was hardly like we were rushing things…I just wanted it out of the way.''

''Out of the way?'' Judith felt a deep, leaden feeling in her chest. ''How romantic.''

''This isn't about romance, Judith,'' Sarah said. ''This just…I don't know. It's what I wanted. He loves me, and he cares about me, and he'll take care of me.''

''And that's what you want?'' Judith couldn't keep the tone of revulsion out of her voice, and realized she didn't want to. She wanted to shake Sarah. If she'd been standing there, she would have. ''You want to settle for a guy who'll take care of you?''

''I said he loves me,'' Sarah said, her voice getting sharper. ''I thought you'd be pleased. You're the one who said I should give him a second chance, after all.''

''That was before…'' Judith took a deep breath. ''That was just before. Now, I know you're making a mistake.''

Sarah sighed. ''I take it you're not going to be my maid of honor, then. Would you even consider coming to the ceremony? It'd be nice for somebody I know to be there.''

Sarah sounded lonely—and this whole thing

sounded *awful.* "Sarah, you really need to think this over, very carefully. This isn't right. You need more out of your life than just security and a to-do list. You need passion. Trust me on this one!"

"Judith, I'm pretty sure I know what I'm doing," Sarah said, cutting through her impassioned argument. "It's going to be at the Excalibur, at five o'clock, on Friday. We're flying out tomorrow night. If you want to be there, that's fine. If you don't, that's fine. I'll call you when I get back."

"Sarah," Judith made one last-ditch attempt, "don't *do* this!"

"I'll talk to you later," Sarah said simply, then hung up the phone.

Judith blinked. When it rains, she thought, it pours. She wasn't ready to deal with Sarah's problems when she had more than enough of her own.

Judith stood there for a moment, then realized the beef was starting to smoke slightly. She tossed the phone on the counter and yanked the roast out of the oven, narrowly rescuing it.

"Judith?" David's voice called out to her from the dining room. "Something smells good. Dinner ready?"

"I'm almost ready," Judith replied. The side dishes were on the table. Now it was just up to her to serve the main course.

"Judith, this is great steak. Where did you get the beef? Whole Foods?"

"There's a new meat place, a real butcher, that opened up on Olympic, closer to Santa Monica," Judith said, pushing at the food on her plate mechanically.

"Well, it's fantastic. You know, I was thinking of inviting Henderson over for a barbecue. Do they do ribs? They've got to do ribs."

"David, I've had an affair."

He frowned at his plate. "Say, is corn in season? That would go well. That, a salad…no problem. Barely any trouble."

"I said, I had an affair."

He blinked at her. His knife clattered to the plate. "I'm sorry. Did you just say you had an affair?"

She nodded, then picked up a piece of her potato, delicately eating it off the fork.

He seemed to be digesting both meat and this bit of news. "So. Anyone I know?"

"No." She swallowed the potato with difficulty. "Nobody I know, either, to be grossly technical."

His brow furrowed. "What the hell are you talking about? You, what, propositioned some stranger?"

"No." She took a deep breath. "I met him on the Internet."

He blinked. Then, to her disgust, he started laughing. "This just gets better and better. How long has this been going on?"

"We've been writing to each other." She tried for another forkful, finally put it down. She couldn't keep up the facade. It was ridiculous to try.

His eyes narrowed. "Judith…have you actually met?"

"Yesterday." She took another deep, calming breath. "We finally met yesterday."

"So you've only slept with him once."

"Actually, we've never slept together."

"So where does the affair part come in?"

She stared back at him. "David, don't you understand? I've been talking to another man. I...I thought I'd grown to care about him very much."

"And now you don't?"

"Well..." She was not going to explain the incident. "Let's just say that when I met him, in person, he wasn't what I thought he was."

He grinned...there was a malicious edge to his smile. "I see. Ugly? Balding? Grossly obese?"

She simply kept silent. It was easier to let him think those things—easier to save his pride.

And why bother saving his pride? Hadn't she done that enough all these years?

Easier to save my own pride, then.

"The point is, I think we're having problems. You and me, that is. I think...I think maybe we should go to counseling."

"Why?" He sighed, deeply. "Jesus, Judith. You know I don't have time for this. Do you have any idea how close I am to making partner? How long I've worked for this?"

"Of course I do," Judith snapped. "Haven't I been there, doing everything I possibly could to help you out?"

"Oh, please. Get off the cross, somebody needs the wood." He got up, and started stalking around the dining table like he was addressing a jury. "Judith, I think what we have here is a classic case of you thinking I should be paying you more attention. Well, you knew it when I went to law school, you know it now—I haven't changed a bit. I'm not going to miraculously have time to shower you with roses every time you feel neglected. We're both adults now, remember?"

"Could you be a little more patronizing?" she asked in a conversational tone.

"Could you be a little more unreasonable?" He shook his head. "Cyberaffair. Jesus. Do you know how pathetic that sounds, Judith?" He sent her a humorless grin. "If you were someone else's wife, I'd be laughing my ass off right now."

"Well, I'm not somebody else's wife, am I."

Why had she thought this was a good idea? Because she'd been unhappy. She was, and continued to be, unhappy. It was that simple.

Did she really think he'd change into something that made her happy? Did she think telling him would wake him up? How codependent was she? In this day of Oprah and Ricki and...and Jerry Springer. She should have known better, for pity's sake.

"I really, really don't have time for this," he said. "If you really want flowers, I'll send them, but Jesus, Judith, you know better."

He retreated to his study, muttering about cyberaffairs and how funny it was. She watched his retreating back. Then, methodically, hypnotically, she started clearing the table, cleaning the remains of the meal they'd shared.

What else can I do?

She thought about it.

I could leave.

She paused in the act of wiping down the surface of the table. Leave? What would that accomplish? How embarrassed would her family be? How hurt would David be?

He was right, now wasn't really the time. She'd bide her time, wait for him to make partner. Then he'd be too busy to even notice she was gone.

She looked at the remains of the food, thought about her parting words.

And what would waiting accomplish, really?

She left the mess on the table. She left the room.

Chapter 18

Ship of Fools

Another temp assignment. Different color gray, same fabric-covered cube walls. Thank God this was an easy assignment. Sarah felt like she could do Power-point presentations in her sleep. Now that she thought of it, reflecting on her agency days, she *had*. That seemed like such a long time ago now.

Married. She was getting married. How weird was that? To Benjamin, of all people.

If Martika would show up at the apartment, she might tell her about her impending nuptials…then again, she might not. Mother Hen probably wouldn't like one of her scout troop wandering off to marry "the enemy," get a life and some direction. It was just as well they were getting married in Vegas. She certainly couldn't see her own mother attending—suddenly, it would be another drama of how-can-I-make-this-about-me. No, having Mother there was certainly not an option. Like her father would even take the time, and certainly not to attend anything so spontaneous as a Vegas wedding. He'd probably approve of Benjamin, though.

She stopped. Okay, *that* thought was vaguely disconcerting.

She stopped thinking about it, dropping clip art strategically on the slide she was building, then typing in more text. Still, it'd be nice to have *somebody* she knew there. Obviously not any of the crew—they wouldn't understand.

She thought of Kit, and quickly blocked it out. She hadn't mentioned her day with Kit to anyone, especially not Benjamin. Of course, after Jessica, it was hardly like he could say anything. Still, that was all behind them now.

She quickly moved to a different mental topic.

Judith was being judgmental, she realized. Still, Sarah really wished Judith or Martika would bend and accept this. If nothing else, a girl ought to have brides-maids…

"How's that presentation coming?"

Sarah eyed the man looking at her impatiently. "I'm almost done."

"You are?" He sneered. "You can't be. There were eighty pages there."

She shrugged and gestured at the screen. "I dressed them up a little."

He looked, and he didn't look pleased. *Oh, so you're one of those,* Sarah thought. After the dual polarity of Becky the acerbic and Richard the chaotic, nothing phased her. Certainly not some bossy little prick who didn't have enough seniority to push around anybody but a temp.

"Well, we might need more changes on Friday," he said, obviously needing to say something negative.

She shrugged. "I won't be able to be here on Friday."

His eyebrows went up. Obviously, this was a tidbit he could work with. "This is a long-term assignment! You should have…"

Sarah put up a hand and interrupted. "I told the agency this week—I am getting married on Friday. They cleared it. And I should be moving fairly soon— I'm only booked through the end of the month. They cleared that, too. If that's a problem, I'm sure you could get someone else."

His mouth worked like a fish. "Buh…buh…"

"She's quite right."

Sarah looked at the new participant. A woman, wearing a red power suit and a short, dark brown haircut that made her look like a futuristic fairy…a gamine cut that was a little spritely and sharp. Her smile matched the attitude.

"In fact, her agency called here looking for you, according to Marcy. How late did you come in this morning, Bob?"

Bob now had bigger issues to worry about, obviously. His tone went from aggressive to obsequious.

"I…was down on the fourth floor…talking to the guy in the mailroom…" He was working up the excuse, Sarah noted, and badly.

The woman ignored his blathering, walking directly to Sarah.

"I'm Erica Ross," she said, shaking Sarah's hand.

"Sarah Walker," Sarah replied. "Nice to meet you."

The woman's eyebrow went up, sharply. "You don't know who I am, do you?"

Sarah narrowed her eyes, studying the woman's face. No bells were ringing—she wondered if the woman had been on TV or something.

"I'm the director of this department."

Sarah waited. Okay, no TV appearance. She didn't know whether she should congratulate the woman or what.

The woman took her appraisal with a smile, then glanced through the slides. "This is good work," she said, clicking the mouse through the presentation at lightning speed. "This is something I'm presenting to the Strategy and Operations committee on Monday. I frankly was surprised you got it done in one day."

Sarah shrugged. "It wasn't any problem."

"I like you, Sarah," Erica said, with a nod. "I don't suppose you're looking for a permanent position?"

Sarah felt a surge of…happiness? Excitement? And

just as suddenly as she felt it, it was gone. ''I don't think so.''

The woman blinked at her. ''Why not? We offer very competitive salaries, and excellent benefits. I'm always looking for talented workers.'' She sent a quick, disapproving look to Bob. ''Some positions should be opening up soon.''

Bob went white as a sheet.

''I...my husband is probably getting a job in Northern California.'' She paused. ''And besides, I prefer the freedom I have now.'' *Now, why did I add that?*

The woman's smile, if possible, sharpened, and her eyes glinted brightly. ''I see. Well, we'd really like to keep you around. I like someone who doesn't just put on a good face for management and is interested in more than covering their own ass.'' Bob was practically having a seizure at this point. ''If your—husband was it?—winds up staying, and you want a job, you come and talk to me.''

Sarah's smile was noncommittal, but her thoughts were chaotic. That was it? She wasn't trying to please, she was just doing her job and telling off some guy who was trying to push her around...and she was offered a job?

''Thanks,'' Sarah said, bemused. ''I will.''

Judith felt her heart beating as if she'd just taken speed. She stood waiting in the lobby of Sarah's building, her suitcase sitting by her heels. Thanks to careful packing, she had two weeks worth of clothes, all of her makeup, and in her briefcase she had all of her pertinent paperwork. Even if she had to camp out on Sarah's couch, even if she had to share a bathroom with that…what had Sarah called her? A "Glamazon"? She would make this. At some point, David would realize she'd left.

Perhaps she should have left a note.

The ancient elevator doors opened, and she walked in. Why leave a message? She doubted he'd read a note, anyway. He was in the office all day today, at any rate.

She got to the door, and heard a commotion going on. It was the Glamazon, she thought, hearing the vitriolic voice go up and down like an opera singer practicing scales.

"You have got to get over here!"

Judith knocked several times—she knew she should have called. It was unlike her to be so ill prepared.

The door flew open. "Sarah?"

Judith blinked. Martika's curls flew haphazardly around her head. She looked like a voodoo priestess. She held a cell phone to her ear.

"Um, hello," Judith said.

Martika waved at her impatiently. "Have you heard from Sarah?"

"No…"

"Dammit!" Martika strode back into the living room, leaving the door wide-open. "Taylor, that does it. We're going to Las Vegas." She paused. "I know there are a thousand fucking wedding chapels, but we'll find her. I don't know! Hire a detective or something!''

Judith tentatively rolled her suitcase in. "Did I come at a bad time?''

Martika paid attention to her for the first time. "Oh, I don't know. Sarah's left me a note saying that I need to get my shit out of here before the lease expires, because she's *getting married*...to that asshole exboyfriend of hers. Sounds like a bad time to me. What do you think?''

Judith's mouth dropped open. "She isn't really going through with that, is she? I thought she was just talking!''

Now Martika gave her the full force of those Glamazon eyes. "Wait a sec. She talked to you about getting married?'' There was a frenzied squawking on the other side of the cell phone line, and Martika said, "Taylor, hold on a second. Judith seems to know what's going on. Judith. Yeah, that's the one.'' She put the phone against her chest. "What did she tell you? When did you talk to her?''

"A couple of days ago. She asked me if I wanted to go to Vegas to see her get married to Benjamin. I thought it was just a joke. I mean, I figured she'd come to her senses by now.''

"Doesn't seem like a joke now, does it?'' Martika sighed. "Did she tell you where?''

"At that medieval-castle-looking-one... Excalibur,'' Judith said, running it over in her mind for a minute.

Martika looked supremely offended. "She told you, but she wouldn't tell me?"

"She wanted…" Suddenly, it struck her as prudent *not* to mention that Sarah had asked her to be maid of honor. "She wanted me to be there. I guess she thought I'd understand more."

"So why didn't you go?"

Judith glanced down at the carpet. "I'm afraid I didn't handle it very well. The past couple of weeks have been very…unsettling for me. I barely listened to her when she told me, I'm afraid, and then I yelled at her. I don't really…I didn't express myself very well, let's say. I was busy with domestic problems of my own." She leveled a glance at Martika, now, challenging her to pry.

Martika's eyes lit on the wheeled bag…on Judith's naked left hand.

"I see." To her credit, in her outlandish outfit, she managed a look of elegant understanding that would have looked more at home on a fifty-year-old in a St. John's suit. "Well. You wouldn't happen to know *when* she's planning on getting married?"

Judith frowned. "What day is today?" God, she'd gotten far afield.

"Thursday."

"They're getting married on Friday. Night. They're flying out tonight."

Martika grabbed the phone from its resting place on her bosom. "Taylor. Did you hear that? No? She's getting married at the Excalibur tomorrow night. Taylor!'' Martika's ruby-red lips pursed. "I think being tacky is the least of her problems right now!"

Suddenly, the tall woman's eyes fluttered, and she lurched toward the nearby settee.

"Hey!" Judith flew to her side, propping her up. "Are you okay?"

"Little morning sickness," Martika said, gritting her teeth. Judith's eyes flew down to the barely discernible bulge in her otherwise smooth midriff. "Dammit. I don't have time for this."

The squawking continued, and Martika sighed. "Taylor, sweetie, it's fine. We're road tripping. Get packed." She hung up the phone with a punch of a button.

"Are you sure you should be traveling in your condition?" Judith said, sternly. "You went quite pale there for a second."

"It happens. This is just first trimester, anyway," Martika said stubbornly. "And I'll bring the boys as backup. I certainly won't be able to drive it."

"This is very ill-advised," Judith remarked, nudging Martika onto the couch and, for lack of anything better to do, getting her a glass of tap water from the kitchen. Martika frowned at it, then got up and headed for her bedroom. "Where are you going?"

"To pack."

"Honestly! It's not like Sarah even wants you there!" Judith stopped. She hadn't meant to be that rude—at least, not that blatantly so—but this was ridiculous.

"That's fine. I'm sure she doesn't want me there. We're going there to stop her."

Judith blinked. "Stop her? You mean...just ruin her wedding?"

"That's the plan, yes," Martika called from her open bedroom door. Judith saw her haphazardly stuffing a black duffel bag full of clothes.

"But...?"

Martika stopped, a fistful of bras in her hand. She glanced at Judith, her mouth working for a second, then she nodded meaningfully at the bag at Judith's feet.

"I just want her to really think about what she's doing," Martika said. "He's an asshole, but if that's what she really wants...well, we'll see. I think she's just doing this out of a misguided sense of comfort, but hey, I could be wrong."

Judith thought about it. Comfort. Duty. Direction.

Why in the hell had she married David?

She watched, fascinated, as Martika's eyes flashed, cursing as she zipped her bag shut.

And what would she have done if friends, people who had cared about her, asked her if she really knew what she was doing when she married the newly graduated law student?

She glanced down at her bag, then walked to Martika's doorway.

"I'm going with you," she said.

Martika's eyes widened, then she smiled. "Great. You get first shift."

* * *

So this was Las Vegas. Sarah had been once before, when her parents were still married. She thought. Actually, that might have been Reno.

At any rate, it was bright, exciting, and the perfect way to start her married life. Martika would be proud...

She stopped. No, actually Martika would *not* be proud, but hell...she'd still be the Las Vegas type, Sarah could just tell. The garish, kitschy quality of it, the fact that it never shut down. *The legalized prostitution,* a little, cruel part of her pointed out. She ignored it. She was getting good at shepherding her thoughts lately.

She wished that Martika could have come anyway. Or Judith.

Or anybody, really.

Staying happy, staying happy. This was the way she wanted her life to work, after all. They'd be moving back up to Northern Cal. No more roommate mess. No more job weirdness. She was finally back on track. She had direction. She had a purpose to her life.

They checked in to the hotel. "I'm looking forward to exploring. The Luxor's right next door—I mean, it isn't new anymore, but I've always wanted to see it."

He quirked an eyebrow at her. "That pyramid thing?"

"Yes! I heard they had a dance club. It's nothing fantastic or anything, but it looks like fun, and I could really blow off some steam. What do you say, Benjamin? It'd be fun."

"I was hoping we could just spend the night in the

room. You know—relaxing. It's been a hell of a week for me. I figured I'll take a few weeks off after I finally quit. This is sort of an early vacation for me. Why don't we just rest?'' He nuzzled her neck. ''We'll probably spend tomorrow running around, handling wedding stuff. Or by the pool.'' He backed off, grinning. ''Just swimming.''

But she hated swimming, and she really was feeling restless. ''Well, how about gambling a little?''

''Well…''

She could *feel* his reluctance, and she felt petulant. ''Okay, *I'll* gamble, how about that? Then I'll catch up with you later.'' There was a crisp sassiness to her voice, she noticed, and grinned.

He frowned more deeply. ''You don't mean you'd be wandering around Las Vegas without me?''

''It's no big deal,'' she assured him, as they headed to the bank of elevators that led up to their floor. ''I mean, I've wandered around worse parts of L.A. practically by myself.''

''And you're lucky you didn't get killed,'' he chastised. ''Why don't we just hang out?''

Because that's boring! She clamped down on the attitude. She was just a little restless. Ordinarily, her prescription for that would have been a few hours at Oval or Pointless Party. Not that that had helped in the long run, she reminded herself.

Maybe what she needed was rest, she thought, as she saw the flashing lights of the slot machines disappear behind the closing doors of the elevator. She sighed. ''So, when do you think you'll quit?''

"Next Monday. That ought to give us enough time to get packed up. I figured we could live at your mother's until I get a new job."

She shot him a look of horror. "You're fucking kidding me."

He hugged her. "Of course I am! I mean, this is impetuous, but I'm hardly rushing into *everything*." He kissed the top of her head, and she felt the anger recede. "You might want to watch that vocabulary, though. We're not with those club freaks you called roommates."

She didn't like his tone. What had happened? Was she channeling Martika, here?

"Sorry. I've been really on edge here."

"I understand," he said. "It's been tough on both of us. This will make all the difference, believe me. I didn't realize how crazy my life had gotten until I moved to that hellhole. Now, I'm looking forward to having a normal life. A house, a couple of kids, going out to the movies every now and then, having a normal book of business…"

She listened to him describe his idyllic picture, and she felt a little prickle of apprehension. She wasn't sure she was ready for kids anymore, actually. She wasn't sure at all. She was twenty-five after all…she was in no hurry. But she was sure he meant the kids were an eventuality, not an immediate result, like he was going to slip the ring on her finger and then instantly assert his fertility or something.

"And we could go out every now and then," she

added, when he took a contemplative breath. "You know. Dinner, maybe some dancing."

"Well, I'd go to watch you dance," he said with a laugh. "You know I hate that sort of thing. And dinner—we'll probably be doing plenty of that. You know how much I'm going to need to schmooze."

She bit her lip. Oh, right. She remembered that. But it wasn't quite the same when you had to choke down really good food as an old geezer stared at your tits and asked you what you did for a living—"besides being Benjamin's better half! Ho ho!"

"You know, I think I'm going to break into the minibar," she said, when Benjamin finally got the door open.

He frowned at her. "Those things cost an arm and a leg."

She kept her smile on. "That's okay. I'll spring for this one."

Chapter 19

Five to One

"**W**here the hell *is* she?"

Martika led the charge with Taylor, his new boy-friend Arthur, and Kit in tow. Judith made a beeline for the front desk, while Martika yelled "Sarah! Sarah!"

Judith headed back to them. "Stop that. I know where they are. They're in something called the Knight's Grotto. Small private wedding. I don't know where it is from here, but the lady at the front desk said that there's a window overlooking it, and she gave me a map…"

The five of them huddled around the black and

white photocopy that Judith held. Martika frowned. "Fuck. Which floor is it on, first or second?"

The copy was smudged. She glanced at the other faces. Judith frowned. "I'm betting first floor," she said, "but it's private. We're going to have to figure out how to get in there."

"I think it's second," Taylor protested. Arthur, his new boyfriend, nodded loyally.

"Fine," Martika finally said, with a huff. She glanced at her watch. She was punchy, she'd been up too long, she was tired. She wanted a cigarette and/ or a drink, and her nausea put a razor edge on her bitchiness. She wanted a bouncer to *try* stopping her in this present mood. "Judith and I will hit the first floor, you boys hit the second floor, and either way we try to get in. Even if you can't, try to figure out how to stall it. Got that? Break!"

She grabbed Judith by the arm, to the Asian woman's surprise. The boys went off, Taylor and Arthur looking bewildered, Kit moving with lanky, languid purpose behind them. Stall them, she thought. Stop this wedding. What was the kid thinking?

Good thing she had Mama Martika looking out for her, she thought with a minuscule grin.

After about five minutes of dedicated searching, she and Judith finally found the chapel doors. She tugged at them. "They're locked!"

She heard organ music starting—very electronic, very cheesy. *If nothing else, we're going to have words about the tackiness of all this,* she thought desperately.

Judith started pounding at the door. "Open up!"

After a moment, a beefy looking security guard walked up to them. "Is there a problem, ladies?"

"Yes, there is," Martika said. "My friend is in there, marrying a total asshole. I need to object. I have reason to put this marriage asunder. Or whatever that official sounding bullshit is. I want in there right now!"

"I'm sorry, but that's a private wedding," he said, not sounding sorry at all. "We can't just let anybody go in and disrupt the weddings we have here. We've got a reputation to uphold, after all."

"Reputation?" *As if I were just anybody!* Martika was incensed by the very thought. "Listen, you jackass, either you let me in or I rip that fucking door off its hinges…"

"Excuse me." Judith's voice was like a knife that had been in the freezer, cold and sharp. "I'm Judith Anderson, and the bride is my client—rather, her family is my client. I have reason to believe the bride is underage, and want to consult with her and check any paperwork she may have provided. It is undoubtedly forged. Her family would not have given her permission to go through with this. I believe your hotel would be participating in a fraud by allowing this wedding."

This caused the man to stop, and his face was skeptical. "She did look sorta young."

Judith nodded. "This is a travesty. This wedding needs to be stopped immediately."

Martika stared at her. The woman never broke a

sweat. She looked as if she were discussing a golf game.

Looks like I'm going to have to reevaluate this one, Martika thought, with a grudging admiration. Especially if it got them in there.

The man looked nervous, and somewhat confused. "Do you have any papers or anything backing this up?"

Judith glared at him. "No, *you* would have any documentation. Perhaps you should get the person in charge of weddings." She frowned. "And maybe your supervisor."

"Let me see…" He walked off to one side. Martika made one more tug at the door. He spoke into his little walkie-talkie thing. "Hey, does anybody know where Michele is? The wedding chick. Dammit. There's a problem here in the Knight's Grotto. Something about…forgery or something. There's a problem, I'm telling you!"

"Chuck, get in here," a voice growled over his walkie-talkie thingy. "What the hell is going on?"

The security guard ("Chuck") looked at them apologetically. "I'll get somebody here in a minute. Don't worry. Just stay right here." With alarming speed for someone his size, he sped off down the corridor.

Martika studied the door. How the hell was she going to get in there?

"I think I bought us five, perhaps ten minutes," Judith said critically, also studying the door. "How are we going to get in there?"

She glanced around. "Find a maintenance guy.

We'll bribe him. We probably should have bribed the security guy—but they make more money, anyway."

Suddenly, there was a noise…something weird, that could be heard over the keening wail of the organ.

She glanced at Judith. "Do you hear that?"

Judith cocked her head. "What the hell?"

"We are gathered here today…"

Sarah felt her palms sweating as she clutched the bouquet of…she didn't even know what the flowers were. Carnations, she recognized those. And roses. Lots of white. She was wearing a simple white dress, she had a ring of white flowers on her head.

It was rather like a funeral, actually.

Ooh, that probably wasn't a good analogy.

Benjamin was wearing that awful cream-colored suit of his, the one she'd dubbed "Miami Vice." He liked it, though, and he looked pretty good, with his white shirt and blue tie. He smiled at her. In fact he was staring at her. It was romantic, the flowers, candles. At least he wasn't wearing the costume the hotel staff had volunteered to provide. If she saw him in a chain mail shirt, she didn't think she could go through with it.

She realized she was hyperventilating a little, and forced herself to breathe a little more slowly. This would work out just fine, she told herself. She was finally doing what she was supposed to be doing. This was direction. This was purpose. This fear, this nervousness she felt was normal, and she felt sure it was going to pass.

Any minute now, in fact.

She frowned. The justice-of-the-peace-type-guy they'd hired was going on and on, speaking as if there were a group of onlookers. *Get on with it, get on with it...*

It probably wasn't taking that long. The guy looked at Benjamin. "Do you, Benjamin Slater, take this woman..."

She glanced into Benjamin's eyes. He looked so sure. He looked...relieved. "I do," he said, in a clear voice.

The official looked at her. "Do you, Sarah Walker, take this man Benjamin to be your lawfully wedded husband?"

He looked at her expectantly. They both did.

She opened her mouth.

"I..." She paused.

She apparently paused for a long time. The man looked gently expectant still, but Benjamin was beginning to look irritated.

She tried it again.

"I..."

Maybe she needed water. Why didn't they have water in places like this? You always saw public speakers with a little table and a pitcher of water...

"Sarah?"

Benjamin's voice was curt. More than curt. It was peremptory.

She took a deep breath, and looked into his eyes.

"No way in hell."

She blinked.

Benjamin blinked back at her.

The justice-guy laughed, nervously. "Oh, you kids."

Benjamin glared. "Sarah, this is serious."

Sarah grimaced. This couldn't be right. She'd been sure that this was what she needed, but it couldn't be right. It was too...

Suddenly, she heard it...a loud pounding. She glanced around, not sure where it was coming from.

The pounding continued. "Now what?" the justice said, losing some of his calm composure. Benjamin looked more than irritated—he looked *pissed*.

She glanced up, to the glass windows that let people on the second floor look down into the grotto...

Kit was there. He was banging on the window, his shirt half out of his pants.

"Elaine!" he yelled, the sound muffled. *"Elaine!"*

She started laughing.

"Who the hell is Elaine?" Benjamin said, bewildered.

Sarah glanced at him. "Today, I guess I am."

And with that, she walked down the aisle, stopping only to grab her purse and tear up the license they'd just purchased.

He grabbed her arm, painfully. "We're getting married!" he growled.

She yanked her arm away, and stepped up to meet him. "Not this way. Jesus, Benjamin, can you honestly tell me that this is what you want? You don't even know me anymore."

His face was ugly, red with rage. "Now? You're

just telling me this now?'' He shook his head, and tried to plaster his smiling salesman face over the anger. It didn't work. ''Come on, Sarah. You know we're right for each other. Didn't almost an entire year apart prove that to you?''

''No, it proved that I'm right for you...and it proved it to *you*. I'm just starting to figure out what I want. If you really love me, you'd wait...''

''Don't give me these bullshit ultimatums!''

She shook her head. ''But it doesn't matter. *Because I don't love you.*''

She took the wreath off her head, feeling lighter already. ''Sorry, Benjamin. I think I know what I'm doing now.''

She walked out the door, right into Martika and Judith.

''I couldn't go through with it,'' she said, as Martika enveloped her in a hug. Judith was talking with a security guard, who shook his head and walked away with a supervisor-looking fellow. ''I just couldn't go through with it.''

''Honey, I'm sorry we argued, I'm pregnant and the mood swings have been killing me,'' Martika said in a rush.

Before Sarah could process that, Judith walked up to her. To her surprise, she was wearing a broad grin. ''And I should have listened,'' Judith said, in her quietly calm voice, ''but I was in the process of leaving my husband.''

''Jesus,'' Sarah said. ''I thought just getting married was a big deal.''

"Judith's going to stay with us for as long as she likes," Martika said, nodding. "Hell, maybe we should look for a bigger place. If you don't mind sharing it with a tyke for a while. I think that means sleepless nights for all."

Benjamin stalked out, his eyes burning. Martika glowered at him, almost pushing Sarah behind her. Sarah stepped forward.

"I really am sorry, Benjamin."

"Stay with your loser friends," he said, with a tone of finality. "I'm sick of the sight of you."

Taylor, Arthur and Kit had run up to them at this point. Taylor and Arthur were a little out of breath. Kit's eyes seemed a little more intense than usual, however.

"Don't try to contact me again," Benjamin said. "I don't know what I was thinking. You still want to fuck around with your slutty roommate and her band of freaks, who am I to stop…"

Because he was so intent on Sarah, he didn't see Kit coming…or the punch, really. He went down like a shot rhino.

They stared at Kit for a moment. He was rubbing his hand, still not out of breath.

"Sarah, are you all right?"

She stared at him.

"Do you have anything up in the room that you absolutely can't part with?"

She paused. "Nope. I've got my purse here."

"Then let's get the hell out of here."

To her surprise, he held out his hand. She grabbed it. And the whole lot of them ran out of the lobby, laughing like little kids, into the sweltering hot sunlight beyond.

Chapter 20

L.A. Woman

The invitations said "A Little Sumptin'-Sumptin'" and looked more like a club promotion than a shower invitation. The only difference was the text, "bring baby type gifts." Martika had announced her new arrival in grand style. Their new town house was packed. Judith's friend had really hooked them up with a find: two bedrooms and a guest house, which was where Martika stayed. They would figure out the kid situation—Judith, strangely, was sort of looking forward to it. Now that she'd broken with David (who apparently was serving her with divorce papers any day now), she was reevaluating with the grace and aplomb of Ingrid Bergman. She'd even taken time off of work. Sarah thought Judith's mother would have a heart attack. Unlike David, Judith's parents called all the time.

Martika's mother had entered the picture, as well, and had promised to help with baby-sitting or "whatever you girls need," which was another weird situation. Martika seemed either disgruntled by the offer of assistance, or uncomfortably sentimental—something she kept blaming on her hormones. She'd been back to her childhood house for dinner twice, but had no intention of moving there. In the meantime, Martika was approaching motherhood with the same confident aplomb that she approached everything—full bore.

"Okay, who found baby vinyl clothes?" Martika said, holding up a miniature vinyl dress and laughing.

"We did!" Taylor and Arthur raised their hands.

Judith, who was sitting on Martika's left side and jotting down who had given what in a baby-shower type notebook, stared at the outfit bewildered. "What do I say that is?"

"Baby Goth outfit," Martika said, putting it aside with a leonine laugh.

Sarah smiled, then decided to go to the kitchen and get a refill on her soda.

Kit was leaning against the counter.

They hadn't really talked since Las Vegas, even though he'd helped with the move to the town house. She wasn't sure what to say to him, actually.

"So...looks like you're settled in."

"Yeah. The drive's not so bad, either."

He tucked his hands into the pockets of his blue jeans. "Understand you took that job as a permanent."

She shrugged. "For now. They seem like a pretty good company. I think I might go back to school, though."

"For what?"

She smiled. "Haven't decided."

He smiled back, and took a step closer to her. She stared at him, studying his shy smile.

"I'm glad you stayed, Sarah."

She felt her heart race a little, and tried to slow it down. "I'm glad I stayed, too."

"I was wondering…"

She held up a hand. "Let's get one thing straight. I just got over a guy. I don't need to walk into another mess just like it. I've finally got a job, a roommate situation that doesn't look like it's going to completely explode on me…"

"At least not until the baby comes," he added.

"Well, yes, and I'm finally getting my head together. And I have some really, really great friends."

"I'm all for friends."

"So…." She looked at him expectantly.

"So, what?"

She blinked. "Weren't you going to ask me out?"

"Hell, no."

She felt the tinges of embarrassment heat up her cheeks. "Oh. Sorry. So what were you wondering?"

He smirked, then leaned down and kissed her. Thoroughly.

"I was wondering whether you'd figured all of that out," he said, and laughed at her bemused expression.

"Well." She smirked back, then leaned in and planted one of her own kisses on him. "Glad we got that straight," she said wryly.

He put an arm around her shoulder, and they walked back into the crowded living room.

SPOTLIGHT

**Every month we'll spotlight
original stories from Harlequin
and Silhouette Books' Shining Stars!**

Fantastic authors, including:
- Debra Webb
- Julie Elizabeth Leto
- Merline Lovelace
- Rhonda Nelson

**Plus, value-added Bonus Features
are coming soon to a book near you!**

- Author Interviews
- Bonus Reads
- The Writing Life
- Character Profiles

SIGNATURE SELECT SPOTLIGHT
On sale January 2005

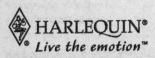

Escape with a courageous woman's story of
motherhood, determination...and true love!

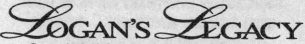

LOGAN'S LEGACY

Because birthright has its privileges and family ties run deep.

Coming in December...

CHILD OF HER HEART

by

CHERYL ST.JOHN

After enduring years of tragedy, new single mother
Meredith Malone escaped with her new baby daughter
to the country—and into the arms of Justin Weber.
The sexy attorney seemed perfect...but was he
hiding something?

Where love comes alive™

The men and women of California's Courage Bay Emergency Services team must face any emergency...even the ones that are no accident!

code**RED**

Coming in December...

BLOWN AWAY

by

MURIEL JENSEN

Being rescued by gorgeous K-9 Officer Cole Winslow is a fantasy come true for single mom Kara Abbott. But, despite their mutual attraction, Kara senses Cole is holding back. Now it's Kara's turn to rescue Cole—from the grip of his past.

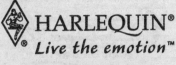

HARLEQUIN®
Live the emotion™

www.eHarlequin.com

CRBA

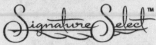

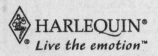